Get a grip, she chided herself. You are here for the conference and to finally meet the man who has been on the other end of the phone and the computer for two years. She peered through the darkness trying to make out the faces of the other participants, straining to find Cord McCune. Cord. The very thought of him filled her with a joy and lust she hadn't felt in all her thirty-six years.

Meant to Be

JEANNE SUMERIX

LOVE SPECTRUM

Love Spectrum is an imprint of
Genesis Press, Inc.
315 Third Avenue North
Columbus, Mississippi 39701

Meant to Be

ISBN 1-58571-020-2

Manufactured in the United States of America

FIRST EDITION

Acknowledgements

I have to thank Cordelle (yes there really is one) for being the great man that he is. He is the inspiration for the character in this book. And he is one of the best Emergency Room nurses I have ever encountered.

A very special thanks to Irving Dickerson who helped with the research and kept encouraging me to continue.

Thanks guys. Without you, *Meant to Be* wouldn't be.

To all multicultural couples who know true love and are willing to suffer and win from their experiences

One

"I can't believe we are finally going to meet." Amy Summers pressed the telephone receiver closer to her ear, waiting to hear the soothing tones of Cord McCune's rich baritone voice. She smiled as she heard his breath catch in his throat.

"I can't wait." His voice broke with huskiness. "Do you want to go to the conference, or right to bed?" The humor of their mutual joke hung in the air.

She giggled lightly. His sensuous suggestion sent rivers of hot blood on a fast course through her body. "I never thought we would be together..." She didn't finish her thought. Putting into words just how much his friendship meant to her was difficult.

"Do you want me to wear a red carnation or something?" he chuckled.

"No. I'm sure I'll know you." Her mental picture of him had formed over the past two years. She was sure she could pick him out anywhere.

"I might be a little late. If not, I'll save you a seat because you always are."

"I'm not always late. I just measure my time a little closer than others." She enjoyed the gentle sparring as much as he did.

"Okay, let's see who is on time tomorrow. Drive carefully. Bye babe."

She dropped the phone receiver into its cradle and stared out the window at the beautiful spring day. But then, it could have been pouring rain and she would've thought it wonderful. Today her life was full of happiness that had long escaped her.

She was in love with a man she'd never met. No, she'd never met him, but she knew him. His kindness, sense of humor, and now the sensuality that glowed in every word he spoke. At times she wondered how they could be so much in love because they had not met. Other times she was sure it was something that was just meant to be. A warmth flooded her as she reflected on their beginning.

Cord McCune, a Michigan Department of Public Health accountant, was assigned as the liaison for the regional offices. And she worked in a regional office. She smiled to herself. Remembering at first he was just her contact. She closed her eyes and let the memories wash over her.

On the day they became friends, she had sought the peace and quiet of her office, her emotions in an upheaval. Every day she left her ailing mother with a nurse. Though she knew she had to earn a living, guilt had consumed her as she reached to hang up her coat. "Not today," she had groaned when her phone buzzer pierced her thoughts.

She'd grabbed the phone to stop the noise. "Yes, Shelley," she spoke abruptly to her assistant. She was immediately ashamed of her tone. She turned and stared out the window at a late spring snowstorm, which did nothing to lift her spirits.

"Good morning, Amy. How's your mother's rehabilitation coming?"

"I don't know. She acts like she doesn't want to recover from the stroke. She says she's too tired."

"I'm sorry. If there's anything I can do."

"No, but thanks. You've been a rock through all of this. First Dad's funeral and then Mom's illness..." Amy couldn't ask for a better friend than Shelley.

"That's what friends are for." She paused for a moment. "Oh, I almost forgot. Cord McCune is on the line. Apparently our April financial status report hasn't reached his desk."

Amy was hardly in the mood to tolerate anyone's incompetence. The strains of a being a single mother working to save enough to put her daughter through college, and at the same time caring for a bedridden parent, were taking their toll.

She rolled her eyes. "I sent it both by computer and hard copy. Maybe he should go down to the mail room and look for it." Her voice was filled with sarcasm. Then she realized she was being surly with her assistant and an even better friend. After all, she was just the messenger of the bad news. Her voice softened. "I'm sorry, Shelley. Thanks. Which line is he on?"

"Two."

Amy punched the phone button as she flipped on her computer to check the date she'd sent it. "Amy Summers here. What can I do for you?" She made an effort to bring civility to her voice.

"Hi Amy. We haven't received your financial status report for April yet. You've always been so punctual, I'm sure the problem is ours. Could you send it again?"

Amy leaned back in her chair and released the breath she was holding. Though she had been ready to do battle, he completely deflated her anger. "Sure, no problem." She sent her computer on a search for the report. File Not Found popped up on the screen. An uneasy panic crept up her spine to the hair roots at the base of her skull. "Cord, I seem to be having a computer problem," she lied. "I'll get back with you."

"I'm in all day, just give me a call. As long as you can send it in before five, I'll process your program's monthly check."

"Thanks Cord, I'll get back to you." She dropped the receiver on its base. Though she searched frantically, clicking the keyboard in a frenzy, she couldn't find the original entries. Tears of frustration streamed down her cheeks as she realized the truth. She hadn't done the report this month. She couldn't believe it. Her job was the one thing in her life she could control and now she might have lost that too. If she didn't get it done, her office wouldn't receive its monthly grant check and the executive-director would come unglued. Just what she need-ed...more anxiety added to a day already crowded with it.

Swiveling back to the window, she stared at the ever-increasing snowfall. New snow blanketed the spring grass and the few flowers that had sprouted. The weather was cooperating fully with her mood. Resolutely, she pushed up her sleeves and brushed her hair from her face. It would take most of the day, but she could do it.

Amy pushed Shelley's buzzer. Her assistant's cheery voice came on the line. It seemed an eternity since Amy had felt as buoyant as Shelley sounded. "Shell, screen my calls. Unless there is a national emergency, take a message."

"Sure thing. Is there anything I can do to help?"

"No...yes. Keep the coffee coming." Amy had never asked anyone to get her coffee and she hated to do it now. Even though Shelley had volunteered to do it many times, Amy had always refused, not wanting to be one of those executives who did that to prove their importance. Today was different, however. A two-day task to complete in one day and that wouldn't allow time to break for anything.

"Sure thing. And I'll have lunch brought in."

"Thanks, Shell, I'll make it up to you." She replaced the phone in its cradle, thanking her lucky stars for her friend.

The hours flew by as she worked furiously. Finally she breathed a sigh of relief and reached for the phone, pushing memory one. "Cord, Amy Summers, I am ready to send."

"Amy..." He hesitated, surprise filling his voice. "When you didn't return my call from this morning, I processed the checks without yours."

"I told you I would get it to you today. For God's sake, doesn't your office stay open until five?" Her voice had grown to a fevered pitch. The last thing she needed was to deal with an irate boss.

"Amy," Cord's voice had an infinitely compassionate tone, "it's seven o'clock. I'm staying over to catch up on some work."

Her long lashes swept open as she gazed up at the clock. "Seven! Oh my God. Could you hold on a minute?" Without waiting for Cord's answer, she put him on hold and punched memory two, praying the home-care nurse would understand. When the curt voice came on the line, Amy knew she was in trouble. She offered apologies, promising to be home soon. Though unhappy, the nurse agreed to stay for another hour. Amy punched the button to return to Cord.

"I'm sorry. I didn't realize it was so late." Tears were threatening. She tried to choke them back and to act halfway professional.

"Amy, is there anything wrong? Can I help you with anything?" His deep voice carried a totally sympathetic edge.

A hot tear trickled down Amy's cheek. "Cord, I...that is..." Her voice broke miserably. Between sobs she dumped all her troubles on a person she knew only professionally, and long distance at that, almost a complete stranger. Once the floodgates opened there was no turning back. She couldn't believe how good it felt to have someone listen to her. And she knew he was listening.

"Shh. Amy, there's nothing done that we can't fix. I'll process the check tonight and hand carry it for signature in the morning." His deep, velvety voice lulled her into a more relaxed mood.

"I don't want to put you out. It's my mistake...my problem." She felt foolish at having burdened another person with her problems and continued apologetically. "I'm sorry. I guess I was ready to fall and you were the one in the way."

He chuckled. "I don't mind. I've had a few of those days in my past. I understand how it is to be swamped. You have to believe there is a light at the end of the tunnel. This one is on me. Let's just say it's for all those times when you made my job easier."

That was the beginning. Even then Amy was drawn to his kindness and willingness to help a stranger. After that fateful day he was her lifeline. Their conversations steadily became more personal until they exchanged home phone numbers and began talking into the wee hours of the night. Yes, That was the beginning. Reliving it always made her appreciate the hand of destiny. And now tomorrow would be a beginning of another kind.

■ ■ ■

Amy arranged her hair, tousled by the spring breeze, and sat her briefcase on the ground. Staring at her reflection in the dark-tinted window, she straightened her dress and tried to compose herself. Butterflies were dancing in her belly in anticipation of at last meeting her dear friend and the man she cared for so deeply.

She tucked her briefcase under her arm and pulled open the door to the conference center. She was late.

Damn it, he was right. I should've spent less time linger-ing. She cursed to herself. Yet the drive along the bay in the warm sun had felt so good after the long winter. It made being late worth the embarrassment.

Next time she would allow more time for the drive from Sault Saint Marie to Traverse City. But that doesn't do any good this time. She did a fast walk through the lobby, as if she could make up time lost in the five-hour drive. A drive that should have been four hours, she scolded herself.

The conference room she entered was dark except for the filtered light from the large television screen. She edged her way along the mahogany-paneled wall. Thankfully, all eyes were on the speaker's video presenta-tion. She searched for a place to sit in the full room. The aromas of perfume, cologne, and after-shave tickled her nose. Grabbing a tissue from her purse, she headed off the impending sneeze that would have drawn eyes in her direction, and slipped into a seat between a distinguished, elderly man and a rather handsome man about her age.

When the clunk of her briefcase brought quick looks from the men on either side of her, Amy offered both of them an apologetic smile. Though the elderly man gri-maced, the younger man offered her a smile that sent blood rushing to her head.

God, was he handsome. His face was symmetrically perfect, right down to the flashing dimples on either cheek as his smile widened. Charming angel kisses, as her moth-er would say. Embarrassed, she glanced away, praying the heat she felt in her face did not reveal her thoughts.

Get a grip, she chided herself. You are here for the conference and to finally meet the man who has been on the other end of the phone and the computer for two years. She peered through the darkness trying to make out the faces of the other participants, straining to find Cord McCune. Cord. The very thought of him filled her with a joy and lust she hadn't felt in all her thirty-six years.

She scanned the dim room again. Here she was, but where was he? Her heart sank. Maybe he wasn't coming. No, they had talked of nothing else for two months. Talked? she thought to herself. Her face flushed hot thinking of their conversations. Sometimes they were akin to phone sex, she thought, but I'm sure the real thing will be much better. Then she cringed, realizing she sounded like a shameless hussy, even to herself. She glanced at the men on either side of her to reassure herself that no one saw her flaming cheeks. They were doing what they were supposed to be doing, listening to the speaker, something she should be doing. Unable to concentrate she resumed her survey.

Her gaze landed on a man halfway across the room. After studying him she ruled him out. He was too young. Although they had never specifically discussed their age, they had discovered they had both graduated from the same college fourteen years before. Amy often wished they had met then, sure they would have hit it off. But at that time he was a married man and she a single mom, just divorced from Tom. Tom, the high school sweetheart who had left her right after their daughter's birth. The bitter experience had made her want to put men out of her life and except for an occasional date, she had succeeded, until Cord. Disappointed, she sighed and ended her survey. No one fit her image of him.

When the lights came on an hour later, the speaker announced a fifteen-minute coffee break. Again, this time in full lights, Amy looked around the room. He was not at the conference. And after he promised to take me to dinner. He said he might be late, but not this late. She began to worry. What if he had been in an accident? What if something had happened to a family member? No, she told herself. He'll be here. Cord was always laughing at her because she immediately thought the worst. He teased her about worrying so much. She smiled. He will be here.

Amy looked up to find Mr. Tall-Dark-And-Handsome gazing at her, as if he'd read her mind. She colored, wondering if she had spoken aloud. "I'm sorry if I've been disturbing you." She offered a wan smile. "I'll try to do better after the break."

"No, no. I was just wondering if you would have lunch with me."

Tempting, Amy thought, but she shook her head. "I'd love to, but I am expecting someone momentarily." She glanced around.

"Of course. Maybe another time."

Something more than mild disappointment showed in his eyes, but she couldn't put her finger on it. Amy grabbed her purse. "I've got to run. See you after the break." He nodded. What was it she saw in his eyes?

Could he have thought I turned him down because of his race? Oh, God, she groaned inside. That was the last thing she would do. She hurried to take advantage of the break, rushing to fix her hair and makeup, cursing her insensitivity the whole time.

When she returned, she found a note from Cord on her briefcase. Mr. Tall-Dark-And-Handsome was just seating himself. "Good news, I hope."

She smiled warmly at him and then scanned the note inviting her to lunch. Her gaze traveled the room in search of Cord. Why didn't he asked her in person? Maybe he's started a middle-aged spread and is losing his hair. She shrugged her shoulders. None of that really mattered to her. He was her friend and more, much more. The chemistry was there, no matter what he looked like.

Amy smiled to herself as she glanced at the clock. "Two hours before I meet him," she grumbled. It was just like Cord to keep her guessing. He loved to tease her. His sense of humor had been a Godsend. It had helped her to maintain her sanity throughout her mother's recovery.

Again the man flashed her a bright smile. "Is there a problem?"

She realized she had spoken aloud and brought her gaze up to meet his. She shook her head and stared at him, uttering a barely audible, "No."

Something about him was familiar but she couldn't figure out what. He was African-American. There weren't many African-Americans in Sault Saint Marie or anywhere else in Michigan's Upper Peninsula. Except for the vacation spots and casinos they were almost non-existent. She rarely traveled south of the Mackinac Bridge and really had no reason to visit the lower peninsula. So she was sure she had never met him. Besides women, the only minorities she had ever dealt with were Native Americans. But somehow Native Americans didn't seem like minorities. In the neighborhood where Amy had grown up, the two races lived together with little problem. And the problems that did exist weren't racially-based. Her mother had always told her a bad neighbor is just that. A bad neighbor.

As she pulled her gaze away, she couldn't help admiring him, and not just for his looks, though they were quite sufficient. His whole demeanor exuded self-confidence, self-respect, and damn it, he was downright sexy.

The speaker brought her attention to the front of the room. Her eyes widened. A handsome man, in the right age bracket, stood at the podium. He glanced in her direction and smiled. She returned the smile. Damn him. It would be just like Cord not to tell her he was the speaker. She hadn't caught his name because she had been gawking at the man next to her.

"Now," the speaker announced, "team up with your neighbor to work on the project." Amy listened closely to his voice but not his words. In person it didn't carry the same richness that it did on the phone. Maybe it wasn't him. Still he had offered her a big smile. When she got her hands on Cord she was going to wring his neck for keeping her guessing. Her gaze flew around the room. He was somewhere here laughing at her. She returned her gaze to the speaker. But then, it could be him.

Mr. Handsome nudged her. "Everyone else has teamed up. I guess that leaves you and me."

Her lashes flew up. "For what?" Her cheeks stained fire-engine red at being caught daydreaming.

"To work on the budgeting procedure. You know, the one we came to the conference to learn before the new fiscal year begins." He spoke in hushed tones. His face carried a stern look but his eyes twinkled as he gazed down.

"Yes, of course." Mercifully someone spoke to him, pulling his attention away, giving her time to recover.

Amy was drawn to the man like bees to honey. A veiled glance at his left hand showed no open commitment. Her inspection continued as he leaned way over the table to accept the packet being handed across. He stretched to receive it, his long body virtually suspended above the table. His thigh hung inches over her hand that rested on the conference table. Amy marveled at his long lean, sinewy body. His thigh now hovered no more than an inch over her fingers, which had taken on a mind of their own, twitching involuntarily. It was obvious she had been away from men far too long. Still she didn't move her hand. She chided herself. Get a grip on yourself, you are here to meet Cord. Besides, this guy is probably sought after by every female he comes into contact with. He certainly isn't going to be interested in an average-looking white woman.

This time her quick survey of the room spotted several extremely beautiful African-American women. She sighed. Even if she wanted, she couldn't compete with them. She looked like a country bumpkin and they were perfectly put together. Besides, she couldn't have a serious relationship with him anyway. Her mother would probably have another stroke. There, she felt better. He wouldn't want her. And she couldn't have him if he did.

Amy forced her gaze to the materials he had spread in front of her, suddenly feeling guilty. Somehow she felt she was being disloyal to Cord, the friend who had stuck by her through thick and thin. She drew in a long, deep breath and tried to ignore the sexual magnetism of the man next to her. Soon she would be with Cord and all of this nonsense would cease. She concentrated on the budget procedure. She read the caption, "Zero Based Budgeting." This should be easy, she thought, it's a lot like my check-book.

Her teammate pushed sample spread sheets in front of her. In a soft, rich voice that would pull on anyone's innards, he asked, "Are you ready to begin?"

She swallowed hard and nodded. But she thought, yes-yes-yes. Anytime, anywhere. A soft giggle escaped her lips.

The man smiled at her. "Private joke or can anyone share?"

She didn't want to rebuff him or let him know what she was really thinking, so she covered her desire for him with a half-truth. "I was just thinking that my checkbook would be a good place to begin with a zero base."

His rich, deep laugh brought her attention to his face as he spoke. "I know just what you mean." They laughed together but Amy was uneasy. Somehow, somewhere, she'd had contact with this man. But she just couldn't place him. Although she wanted to ask if he'd ever been to her office, she resisted. He would probably think she was coming on to him. Not that she didn't find the idea intriguing but she had other plans. Most of all, she hated the look of a man who was trying to let a woman down without saying, "You're not my type."

Somehow she managed to shove her hormones back into their proper place and concentrate on the task in front of her. Soon they were working on the process as if they had worked together forever. Still, his rich, soft voice and spicy cologne sent shivers through her body.

When lunch break was announced, she was more than ready to remove herself from the onslaught of emotions brought on by her handsome work partner and the absence of the man she came to see. Sliding her chair back, she slid right into the older man's briefcase. The abrupt stop thrust her forward and before she knew it, she had jolted the table, spilling the remains of the coffee in several cups. "Damn it," she spat as she began cleaning up the mess. The young man who had been serving the coffee rushed to her aid. "Thank you," she smiled weakly. "I'm sorry for being such a bother."

"This is my job, ma'am." His young face showed stress as he averted his gaze from her. "Why don't you go to lunch...I'll take care of this."

Amy hesitated, wondering if she should help or leave. Totally distracted, she wheeled to leave and ran right into her work partner whose foot was propped on a chair while he dabbed at a coffee stain on his pants leg. Her eyes grew wide watching him wobble on one leg until he caught his balance. He returned his foot to the chair and began rubbing the spot again, giving her only a cursory look. Her face flushed with humiliation and anger at herself, and her hand flew to her mouth. "I'm so sorry."

Amy dabbed a napkin in the ice water she hadn't spilled and bent to work on the stained pant leg. "If you could take your pants off..." She stopped, realizing what she had said. Her face had been a hot bed of coals all morning and this did nothing to change it. She watched as his eyes grew openly amused. Somehow, she, a usually mature, normal woman, had completely lost control. "I mean, if you send them to the cleaners I'll gladly pay the bill."

He stared at her, then released a low chuckle. "I think maybe I should take care of my own pants — whether they are on or off." He removed his foot from the chair and set it firmly on the floor. "I have to grab some lunch before the afternoon session. I suggest you do the same." He turned on his heel and left.

Her gaze followed him from the room. There was something warm and enchanting in his humor. Any woman would be lucky to latch onto a man like that. She couldn't believe she had made such a fool of herself. At the afternoon session she would try to avoid him for his own good—and to remove herself from the emotional roller coaster.

After lunch she would hopefully find Cord and work with him, and try to keep her eyes off this man. "Shoot," she murmured. She watched as his strong back and wide shoulders disappeared through the door. "I didn't even ask his name." Ruining his morning and destroying his pants wasn't enough. She had neglected to offer him the common courtesy of an introduction.

If she could, she would make it up to him, but she had no idea how.

She hurried to the lounge. Stepping over the threshold, she hesitated while her eyes adjusted from the brightly-lit pastels of the lobby to the lounge's dimly lit decor of deep forest green and burgundy. The lounge was empty except for a couple of women who were chatting at the bar. She breathed a sigh of relief. Cord hadn't arrived yet.

Amy slipped past the women and slid into a booth in the back, the darkest one she could find. The last thing she needed was for Cord to see her in her chronic state of embarrassment. She wanted to be calm and somewhat normal when she met the man on the other end of the telephone line. All she had to do, she told herself, was put the disastrous morning out of her mind.

Amy took a long drink of the Diet Coke she had ordered. Inhaling deeply, she rested her head against the high back of the cushioned seat and closed her eyes, willing herself to come down off her hormone bonanza and compose herself. The soft music and dimly lit room lulled her into a more relaxed frame of mind.

She could even laugh at herself. What an impression she must have made on her teammate. She'd never before been klutzy and what a heck of a time to begin. And her thoughts this morning! She was glad no one could read her mind, especially what's-his-name.

Amy could still smell the spicy cologne Mr. Handsome had worn this morning. It made her feel warm all over. In fact the aroma was very strong, as if she had leaned against him and now she would wear it all day. However, she wasn't sure she was up to having a constant memory of this morning. After lunch she would run up to her room change her blouse and impose an iron control on herself. There would be no more of this teenage hormone stuff. After all, she was an adult woman here to meet the man she was sure she had fallen in love with.

Filled with a new resolve and ready to face the rest of the day, she opened her eyes. She was staring into the richest chocolate eyes she'd ever seen. And how she loved chocolate. Her resolve weakened. Her gaze darted around him, frantically searching for Cord.

Mr. Handsome offered her a bright smile and spoke in his rich baritone voice, "Mind if I join you?"

Amy's throat constricted. "Are you sure you want to?" She could barely get her voice above a hoarse whisper. This man was having a major effect on her. If he sat down she would lose the precious control she had gained. Cord would be sure to notice. Yet she couldn't be discourteous. Her fidgeting had disturbed his whole morning. And the truth was, she really did want him to join her.

"No, please sit." She watched as he slid his marvelous body into the booth across from her. "I am waiting for someone but I'm sure he won't mind," she added feebly.

He smiled warmly. "I'm waiting too."

Regaining some of her composure, she continued, "I'm afraid I neglected to introduce myself this morning. I'm Amy Summers. I work in the Sault Saint Marie office."

Mr. Handsome stared at her from across the table. "Amy Summers," he repeated.

His voice, deep and sensual, sent a ripple of awareness through her. She stared wordlessly at him, her heart hurling at a rapid pace. She cringed inside. Could this be Cord? Had she sat by him all morning and not known him? Oh God, he must think she was an idiot or worse yet, a racist.

He continued, "I've wanted to meet you for a couple of years now." He held out his hand, "I'm Cord McCune. It's a pleasure to finally meet you."

Amy tried to hide her surprise and embarrassment as he confirmed her thoughts. This strong, velvet-edged voice did indeed belong to Cord, her Cord.

How could she have spent the morning drooling over him and not have recognized his voice?

"Oh, Cord, I'm so sorry. I didn't expect...I mean, I had you pictured differently." Amy could have kicked herself for being so insensitive. Trying to recover and restore their relationship, she accepted his proffered hand. "It's truly great to finally meet you. Why didn't you say something this morning? Did you know me?"

Cord narrowed his eyebrows. "Yes, I knew. But when you didn't recognize me or my voice, I realized you didn't know everything you should about me." He paused and then smiled. "I guess the red carnation would have been a good idea."

Amy's blood raced to her face, announcing her embarrassment. "But...I mean, how would I have known? I've never seen you before."

Her desperate plea brought a smile to his long face, displaying his perfectly charming dimples. "I'm sorry, Amy, I thought you'd do what I did. I asked people who had been to your office to describe you. I was told that your shoulder-length hair is always in your face. I was also told your eyes were silver-green. I couldn't imagine them that way, but it's true." He stared into her eyes as if trying to decide if they were real or not.

Subconsciously pushing her hair away from her face, Amy stared back. He did look as she'd thought. He was definitely tall, dark, and very handsome. She was as physically attracted to him as she had been mentally. The silence stretched between them as two years of intimate phone conversations settled inside their hearts.

Many times they had joked about their first meeting. They'd laughed, saying they knew each other so well that they could avoid the social amenities and go right to bed.

She felt the heat rise as she remembered. She couldn't believe she'd been so blind that she hadn't seen him.

Amy let her gaze drop to their hands, which had not parted after the handshake. She finally found her voice. "It never dawned on me to ask anyone what you looked like. Our telephone friendship was so warm and good, and— well, I was sure you were everything that you are."

Cord squeezed her hand. "Amy, look at me." When she didn't lift her eyes, he took his free hand and lifted her chin. Their eyes met with Fourth of July fireworks. The telephone relationship had been warm and caring but this was definitely hot and sensuous. Cord sucked in air. "If you don't want to continue our friendship I'll understand."

Eyes widening, Amy slowly shook her head, and answered, "If you don't know me by now, then you probably never will. I value our friendship, and the truth is, when you asked me to have dinner with you, I was sure we were ready to move to another level." Feeling herself a bit too brazen, Amy stopped.

Cord squeezed her hand again, holding her attention, "And now?"

Amy placed her other hand on top of his, feeling the firm, smooth skin. "And now," she parroted him in a hushed voice, "maybe we should keep our date and find out."

Cord's warm smile carried Amy through the afternoon in high spirits. In the conference room they were all business except for an occasional stolen moment. They worked diligently on the procedure, and by the time the afternoon was over, both understood the new process and needed to rest their minds. As Cord finished dropping in the rest of the numbers, Amy smiled seductively at him. "You've given me every number except your room number."

Cord moved his pencil and wrote 548 on the top of the paper she was working on. "This is the only number you will need for the evening, or would you rather eat out?"

Amy wanted nothing more than to spend the evening alone with him. Letting her knee touch his, she felt shock waves course through her body. Instinct told her she wouldn't have any control alone with this man and she felt they should explore their feelings on neutral ground. I'll come to your room at seven but I think we should go to a public place and talk." Her mind swirled with the vision of moist, naked bodies tangled in lovemaking. Being alone with him was all she could think of.

She finished weakly, "I'll see you at seven and then we can decide."

The elevator ride to their rooms seemed entirely too quick. They unwillingly parted, when Amy exited on the fourth floor. She wanted to be with Cord more than she had ever wanted anything but their race difference could cause a problem. Not for her. But she did have to think of her mother and her daughter.

Amy should have known it was too good to be true. After all these lonely years, her knight in shining armor had ridden in, but on a horse of a different color. She shivered as a cold chill ran over her.

She shoved the key in the door. Why in the hell should other people dictate who she loved, or who she chose to be with? She closed the door and leaned against it. What was she going to do? She was sure she was in love with Cord. It had been a year since she'd realized it. At the time she'd scolded herself for being so romantic. She had told herself his looks didn't matter, that she was in love with his heart, voice, sense of humor and the way he made her feel. She truly hadn't expected him to be so damned handsome. Or African-American.

Two

Cord threw his briefcase on the bed and watched as the black leather case bounced to the floor. "Damn it!" he cursed. He knew he should have told her. He retrieved the briefcase and placed it on the table by the phone. They should have left well enough alone. At least they both had had a shoulder to cry on and that was cheaper than a therapist. Hell, he thought to himself, I didn't mean to fall in love with her. But then maybe it isn't love, he argued with himself. Seeing her today had almost removed any doubts he might have had. His feelings for her didn't involve only her physical beauty. No, he could get that anywhere. It was the beauty that glowed from within.

At first, he hadn't given her race a thought. By the time he realized he could be falling in love, it was too late. He knew that eventually they would have to deal with their families and society but he thought Amy knew his race. He thought she knew and just decided it wasn't important. She hadn't brought it up so why should he? Being just a voice on the phone was the perfect way to discover another person's real self. At least that's what he'd thought.

Her actions this morning told the whole story. Amy was looking for him but she wasn't expecting a black man. She hadn't been able to conceal her overwhelming surprise. When she had realized the truth, she acted as if it didn't matter. He was sure that would change once it sank in. Or maybe it already had and she was just pretending.

What would she do when she discovered he was taking the temporary assignment as her agency's director? He loosened his belt and let his pants fall. Grabbing them, he stared at the coffee stain. He couldn't help smiling when he thought about her mortification this morning. Somehow he had thought their friendship would transcend any barriers. Now he felt the coffee stain was indicative of what was to come.

He pulled off his dusty-blue, Italian silk tie and hung it over the bar in the closet. After hanging his suit coat, Cord unbuttoned his shirt, making a different decision with each button he slid out of its hole. He would pack and leave. He would turn down the directorship of her office. That way they could continue their long-distance relationship. No, he would stay and see if she was the woman he thought she was. If he didn't love her so damned much, he would seduce her and leave her. No, he knew he'd never do that, even if he didn't care about her. He half-laughed and half-grunted to himself. *Like I could seduce anyone.*

His wife leaving him for someone else stung even more now. Five years had helped to get over her, but not the blow to his manhood. He didn't need or want to deal with another rejection. Involuntarily he winced at the thought. Then he folded the shirt and placed it in the bag he had brought for soiled clothing.

Cord stood naked in the bathroom and turned on the shower until it ran warm. Visions of Amy's glowing eyes and sweet face played in his mind. Her voice asking for his room number sang its song of seduction. Perhaps it might be better to take a cold shower and have an equally cold dinner with Amy. If he didn't, they would either end up in bed or hating each other because they couldn't.

If he wanted to become involved there were plenty of fine looking women at the conference who might give him the time of day. His mind returned to the morning session where he'd spotted a couple of onyx beauties. But he didn't love them. He stepped into the shower and turned the faucet to cold water. No, he didn't need any more rejection.

■■■

Amy plopped on the bed and slowly, thoughtfully, dialed the eleven digits to her home.

"Hello," Mrs. Summers answered cheerfully. Amy smiled as her mother's warm voice touched her ear.

"Hi Mom. How's everything going?"

"Everything is just fine dear. Don't you worry about me," she scolded and then continued. "I'm going to watch a little television and go to bed early."

At least everything at home sounded normal. Amy's mother had recovered completely and now was enjoying her role, in taking care of her and Sara. Amy was thankful for that blessing. One problem at a time was all she could deal with. For the next three months she would be extremely busy filling in as her agency's director. Of course the board of directors hadn't asked her yet, but she was the logical choice. She breathed a sigh of relief. At least some things went as planned.

"So you're gong to take advantage of a little quiet time," she teased.

"And I'm guessing you will be having dinner with that fellow you took so much time to prepare for."

"Mom, I told you that there is no fellow." Her mother was too close to the truth for Amy's comfort. "I'd much rather be with you tonight." She gave a regretful sigh and changed the subject. "Did Sara get off on her senior trip, okay?"

"All right, dear. Whatever you say. And yes, Sara got off just fine. Don't worry about me. You just learn all you need and then come home safely."

"I will. See you tomorrow night." She knew she hadn't convinced her mother but she wasn't going to drop the bomb until it was absolutely necessary; if it ever was. At this moment she wasn't even sure of her name.

"All right, dear. Sara said she'd probably call tomorrow night."

"I'll be home by then, Mom." Amy could hardly believe her daughter was a senior in high school and would be beginning college next fall. She breathed a long sigh. Her life had been so busy she hadn't had time to live it. "Good night, Mom."

"Good night, dear."

Reassured, Amy undressed, quickly dropping her clothes as she headed toward the bathroom. She slid her panties to her ankles and kicked them into the corner, promising herself she would pick them up later.

Right now she needed to think, and she couldn't think of a better place than the shower. Amy eased into the steaming box and let the hot water run over her, relaxing muscles made tense by her time with Cord.

Every nerve in her body vibrated. She couldn't think of anything except the handsome man who wanted her, and she undeniably wanted him. Visions of his long muscular body tripped through her mind. No. I can't think of that, she told herself. If we go down that path, we'll lose everything we've had. But his dimpled cheeks were so inviting, she wanted to kiss each until her lips burned an imprint on his cheek. Stop it, she scolded herself. Calm down and think rationally.

She knew people crossed racial lines, but she didn't know if she was up to the pressure from both communities. She'd watched her secretary struggle with her mixed marriage to Leo Pine, a Native American.

While Native Americans had made great strides in Northern Michigan, that didn't change the fact that they were another race. Racial prejudice was not her personal feeling, and there were many in her community who thought like her. Still, there was that unspoken feeling in the community that caused Amy to shudder. Sometimes she was ashamed of her race for being so intolerant. But then, she thought, it's not like the other races like the mixing any better. And she loved Cord so much, she didn't want him to suffer. As much as she wanted to wrap her arms around that big strong body, she knew it would bring nothing but trouble.

This relationship could go no further.

Their conversations over the past two years drifted through her like a familiar melody. She thought they had left no rock unturned. They'd discussed work, school, family, and fun. They had seemed so compatible that she wanted to jump headlong into the relationship and forget everyone and everything else. But that would be impossible. It wouldn't work.

Not for her and not for him either. The rock she hadn't turned was the one she felt sitting on her chest.

She slipped a mauve, cotton cardigan sweater over her head and slid her jeans over silk panties. She told herself it was her way of letting Cord see the real person, not the one dressed for the office. Yet, she knew the silk panties and bra had been purchased especially for this trip. Her face flushed as she realized her mother knew it too.

Amy stared at herself in the mirror. Remembering the beautiful black women she had seen this morning, she looked away. She couldn't compete with her city sisters and she knew it. That was another problem. He was city and she was country. If they were going to continue a friendship, just a friendship, she reassured herself, it would have to be honest. Cord would have to see her as she was, not as he had imagined. Still, he was more than she had imagined.

The picture of his thigh hanging inches above her fingers this afternoon as he had leaned to receive the folder sent the blood rushing to the pit of her stomach. She knew she wanted him more than she had ever wanted any man. Somewhere in the back of her mind she hoped all her worries were for nothing. Maybe she could have him. No. Neither of them needed the grief.

She walked slowly, giving herself time to change her mind. Room 548 loomed in front of her eyes. She feathered the raised gold letters with her fingers. I can't do this, she thought. But then, as if her hands had a mind of their own, she tapped lightly on door. She hoped he wouldn't hear. Then she would have an excuse to leave. Placing her fingers on the smooth wood finish, she held her breath. He wasn't coming. He hadn't heard. Well, she'd tried. She lightly shrugged her shoulders.

Slowly Amy backed away from the door, telling herself she had done the right thing, praying he would come and hoping he wouldn't. She hesitated. Should she knock again? No, maybe he didn't want to hear. The door opened with a swish, startling her. "Cord." Her eyes grew wide.

"Who were you expecting? You knocked on my door." He stared at her and then burst out laughing. "You look like you got caught with your fingers in the cookie jar."

She loved his easy rapport, his subtle wit. She offered him a warm smile. "If you are the cookie jar, then I have."

Leaving the door open for safety, she stepped in. Her gaze shifted from his face to travel the full length of his body, appraising him. He had dressed in a light blue, cotton sweater and blue jeans. Blue jeans that could only be filled this nicely by his genes. The sweater enhanced his deep, dusky-bronze complexion.

She thought they must look like a couple who had discussed what they would wear. Apparently Cord thought so too. After scanning her critically, he threw back his head and laughed. He then beamed his approval. "I see we've both dressed for the same occasion. Can you believe it?"

"No," she smiled nervously. Her plan to show him the real person, whoever that was, floated off into the air. Unfortunately, her resolve to maintain only a friendship was going the same way. She watched as he moved fluidly across the floor and carefully filled his pockets with the contents left on the nightstand. His liquid movements as he returned to her were mesmerizing. Heat came from everywhere in her body and settled in the pit of her stomach. She waited for him to speak, to offer direction to her muddled mind.

"I thought we could go for a drive along the Grand Traverse Bay. Maybe a walk on the beach and then grab something to eat before we come back."

A chuckle came from deep inside him as he was obviously amused by her reaction.

His deep voice jarred her enough to allow her to speak. "The evening sounds wonderful," she offered breathlessly. Her gaze drifted from his and wandered around his neat room. "It will give us time to talk." Maybe their race and different backgrounds weren't their only differences. His room looked as if the maid followed him around straightening anything that was out of place.

"Yes, talk is just what we need," he smiled at her. "After all, that's what we've been doing for two years...talking."

Amy thought of those talks as she reached for the knob of the door that she had left standing open. They had joked they were all talked out and were ready for action. She blushed inwardly at her thoughts. She didn't want to stay in the room, she was afraid she would not leave. But she didn't want to go because she feared they would not return. She longed to have his arms around her. She glanced up at him. He seemed to be waiting for her to speak. She drew in a deep controlling breath. "Shall we go?" she asked quietly in a neutral voice.

Cord's hand wrapped around hers on the knob. "Sure," he answered hoarsely. A dual intake of air brought their eyes to an immediate locked gaze. They froze in stunned tableau, neither wanting to move. Neither wanting to stay. Their well thought out resolve was melting. They both knew their lives were about to change forever.

Searing fire shot through her hand. Amy's eyes closed as their bodies pressed together in an embrace that was long overdue. The slamming of the door as their bodies jolted against it overrode all logical thought. Amy hungrily returned the passion, casting all reservation aside as Cord brushed his lips over her face. This wasn't what she had planned. Or was it? Would he think she was committing to a long-term relationship? Was she? The questions faded as the intoxicating drug of passion swept her away.

Amy felt herself being lifted to her tiptoes. Cord buried his mouth in her neck and she felt the gentle sucking that knotted her innards. God, she had died and gone to heaven!

Her lips found the angel kisses on his cheeks. She flicked the indentations with her tongue, tasting the flesh seasoned with spicy aftershave. Gripping his neck with her hand she held him tight against her, suspended in air and on a cloud of desire.

Without asking or releasing his embrace, Cord walked her closer to the bed. His deep voice grew husky. "I've wanted you for so long, I can't believe you are finally where you belong." Reclaiming her lips he crushed her to him.

The kiss sent the pit of her stomach into a wild swirl. Amy didn't speak. She couldn't. Her trembling limbs clung to him in anticipation and her heart was pounding an erratic rhythm in her throat. Running her hands over his sinewy chest, she let her body do her speaking. Her fingers crept down, lifted the sweater and feathered over his bare skin. He moaned. Heat from his chest radiated through her fingers and a delightful shiver of wanting ran through her. She lifted her gaze to peer into his rich chocolate eyes. He returned a look that was as soft as a caress. Hot blood pounded in her brain, leapt from her heart and made her knees tremble. Oh my God, she thought, I wish this moment would go on forever.

Cord held the gaze as he slowly unbuttoned her sweater, his fingers fiery hot. He pushed the soft garment from her shoulders and drew his hands down over her small breasts. His breath caught in his throat; her nipples were erect and begging to be unrestrained.

Tenderly he moved his hands over her soft skin to her back and unhooked the lacy fabric that stood between them. As it fell away, he dropped his hands to her waist, taking in the firm smooth flesh under his fingertips. His tongue flicked at a swollen nipple teasing the taut, petal pink-bud.

Placing his large hand on her soft belly, he expertly released the snap and slid the zipper down, then gently pushed her jeans to the floor. Cord held her back, slowly and seductively sliding his gaze downward. A beautiful woman stood before him in a pair of mauve, silk bikini panties. He was transfixed as if he were photographing her with his eyes, as Amy smoothly stepped out of the jeans at her feet.

Amy pushed her hands under his blue sweater and lifted it over his head. Slipping her hands down to his waist, she released his fastenings. Physical evidence of his passion sprang free. She slipped her fingers into his belt loops and slid the barrier from his hips. A shiver of pure delight ran through her. He was even more stunningly virile than she had imagined. She ran her hands over his tightly muscled hips and spoke in a hoarse whisper, "You are absolutely fabulous."

Cord groaned. He swept Amy into his arms. Her taut nipples brushing over his heated flesh jarred his sensibilities. The sweet smell of her vanilla-musk perfume seemed almost physical. He gently eased her down to the bed and slid his long fingers across her silken belly. Hooking one finger in the waistband, he slipped the soft silk from her body.

He looked upon her face and suddenly felt as if cold water had been thrown on him. He saw his friend. He pushed himself up, but not away, hesitating as if trying to make a decision. "Amy," he spoke with a breathless quiet, "are you sure?"

She saw the heartrending tenderness of his gaze. "How can you ask?" Her harsh uneven breathing made her voice sound strange to her. "Cord," she could hardly lift her voice above a whisper, "I want you. I've never been more sure of anything."

Cord lowered himself to her waiting body and gathered her snugly into his arms. "Me too," his hot breath whispered against her ear.

Her body roared with the meeting of hot flesh against hot flesh, man against woman. His kisses moved from her ear to her waiting parted lips. He circled her lips with his tongue and then slid it between the soft flesh and explored the recesses of her mouth. If she'd had any resolve left, it would have been shattered completely. She was lost as she pulled him closer and caressed the length of his back.

Her consciousness seemed to ebb and then flame more distant than ever.

Cord's hands explored the soft lines of her waist, her
hips, and then moved over her thighs to the pulsing, gold-
en-haired mound. His gentle massage sent currents on a
swift course through her body. Under his spell, she
moaned softly as he worked his magic. His lips traced a
sensuous path to find and suckle her breast. Amy gasped
as she felt the fierce pulsating pull on her breast and the tug
grew stronger on her lower belly. She wasn't sure how
much more she could take. Releasing the nipple, his
tongue explored the rosy peaks of her breast, first one and
then the other.

Amy held on. She grabbed his firm backside and tried
to bring him into her. She was on a ride too wild to let go.
Cord responded. He tucked her curves neatly into his own
contours. Amy felt his hot thick manhood slide between
her thighs. She pressed on his back urgently, imprisoning
him in a stranglehold with her legs, welcoming him into
her body. He entered. The two became one, shutting out
the world and their own cautioning minds.

Wave after wave of ecstasy came as they rose and fell
together. Two bodies, strange to each other an hour ago,
now moved to the beat of the same drummer. Two cautioning minds were set aside for their physical needs.

The room grew dark as they lay in each other's arms.
Their bodies, naked and still moist from their lovemaking,
lay spent in mutual contentment. They couldn't see each

other, which seemed normal for them, but they could feel the intensity of each other's emotions.

Amy rose and leaned over him, her hair falling in both of their faces. Cord grabbed a handful and held it to his nose. He inhaled deeply and then released a long satisfied sigh. She could feel her desire building again. Her telltale nipples hardened and brushed over his chest, sending hot messages. She wanted to yield to the burning sweetness within the core of her body. But before that happened, she wanted to talk. It took all of her strength to push herself away to the edge of the bed. Cord groaned at the separation.

She wrapped a sheet around her and slipped out of bed, her mind tumbling with confused thoughts. Embarrassed by her unbridled passion, she said the first thing that came to mind. "I can't believe we didn't take time to know each other." Her embarrassment grew and she continued, "I've never made love like this before." Then reflecting, she asked, "Did we just have sex or were we making love?"

Cord threw back the sheet he had pulled over himself and jumped out of bed. "If you have to ask, then I guess you had sex. I was making love to the best friend I've ever had."

At the chill in his words she bit her lower lip in dismay. Her question had been sincere, not a blow at his manhood or anything else he might have perceived. She felt a tear escape and roll down her cheek. "Cord..."

A sliver of moonlight filtering through the drapes illuminated him as he pulled on his robe and turned to face her. "I think you should get dressed." He moved toward the door as if to open it and turned to glare at her. As he did, he saw her tears and his face softened. He quickly moved to her and wiped away her tears.

"Are you sorry? I mean, do you wish we had not made love?"

Dropping down beside her, he continued, "If you are, then I wish we'd never met, because I know this means the end of our friendship."

Amy brought her eyes to meet his. "I'm not sorry. I'm thirty-six years old, I have a daughter who will begin college in the fall and I think I've just experienced making love for the first time in my life. I wasn't being sarcastic. If this is making love, then I've only had sex before." Moving away from him, she gathered her pile of clothes and quietly continued. "I feel...I don't know how I feel." She moved toward the bathroom, then turned toward him. "I need a shower. Do you mind?"

Cord shook his head slowly as an easy smile spread from his lips to his eyes. "Only if we do it the environmentally-sound way."

She dropped her clothes on a chair. "Is there any other way?" She couldn't believe the way she was acting. She was either a sex-starved or love-starved woman. Whatever the problem, she would worry about it later. Right now, because the man of her dreams wanted to shower with her, her body shook with gusts of renewed desire.

Cord grabbed the hand she held toward him. This might not last forever but he was going to keep it going for as long as he could. He swept her naked body into his arms. "Now it is time to carry my lover and my friend over the threshold." He stepped into the bathroom.

"If this is the threshold to our relationship we are in serious trouble," she giggled.

One long stride brought them to the shower. He didn't put her down as he reached in and flipped on the water. Her nipples awaited his attention. He traced his hot lips down her smooth neck to a breast. Adjusting her against him, he pulled half of her small breast into his hungry mouth and suckled hard. He'd give her something to remember. Well over a year ago he had captured her mind; now he needed to capture her body. Cord stepped into the shower and set her down without ceasing his feeding frenzy.

As warm water cascaded over them, he pulled her closer, his fingers tracing a heated trail between her thighs. She gasped. "Now!" he heard her beg. He lifted her onto him, wrapping her legs around his waist and plunged into her with a force that jolted her sensibilities. She cried out in luscious pain.

He brought her to the peak again and again, the hot tide of ecstasy raging through them. If he never made love again, he would have this night to hold forever.

They dressed, each lost in their own world of thought. Cord watched her as she covered the small body that had given him so much pleasure. "Amy, let's go get something to eat. We need to talk." His deep, rich voice was softened in the aftermath of lovemaking. He joked, "Unless you want to go to your room so I can call you. We seem to talk easier over the phone."

"Maybe we should. We certainly aren't getting any talking done here." Her cheeks stained red. Her lashes fluttered down. "Do you think we can ever talk to each other as we have for the past two years?"

Cord crossed the room in two long strides to stand beside her. Lifting her chin he answered, "I hope it's better. If you want to forget tonight ever happened, I'll do it for you. Having you on the other end of the phone has made my life bearable." He drew in a deep breath. "If you want to know the truth, I'm 37 years old and I have a son who began college last fall. And I feel like this is the first time I've ever really made love." He pulled her into his arms. "So you see, I do understand."

Her lashes flew up. "What about your wife? Didn't you love her?" He looked as if he were weighing the question. She waited, wondering if she should feel guilty for hoping he never loved her.

"I guess I did. As much as one teenager can love another."

She could relate to that. Sara was the result of a teenage romance that shouldn't have ended in marriage. "I know what you mean." Whenever she thought of Tom, a note of bitterness entered her voice.

Cord pulled her into his arms. "When Geraldine left me, I was crushed. Later, I realized it was my ego that had taken the big blow—not my heart." His voice drifted off.

She was surprised to hear him echo her own thoughts. "I guess it's time to let Geraldine and Tom off the hook. They were young too. They've both made new lives for themselves and we should be happy."

He squeezed her tightly. "You're right. That's what I love the most about you. Your ability to see past the physical and into the soul of others."

She cringed. If he had known her thoughts earlier, he'd suck back in those glowing words. Maybe she could see past the physical, but she wasn't sure others could. And she didn't know if she had the strength to face another problem. Her life had just settled into a nice easy pace. Getting back on the roller coaster with another problem didn't appeal to her. "I think you give me too much credit."

"I hope not."

His eyes searched her face.

Amy didn't want to get into what they were both avoiding. Yet tiptoeing around the subject wouldn't be fair to either of them. She had just made love to the man she adored, yet she didn't see how she could have a permanent relationship. "Cord, I..."

"Let's talk later. I'm starving. That was one hell of a workout and I need nourishment," he interrupted as he pulled the door open.

Amy hesitated and then smiled at her best friend. "You know I'm always easier to talk to after I eat. That's why you called after breakfast, lunch or dinner."

"I worked at learning your secrets." His mouth was smiling but his words were colored in neutral shades.

■ ■ ■

The Trillium Restaurant was filled to capacity. Amy and Cord looked at each other, then at the other guests. They laughed and got back onto the elevator. Their casual attire didn't fit. Cord looked at her apologetically. "We could change and return."

Amy shook her head. "I'm glad. It's not private enough for us."

His eyebrows shot up questioningly. "Should we go back to the room?" His eyes grew openly amused.

She colored fiercely. "I mean, after what we've been through we need real privacy."

"And?"

"Stop it. You know what I mean. We need to talk." Playfully she punched his arm.

Cord grabbed his arm and feigned pain. "Oh, oh," he moaned. "I think I need to lie down." His mouth quirked with humor. "Will you help me return to my room?"

She flipped her still wet–from-the-shower French braid over her shoulder and placed her hands on her hips. "If you are in that much pain, I'll call 911." Her lips trembled with the need to smile.

He glanced at the elevator numbers as they made their descent. When they passed the fifth floor he moaned again. "I don't think an EMT can give me what I need."

She smiled wickedly. "After we eat, I'll be the only nurse you need."

Cord slid his arm around her waist as they exited the elevator. "I think you are just what the doctor ordered."

"And is the doctor's name Cordelle McCune?" She glanced up at him as he led her through the lobby and they stepped out into the warm spring night. Her heart swelled with a feeling she had thought long since dead. She was in love. Her vow not to become involved had been shattered by love. And love conquers all, she thought. At least she hoped and prayed it did.

His laugh was triumphant. "It is indeed and his nurse is Amelia Summers." He looked her over seductively. "After we eat I think we should return to the emergency room for a complete work-up." Amy punched him again as they walked from the hotel to the beach. He pulled her to him. "This is no way to start a relationship. I can't have my lady beating me."

"Emm." Amy leaned her head against his chest as he embraced her tighter. His lady, she thought. It's true I am his and he is mine. An uneasy feeling crept in, a crazy mixture of hope and fear. She hoped Sara and her mother would be happy for her and feared they wouldn't. And there was still the huge matter of his family.

They stopped and Amy slid off her shoes. Wisps of her deep brown hair that had escaped the French braid were softly lifted by the warm breeze and caressed her face. She pressed her toes into the cool sand and glanced back to see her footprints. Cord walked beside her, taking in every move she made in case she decided to make this their last date.

At last, unable to endure the silence between them, he stepped in front of her and placed his hands on her shoulders. "Amy, can you share with me what you're thinking?" He watched as she lifted her face. The bright moonlight struck silver in her eyes.

"Yes, but I don't think you will like it."

"Why don't you let me be the judge of that?"

"I think we should continue our relationship."

Cord couldn't believe what he was hearing. He whirled her around. "Why wouldn't I like it? That's what I've been waiting to hear." He lightly brushed a kiss on her forehead. "I know this is a little premature but I really want to have a more permanent relationship with you. One that will last a long time."

"Whoa," she giggled. "Let's take one step at a time. It'll still be long distance for a while. Steve has been transferred to another office on temporary assignment, so I'll be doing both our jobs." She stood on her tiptoes and pressed her lips against his. Dropping back down, she added, "But it will happen."

Cord pulled her back into his arms so she couldn't see his face. He would have to hand off the assignment when he returned to Lansing. She was right. She could do both jobs better than either Cord or Steve. She'd been there when the office was established. He knew one of her greatest frustrations was being overlooked for the position when it opened. He held her back and gazed into eyes filled with love. "I know it will. I can't wait."

Music floated through the air from a nearby cafe. Cord held her and rocked her to the rhythm. He wasn't going to let a little thing like a job come between them. They would have enough problems without that. "I'm starving. The prospect of spending a lot of time with you in person is making me hungry." He squeezed her tightly. "If this afternoon is any indication, I'll need all of the strength I can get."

"For a while I think we should keep it between you and me." She stopped and stared into his eyes. "I mean I don't think your family will be any happier than mine."

"Amy, I want to shout it from the house tops. I can deal with my family." His parents wouldn't be happy but they would try to understand. Wouldn't they? His sister Leah would be the biggest hurdle. She hated interracial relationships and she would do everything in her power to push Amy away.

Three

Amy awoke the next morning curled next to Cord's body. As she gazed into his sleeping face, warmth flooded her. They had spent the night making love. The turbulence of his passion still swirled around her, causing thrilling shivers to travel through her body. Nothing separated them. Her fingers ached to feather over him but she needed to think. Gently she pulled and tucked the sheet between their bodies. Cord rolled toward her but didn't wake.

His nearness brought a tremor inside her, heating her thighs and groin. Don't, she told herself. Look away. Dragging her gaze from his perfect body she stared at the spring rain washing the window.

The light of day always made things look different. In her mind she tossed their relationship back and forth, weighing all of the potential problems against the potential rewards of an interracial relationship. A tear pushed its way to the brim of her lower lid. She knew she couldn't have him; not in Northern Michigan and not with her mother's ill health. Amy's heart ached.

His arm slid around her, spooning her body next to his heated, strong bulk. "How's my lady this morning?" His voice was sleepy but his hands were fully awake, exploring her breasts, her stomach. He buried his face in her hair. "I love the way you smell. Mmmm, so fresh." He paused, rolling her nipple between his finger and thumb.

"When I leave, I want to take that scent with me." His hand seared a path down her soft stomach and onto her thigh.

At his light and painfully teasing touch, her stomach automatically drew in. Her breast ached to have his lips there once again. She needed to stop him. To tell him she knew they weren't good for each other. She tried staring at the window once more. She wanted to tell him they would be happier apart—but she couldn't. Not yet. Just a few more minutes of bliss, she promised herself, rolling into his waiting arms. Her body melted against his and the world was filled with only them.

His fingers burned into her thigh as they traced a path to her moist triangle. She shivered. His gentle massage cast away any thoughts of turning back. "It's a good thing we live so far apart," she murmured, "we'd never get out of bed."

"Mmm..." His mouth covered hers, tasting her.

"Emm." Amy purred sensually.

Cord outlined the tips of her aroused nipples with his fingers. "Do you want to go to the morning session?"

Amy didn't answer, her thoughts too fragmented as his hands and lips continued their hungry search. Passion pounded the blood through her heart, chest and head. She couldn't think rationally.

His fingers traced her mouth, outlining her lips. "I love you," he whispered.

Her body screamed out for more. "I love you too. More than you will ever know."

Cord held her back and stared into her eyes. "I think I know," he whispered hoarsely as he captured her mouth claiming the gift he had been given.

Her short-circuited senses whirled. Tenderly he moved his lips to her swollen sensitive nipples. Lovemaking had left them sore. Amy could feel them swelling even more as his tongue flicked at them. Pain shot through her as he suckled first one and then the other. He pulled back as she jerked. "Are you OK?" His gentle voice caressed her.

She held his face with both hands and led his mouth back to her breast. It hurt but she wanted to feed his insatiable hunger and drench his unquenchable thirst. She had to give him everything she could to make it last forever. She held him closely, running her fingers over the firm ripples of his back. Amy had never felt more in love. She wanted him with all of her being. Cord covered her with kisses, whispering his love for each part of her body. Instinctively her body arched toward him. She moaned. "Cord, I need you." Her impatience grew to explosive proportions. "Cord—"

He crushed her body with his. She whimpered as his full manhood pushed between her thighs and into her screaming for satiation body. She wrapped her legs around him, forcing a deeper entry. A gasp escaped her lips. He was so deeply embedded in her that she knew they had become one. In exquisite harmony, they soared higher and higher until the peak of delight was reached. Amy couldn't restrain her outcry of passion. Love flowed through her like a river of sweet honey.

Cord shuddered like a train screeching to a stop and then dropped onto her, spent but still joined. Her breath came in long pulls. Rolling to one side and cradling her, he spoke, his hoarse voice filled with joy, "This is the way we will always be."

Amy was satiated but ashamed. She knew she should have told him her decision, but she had wanted him just one last time. Cord deserved more. God, what a mess. Again tears came.

Cord held her back. "Hey, was it that bad?" He was teasing but the question was real in his gaze. Brushing a tear away, he asked, "What is it?"

She pressed a smile to her lips and gazed into the beautiful dark brown eyes. "Nothing," she lied. "I was just thinking we have to part today."

Cord gently covered her body with his. "Not for long." He nuzzled her neck. "We'll be together soon."

His gentle reassurance poured over her. She was sure what she had to tell him was the best thing for both of them. Still, it didn't make it any easier with their bodies singing the same song. This is so right, she thought. But so wrong. She cringed thinking of how the "good ol' boys" would react. They might not verbalize it, but the animosity would be there. Amy shivered involuntarily. She couldn't destroy the best friend she'd ever had.

The only honest thing to do was to speak now before it was too late. Amy turned her face in his direction, and as if drawn by a magnet, her parted lips moved over his cheek and sought the heat of his mouth. She was lost in burning flesh.

"We are going to miss the morning session," Cord whispered hoarsely, his lips still on hers.

She smiled at him. "I've never felt so whole."

"Are you always going to cry when you feel good?"

She shook her head. Needing an out, she said the first thing that came to mind. "We'd better try to make the conference lunch."

"Whoa, that is one of the quickest turnarounds I've ever heard."

Amy felt a lump growing in her throat. She had to get control of herself so that she sounded rational when she told him. "It's just that..."

She choked back a sob.

He pulled her into his arms. "What?"

She let the tears flow. She felt his muscles tightening and knew he awaited an explanation. "I want us to be friends but..." she couldn't finish.

He cautiously pushed her to arm's length. "But what? What are you trying to say?" His commanding voice shook her.

Amy gathered the sheet around her and slid from the bed. "I am trying to say that I want us to be friends. Well, more than friends. Maybe we could meet occasionally, but with no commitments." She held her breath and steeled herself for his response.

Cord's eyebrows raised over narrowed eyes. "Are you telling me you want the same friendship we've had with an occasional sexual rendezvous?"

She shivered under his intense gaze. Her face grew hot. "Yes, I guess that is what I am saying." Her eyelids slid down to stave off his recriminating glare.

He grabbed his robe and quickly wrapped it around himself. Abruptly planting himself in front of her, his fist clenched and unclenched at his sides. "I told you I would forget all of this happened but I didn't say I would be your personal stud service." Amy looked away. He turned her face back. "What's the problem here? Are you afraid to tell your family you've got a Look Who's Coming to Dinner? situation in your life?"

She gasped. He'd struck a nerve and made her admit the truth to herself. And that truth was like eating the sand from the beach they had walked on. She saw the pain and anger in his face, and knew she was responsible for both. She wanted to pull him into her arms yet she knew it was too late.

Moving away from his reproachful glare and the heat of his anger, she tried to explain. "We have other people in our lives to consider. My mother is just returning to normal after her stroke. You know that."

Cord glowered at her. As if daring her to come up with something better.

Amy gave a little shiver and continued. "You also know that she lost Dad a year ago. And even though I don't think theirs was a marriage made in heaven, she misses him." She began pacing, gathering the sheet more tightly around herself. She stopped and glared back at him. "You also know she has never forgiven me for divorcing Tom, so how am I supposed to tell her about you?" She stopped for a quick breath and then added weakly, "And what about our children?"

Cord watched her struggle with the prejudice he had fought all his life. This more than anything prompted him to partially agree. "You are right, of course. My parents won't be happy. Who knows what our children would think? And your mother doesn't need any more trouble." Moving to her, he continued in a voice filled with despair, "But when do we stop worrying about others and begin to live our lives the way we want?"

Amy shook her head. "I don't think either of us can be that selfish. Maybe in a few years we −"

"Don't say it, Amy. I'm not willing to wait. Either we brave the storm, or we end what might have been, right here and now." Softening his voice he continued, "We couldn't possibly have a casual relationship, not after this." He glanced toward the bed and then back at her. She didn't respond so he lifted her chin with his finger and continued, "We both know that."

Amy shook her head and bit her quivering lower lip.

Cord stared into her misty silver-green eyes. "If the color of my skin is the only thing that stands between us, then I'll have to accept that. Because I can't change that, and I wouldn't if I could."

Amy ran her fingers over the smooth texture of his face. "Even before I knew who you were, yesterday, I admired the deep bronze of your skin." She let her hands drop to his chest and then returned her gaze to stormy eyes. "The color of your skin is no more a barrier to our relationship than the color of mine. Are you willing to take me to your parents and say, 'Look Who's Coming to Dinner?' She sighed heavily and forged on, "I know you from our conversations. I know how much your parents mean to you. Are you willing to jeopardize your relationship with them?"

He winced as if she had slapped him but he didn't answer.

"I don't think so." Amy cringed a little under his intense glare but she wasn't going to back off. "You tell me what we should do."

Cord took her hands from his chest and held them, decisiveness playing in his eyes. "I think we should lead our lives as it pleases us." He dropped her hands and pushed his fingers into his rich ebony hair. "When I think of how close we've been for the past two years and the last couple of days..." He dropped into the chair at the desk. "I'm willing to fight for it. I know we have a tough battle, but we aren't kids anymore and we only go around once."

Amy stared at his face, his jaw set in determination, his eyes filled with hope. How could she answer him? He was right, they should live for themselves but she wasn't sure she could do that. "I'm not sure I am." Her words seemed final and cold. When he didn't speak she added,

"Cord...Cord, I am sorry that I even considered asking you...you know...to be with me occasionally." Her voice filled with shame and regret as she added, "As your friend, I know it was an insult and I hope you will forgive me."

"Don't worry about it." He stood and walked to her, flashing a full dimpled smile while he finished his thought, "I've had a lot worse propositions and many worse insults." He brushed her hair from her cheek.

Amy forced her face to lift in a smile, but her heart was breaking. She'd done it. She'd given up her best friend—and her lover. His light touch added to her grief. She wanted to take the fingers that moved her hair and hold them, kiss them, but instead she slowly gathered her clothes and slid into the bathroom.

When she was dressed, she inhaled deeply before opening the door. She was prepared to face her decision. Still, she wanted to be with him for a few more minutes. Amy opened the door slowly and looked to where she had left him standing, as if he wouldn't have moved. Her heart sank. His suitcase was by the door but he had left. She knew he was waiting for her to leave.

Tears trickled down her cheek as she closed the door behind her and returned to her room.

Quickly showering, she threw her belongings into her suitcases. She couldn't face him, or any of the other people at the conference. In her heart she felt she was right. Still, being right didn't ease the pain.

She stood in the doorway of the hotel waiting for the rain to subside. Of course her umbrella was in the car trunk. Re-entering the lobby meant she might run into Cord. Amy cursed her inefficiency and pushed the door open with a determination that wasn't heartfelt. She ran through the rain not really feeling droplets that washed her face.

By the time she got her trunk open she was drenched and her hair hung in dripping ringlets over her face. She ducked under the trunk for protection as she arranged her luggage. Pushing her makeup case to the back, she broke a fingernail. "Damn it," she cursed. "What else could go wrong?"

"I don't know. You tell me." Cord reached in and adjusted her luggage to fit in the small trunk.

Amy whirled around and stared at the man she loved. The man whose friendship meant the world to her. The man she couldn't have. Pain of separation burst through her. "Cord, I thought you had gone. I mean..." She slammed the trunk, trying to conquer her involuntary reactions to that gentle, loving look of his. "Who knows what I mean? I certainly don't." She fought to hold back a fresh flood of tears.

He reached out to push her hair back and used his thumb to erase an errant tear. "Baby, you have to know I understand. I've dealt with prejudice all my life. And if I wasn't so selfish I wouldn't have asked you to jump into the struggle."

Amy hung her head. His dark eyes showed the tortured dullness of despair. And she was responsible for that look. Her ears rang with his rich voice calling her baby. She loved the way it sounded. It made her feel so loved. How could she treat this marvelous human being this way?

God, she wanted to throw her arms around his neck and hold him forever and say to hell with everyone else. A war of emotions raged within her. Pulling on her inner resources, she lifted her gaze to his. "Don't do this." She wasn't going to let him take the blame and make her feel worse. "We both know it's my cowardice that is keeping us apart."

Cord slid his arm around her shoulder and walked her to the car door. "I do understand. But I believe that some-day you will see we belong together. As a couple we would be strong enough to fight back the lions. That is something you will come to terms with."

Amy shivered, but not with cold. She wondered if she would ever feel like this again. Could any man make her feel like a whole woman again? She doubted it. Maybe she was destined to live alone. "I hope you're right but..." Her willpower was fading. Amy drew a deep breath and forbade herself to tremble. She leaned against the door for balance.

He bent down to her, brushing a kiss over her mouth. "I'll always love you."

A moan crept from deep in Amy's soul. "Maybe," she paused and then finished in sinking tones, "but I know a man like you won't stay alone for long."

"You're probably right."

She didn't want him to agree with her. Selfishly she wanted him to protest and say he would wait...or something equally wonderful. She dropped her lashes quickly to hide her hurt.

Cord lifted her chin with his finger. "We can't have it both ways, baby. It's not realistic."

His spicy cologne permeated her brain, imprinting him forever. Tentatively she placed her hands on his firm chest. This simple gesture, which was meant to separate them, sent shockwaves on a fast course to her innards. She knew she had chosen the right track. But still...no, she told herself firmly.

He smiled down at her. "It's not easy for either of us. Call me when you have had time to think."

Think? She did very little else but think. But with his body inches from hers it was impossible to think. She had to leave, but she wanted it to be on a friendly note. Brushing her fingers over his face she said the first thing that came to her mind. "You do more for me than a box of chocolates." She giggled nervously as her heart shattered into pieces and fell at his feet.

"Take another look." His grin grew wider. "This is probably the best box of fine chocolates you will ever get your lips on."

Amy swallowed hard as her gaze searched his. She wanted nothing more than to run her lips all over him. Still, she had others to consider. He was right, he was the finest, but she had made her decision. She gently pushed on his chest. "This isn't going to accomplish anything."

Cord leaned back and held her gaze. "It's your call. Don't wait too long."

She opened the car door and slid in. Glancing up at him, she smiled, "Thank you." At least he was giving her room. She averted her gaze from his loving face. "I have a report due next week. I'll call."

He closed the door and leaned in through the window. "You know my home number if you have anything of a personal nature to report." He brushed her hair back from her forehead and tapped her nose with his finger. "You are wrong. We should be together."

Amy waited until he got into his Navigator and then followed him out of the parking lot. She pulled beside him and waved. He returned the wave, flashing her an ear-to-ear grin displaying his angel kisses. Damn it, she thought. How will I ever get him out of my mind? Their cars pulled out at the same time; he went south and she went north.

■ ■ ■

Cord debated with himself. Should he assume the position as her supervisor or find another way to see her? He knew it wasn't over. This was only a delay. She needed time to think. When she'd had sufficient time she would realize they were not only friends but lovers, friends and lovers who should be lifetime mates. He was counting on the strong physical and mental pull to bring her back into his arms.

If he took the temporary position, she would be angry that he had. After all, he knew how much it meant to her. He wasn't quite sure why the department wasn't letting her do it. She was certainly qualified. It was the department's practice to fill in for agency directors as an internal control measure or when there were suspected problems. However, as far as he knew, this agency was running well. So, he told himself, it had to be just a random check. Still, he didn't have to go personally. Maybe he should send one of his assistants. That's what he would do. Then she wouldn't be angry with him.

■ ■ ■

Cord dragged himself to the office on the following Monday. He had spent the weekend willing the phone to ring. And cursing himself for accepting her feeble excuses. Times had changed. Not completely, no, far from it. Yet there had been enough changes so they could have a relationship. How far behind was Sault Ste. Marie or as Amy would call it, 'the Soo'? It couldn't be that much different. It was only four hundred miles north of Lansing.

He tapped on Mark's desk as he went for coffee. "When I return, come on in. I have an assignment for you." Mark was more than qualified to do the job. He was also married and not overly handsome. But his qualification was getting him the assignment, Cord reassured himself. Yet he knew the biggest reason was his marital status and his looks.

After handing the assignment off to Mark, he felt better. He didn't want Amy to think he was pushing himself on her. "Although that's what I'd like to do," he told himself because he couldn't tell anyone else. Thoughts of her nude body played in his mind. He could see the small breasts that had given him so much pleasure. Somehow he would be with her again. But never as her occasional lover.

He settled back in his office chair. He had never told Amy that he had become the department head. If he had, she would be calling someone else. He'd kept her account without explaining it to anyone. He'd also never told her he owned a string of accounting firms. Before the conference he'd promised himself as soon as they met he would quit this position and manage his business full time, but now to keep the contact with her he would have to stay in his position with the state. He stared at the phone. Damn it. This can't go on. I feel like a teenager whose zipper is running his brain. His head jerked up as he heard a knock on his door.

He glanced up as a tall blond man entered with Mark. Cord stood, recognizing him as the head of treasury investigations. "Bob." He held out his hand glancing from one to the other. "What's up?"

Bob took a seat in front of Cord's desk. "I called Mark to ask when you leave for the Upper Peninsula and he told me you had passed it to him."

Cord nodded. "The conference put me behind here and in my business. Mark is quite capable of doing the accountability audit and of handling the job until the director returns."

Bob glanced at Mark and then back at Cord. "I think we need to talk."

Mark cleared his throat. "I've got a lot to do. If you need me, I'll be at my desk."

Cord watched as the door closed behind his assistant and then he turned his attention to the other man. "What is it?"

"It's not just a matter of covering until the agency's director returns. Our investigator has uncovered some irregularities in the finances." He handed Cord a folder. We need you to go on the inside and either prove or disprove what we suspect."

Cord could feel the frown lines crease his forehead. But he responded as if it were just another program. "And that is?"

"Embezzlement."

He felt as if a mountain were crushing him as he realized the implication pointed in Amy's direction too. "Do you have a lead?"

Bob shook his head. "It has to be one of two people. The director or the financial manager."

Cord pulled in a deep breath. He had to go. He couldn't let someone else investigate Amy. He was sure she was innocent. And he wasn't going to take any chances. He mulled the scenario over in his head. No, not Amy.

"Cord?"

He looked up when his thoughts were interrupted. "Yes, I'll handle this personally." He picked up the file folder and tapped it on the desk. "I'll leave in a couple of days." He stood and stuck out his hand. "I'll call you with periodic reports."

Bob shook Cord's hand. "Thanks. The sooner the better. We'll catch that weasel." He shuffled toward the door. "Let me hear from you soon."

Cord stood and nodded. "Sure. No problem."

No problem, he thought. My God. One of the suspects is the woman I love. He dropped back in his desk chair. "Oh, Amy what's been going on?" he whispered.

Automatically he reached for the phone. He needed to discuss the problem with someone. Then he withdrew his hand. For the first time in two years he didn't have anyone to talk to. He pulled all of the files from his desk and put them in the out basket. Shoving the file for Amy's office into his briefcase, he left the office. He was on his way to her. Whether she liked it or not.

Four

Amy plunked in her office chair and slowly swiveled toward the window. "Another Monday," she sighed. It had rained the rest of the weekend, and now the sun was rushing to dry the dripping leaves. If only she could dry her tears that easily. She had let herself into the office in the wee hours of the morning, sleep being impossible.

The staff would want to know all about the conference and she didn't want to think about it, much less talk about it. The whole situation was hopeless. She wouldn't be able to work until she had some kind of resolution with Cord. She needed her friend, now more than ever.

Her hand rested on the phone. Push memory one, she commanded herself, but she couldn't. How could she let him know how sorry she was for being such a coward. Even if she let him know, it wouldn't change a thing. The phone rang under her hand, vibrating her fingers. Her heart pounded heavily. It was Cord. She just knew it.

Sitting upright, she grasped the phone anxiously. "Hello." Her voice came in a breathless whisper.

"Amy?"

"Yes." Her heart sank and she slumped in her chair. "Jeff, how are you?"

"I was great until you sounded so disappointed. Have I called at a bad time?"

"I'm sorry. It's Monday and I'm kind of busy." She drew in a deep breath. "So. What can I do for you?" God, I wish this was Cord. She tried to suppress her thoughts but it was hopeless.

Jeff laughed. "I knew you would forget. That's why I called to remind you."

Amy's mind raced. Remind her of what? "I'm sorry. Does it have something to do with the DARE Ball?"

"No. Well, in a way. That aside, I do want to thank you for that again. It was a great evening, and you saved me from being the only cop without a date."

"I'm sure you could have gotten a date. I was just convenient."

"No. You're wrong. Being a detective has its drawbacks. Especially when it comes to dating."

She could hear his cocksure attitude in his voice. His bragging irked her. Jeff was a nice enough guy but he sure wasn't Cord. "So what is it I forgot?"

"Tonight—Lionel Richie—Dream Maker's Theater—remember? You said you loved him." Jeff's laughter roared through the phone.

She leaned her head in her hands and her elbows on the desk. Not tonight. A silent groan traveled her body. "I'd forgotten," she offered weakly. She did love Lionel Richie, but she didn't want to be with Jeff. Somehow it seemed like something she should do with Cord, but then everything seemed like that.

He laughed again. "No problem. I have the tickets and I'll pick you up around seven. Thought we'd go to the

Dream Catcher's Restaurant for dinner first. Maybe throw a few quarters in the slots."

The last thing she wanted to do was go to Kewadin. The noise of the casino could only make her head worse. But she saw no way out. At the ball, she had told him it sounded like fun, but she didn't mean for them, she meant for him or her with someone else. She felt a twinge of guilt. She wasn't ready to move on. All she wanted to do was go home and curl up in a ball. Yet, if she was going move on, then she might as well get on with it.

Amy drew in a deep breath. She released the air slowly and forced herself to answer. "Sounds fine. See you this evening."

"Great," she heard him say as she lowered the receiver to its base.

She pressed her forehead into her hands. Why hadn't she told him she had a headache. Or anything that would have gotten her out of the date. "Damn it," she cursed. Now she felt guilty. How would she explain this to Cord? She didn't have to, she remembered. They didn't have a relationship, thanks to her. She massaged her temples. I have to get out of here, she thought.

Amy grabbed the bottom desk drawer and tugged it open. She pulled her purse out and then spotted the heart-shaped box of chocolates Cord had sent her for Valentine's Day. She tenderly placed the box on her desktop and opened it. There was one piece left.

Slowly she removed the wrapping and placed it on her tongue. Her eyes drifted closed as she thought of the sender. Tall, dark, handsome, intelligent, sensitive, loving...and of a different race. He was a beautiful specimen of that race. And she wanted him. Her tongue curled around the silky chocolate, savoring its full richness. She smiled slightly to herself. She had been right, he was better than a box of chocolates.

Heat traveled through her as she let her mind slip back into bed with Cord. His firm body wrapped around hers was more than delicious, it was out of this world. Her fingers touched the box. Her smile grew. He was right; he was probably the best box of fine chocolates she would ever get her lips on. She studied the box. Like her it was empty. Maybe she could send a short message to Cord. After all, they had been friends for a long time, she rationalized.

Amy picked up a bright pink sticky note, sprayed a mist of her perfume on it, and placed it in the box. Then she wrote, "This is how my life will be without you." Lovingly she shoved the box in a large manila envelope and wrote his home address on it.

Gathering her purse and jacket, she stopped at Shelley's desk. "Shell, I have one heck of a headache, I'm going home." She handed her assistant the package. "Would you mail this for me?"

Shelley read the address. "This isn't his office address."

"I know." Amy didn't offer an explanation. "I'll see you in the morning." She left before Shelley could pin her down about anything.

Amy watched as Jeff's long lean body made quick strides around the car to open her door. His sandy brown hair was neatly combed and stayed in place even with the light wind. Somehow, she thought, I attract men who are neat. Opposites attract, but I'm not attracted to him. She held out her hand and smiled. I'll be so glad when this evening is over.

"You look beautiful tonight." He possessively slipped his arm around her shoulder.

"Thank you." She cringed inside but couldn't think of a nice way to push his arm away. After Cord's arms she didn't want anyone else's to be there.

Jeff led her to the glass double doors of the Kewadin Casino complex. When he pulled the door open she was assailed by the noises of another world. The quiet of the Soo seemed to vanish. She marveled at the Las Vegas-like atmosphere that the Chippewa Tribe had created in just a few short years.

"It's certainly different than when we were kids." She felt the need to say something, anything.

"Ya." His eyes traveled over the massive complex. "But they're Indians, they'll figure out a way to destroy it." Jeff's face twisted in disdain.

Amy stared up at him. "I think we've done more to destroy things than the Native Americans. I guess if they want to destroy something, then it's their turn." She was seething inside to think he was so bigoted. She'd never noticed that side of him. Or maybe before Cord it hadn't mattered.

Jeff dropped his arm and stared down at her. "I didn't know you were such an Indian lover."

She bit her tongue. After tonight she wouldn't go anywhere with this idiot again. "It doesn't matter. Come on. If we don't hurry we'll miss dinner and I'm starved."

He smiled at her and took her hand. He led her through the crowds to the restaurant. Once seated he took her hand. "I'm sorry. I didn't mean those things. It's just the cop in me. We have to deal with the tribe when they are off the reservation and it isn't pretty."

Amy slipped her hand from under his long fingers and picked up the menu. Had he always been like this? Was she just being sensitive? What was going on? He wasn't the same person she'd known all of her life. Or was he? In her heart she knew the change was hers. But she couldn't face that right now. "I think I'll have the buffet." She closed the menu and smiled.

"Amy," he took her hand again, "I need to tell you something."

She tried to retrieve her hand but he held tight. This wasn't right. Maybe she couldn't have Cord but she didn't want anyone else either. She cleared her throat. "I'm starved. Let's get in the buffet line." She smiled, trying to turn aside whatever he had in mind.

"Not so quick. I've wanted the opportunity to say this for a long time and I'm going to."

She felt the blood drain from her face as his grip tightened. "Jeff, my hand."

He loosened his grip but held on. "Why do you think I accepted the position here?"

She shrugged her shoulders. "So you could come home?"

"Partly, but most of all because of you."

Amy held her breath. Mentally the pieces began to fall together. He had been attentive but she had thought it was because of their history as friends. She gave a silent groan. "I...don't understand."

His gray eyes danced. "I think you do. Come on, Amy. If it hadn't been for that mistake you made with Tom—we would have been together."

Her eyelids shuttered down. She couldn't look at him. He must be nuts. She'd never known he existed, except as a friend. The more she thought about what he said, the angrier she grew. She lifted her gaze to his and glared at him. "The mistake you speak of has a name. Sara."

He winced as if she had hit him. "I didn't mean that. You know what I mean. I'm in love with you and I want us to be together."

She felt like a trapped animal. How could she respond? She inhaled deeply. Someone was wearing Cord's cologne. Her heart pounded its reaction to the aroma.

She glanced up as a shadow fell on their table, fully expecting to see the waiter. What she saw stopped her cold. "Cord!" She jerked her hand from Jeff's. Her mind whirled. She was sure she must be hallucinating. His tan sports jacket covered a white henley which was tucked neatly into his jeans. Was she dreaming? If she was it would soon be a nightmare. God, no. It was real and in his eyes she saw a storm.

"Amy, it's good to see you."

His mellow voice masked the anger she saw. She wanted to explain but the scene he had come upon was all too obvious. She swallowed to remove the knot in her throat. "What are you doing here? I mean..."

"Of course you didn't know. I'm on assignment here." He glanced from Jeff to Amy.

Her face grew hot and she knew it was crimson. "Cord McCune, this is Jeff Delaney. Jeff is a detective at the local state police post." She drew her gaze from Cord to Jeff. "Cord is an associate." Cord's face twitched when she called him an associate. Why hadn't she introduced him as her friend? She finished weakly, "He works in the main office in Lansing."

The two men shook hands and exchanged a few jokes about working for the government. Amy watched as the surreal picture unfolded. Her heart ached for her best friend and for herself. She didn't want Cord to think this was what it looked like. Still if he did, then it would confirm they weren't meant for each other. She was torn. But how could she do this to the man she loved? Oh God, help me. She glanced up to find both men staring at her. She smiled unconvincingly.

"Cord here is going to the Lionel Richie concert too. I told him how you loved the singer."

She had missed their conversation. Cord stared at her, his eyebrows raised in a question. Amy averted her gaze.

She knew him, knew what he was thinking. Speak, she commanded herself. Maybe she could untangle this when Cord left their table. "Yes. I do love Lionel Richie. And if we don't eat soon we'll miss the concert." To her relief she sounded normal.

Jeff laughed and turned to Cord. "She's been starving since we walked in here."

Cord's face broke into a full dimpled grin that didn't take the storm from his eyes. "I certainly know what it's like to be hungry. I just spent a couple of days in a feeding frenzy. Sometimes you can't get enough and then when it's too late, you realized you've overeaten." His gaze roved over Amy. "I'll leave so you can eat. I have to finish checking into my room before the concert."

Jeff laughed as if he knew exactly what Cord was talking about.

Amy knew better. Her ears burned and her skin heated under Cord's gaze. She could feel the arousal of her nipples as she thought of his voracious hunger. She needed to say something. But what?

Jeff rose and pulled Amy with him. "We have to get in the buffet line." He turned to Cord. "Say, there's no sense of you going to the concert by yourself. Why don't you meet us by the doors in an hour?"

Amy tried to wriggle her hand free but she might as well have been handcuffed. She felt rather than saw Cord's questioning look. What was Jeff doing inviting him to join them? What a mess! Here she was spending the evening with a man she would love to be in bed with, and one who thought they were an item for the wedding announcement page. She couldn't be with Cord through the whole concert and not touch him. Why did Jeff have to ask him?

Cord showed no emotion, speaking in even tones, "Well, if it's okay with Amy." He glanced at their hands. "I mean, I wouldn't want to horn in on a romantic evening." His laugh sounded innocent enough, but she knew what he meant.

Jeff laughed. "No. Amy and I have the rest of our lives to be together. Meet us at the concert hall."

Amy felt herself shrinking. She managed to speak but she didn't know how. "There's no sense of you being alone." Then she added, "Of course you probably have someone with you."

Cord had half-turned to leave when she spoke. His back now turned to Jeff, he openly stared at Amy. "No. I'm just coming off a two-year relationship. She broke it off just recently. I thought we would get back together but I'm beginning to see the futility in that."

Jeff hit him on the shoulder. "Bad luck, man. Join us and we'll try to keep your mind off her."

Amy cringed under Cord's scrutiny. She knew she was the two-year relationship. And now, thanks to Jeff, Cord thought she went home and didn't give him another thought. She bit her lower lip as Cord turned back to Jeff. Tears were threatening but she couldn't let either of them know. If she got through this evening, she would rectify some of the damage done to the friendship between herself and Cord.

She dared a glance from Jeff to Cord. They were talking as if they were old friends. Amy could hardly believe what was playing out before her eyes. This was like a nightmare. Except she was wide awake and feeling all of the pain.

Cord turned his back with little more than a cursory, "See you later." Amy's heart pounded wildly in her chest. I'm so sorry, she thought. She wanted to run after him but her feet felt as if they were glued to the floor. Somehow she would make it up to him.

She turned to Jeff. "Why on earth did you invite him to sit with us?"

Jeff shrugged his shoulders. "What harm is there?" His gaze roved over her body. "It's not like we could do anything at the concert." He pulled her toward the buffet line. Leaning down to whisper to her, he added, "Besides, it looks good for a detective to be seen with other races. It makes me look — tolerant. Who knows? Someday I might want to be the post commander."

Amy recoiled at his suggestive gaze. And then shuddered to think this man could be a trusted public servant and yet be such a bigot. Still, was she any better? The only reason she wasn't with Cord, right now, was his race. She stared at Jeff. How could I be like him? I don't feel the way he does. But my actions spell bigot, don't they? Oh, God, did Cord see her as she saw Jeff?

Cord walked through the casino towards the escalator to his room. He couldn't imagine how he had been so fooled. Something must be wrong with him for women to reject him so easily. Well, it wouldn't happen again. He would finish the assignment here and then go home. The last thing he needed was a woman, regardless of color. Geraldine and Amy, the two loves of his life. And they both turned from him.

He stopped in the Bawatan Art Gallery, staring at the picture of a young Native American woman in native dress. She held her newborn child to the starry sky. "If it's a boy he'll need more than a spirit's blessing," he muttered to himself.

His mind whirled with a myriad of emotions. He hadn't expected to see Amy out for the evening. She looked so damned good, from her hair, which she had pulled to the top of her head, to her high heels, which accentuated her long legs. He hadn't imagined her in a black form-fitting dress and now he didn't have to. Her bare shoulders, slightly covered by a wrap, were an invitation for any man to kiss. He recoiled, thinking the smiling idiot she was with would be the one to do it. He pulled his gaze from the painting that he wasn't seeing and glanced around.

"Hey baby. Why's a handsome man like yourself alone?"

He turned to a beautiful, coffee-laced-with-cream charmer. Her ebony hair hung to her waist and her black eyes sparkled. "I prefer it this way." She was fabulous, but he wasn't going to get tangled with anyone else for a long time.

"What a waste. Your mamma didn't make you this delicious for you to be alone." She ran her tongue over her full, deep-violet lips.

Her eyes moved over his body. The invitation in her gaze was a passionate challenge, hard to resist. He took another look at her. She couldn't be much more than twenty—if that. He was tempted but he wasn't going to date someone who could be his daughter. He smiled down at her. "My mamma told me to stay away from cradles."

"Your mamma was right but I got out of the cradle a long time ago." She touched his arm. "Got me a different cradle now, baby." She moved closer and purred, "Are you going to the concert?" She ran her hand over his arm.

He pulled his arm away and stepped back. "Yes." He tried to make his one-word answer as cool as he could.

"Alone?" she hummed.

"No, with friends." Now that was an overstatement.

"Oh." She backed off. "Maybe I'll see you there." She turned and started to walk away and then whirled around. "If you decide you want company, you just call Sibila in Room 110."

Cord grinned coolly at her. "Sure thing."

He checked his watch. He barely had enough time to get to his room and change. He hurried but he wasn't sure why. It wasn't as if he had the date with Amy. I should just stay in my room, he thought. But then, if he did that he would look the coward. It was certain that other than Lionel Richie he wasn't looking forward to the evening.

Cord slowed his pace as he neared the theater. The last
thing he wanted was to look anxious. On the short trip to
his room he had been lost in thought. Now he began to
notice his surroundings. Everywhere he turned in the
Kewadin complex there were slot machines. The din was
almost deafening. Bells ringing. Money pouring out and
more going in. He probably should have chosen a quieter
hotel, but he had wanted diversion from his loneliness.
Losing himself in a crowd was what he had planned; he
hadn't expected Amy to be part of that crowd.

He spotted Amy. His heart pounded heavily in his
chest. How could he have been so foolish? He had given
her his soul and she'd thrown it back in his face. He
watched as Jeff took her by the arm and led her to the theater door. She was looking over her shoulder.

Their gazes met briefly, but not long enough for him to
read anything in the look. He stopped. Why was he going
to put himself through this torture? He should turn and
leave, but he couldn't. If what he was seeing was real, this
time he had learned his lesson. He wouldn't be playing
with fire again. He drew in a deep breath and pushed a
smile on his face. He'd never let her know how much it
hurt. He strolled at an even pace to the waiting couple.
"Shall we go in and get our seats?" He didn't look at Amy.
He couldn't.

"Hey baby." The young woman he'd met earlier sidled
up to him.

"Sibila?" He was questioning her name and her presence. "I see you made it."

"Emm," she purred. "But I still don't have anyone to sit with." Her eyes roved over his companions. "Are you waiting for someone else."

Jeff moved up a little. "Cord, why don't you introduce us."

Cord made the introduction, letting Sibila supply her last name.

Jeff glanced at Amy and then turned to Cord. "Why don't we invite Sibila to sit with us? Then we'll have a foursome."

Cord glimpsed Amy's face. Was that hurt? No, it must be his imagination. He moved his gaze from Amy to Sibila. "Would you like to join us?" What the hell? He might as well look like he didn't care.

Sibila laid her hand on Cord's arm. Her black eyes sparkled. "I'd love to."

Cord couldn't help smiling. The little imp had planned their meeting and it was working. But she was still a young woman and he wasn't going to date his daughter. He wasn't that desperate.

Amy followed Jeff down the aisle. The warm-up band was playing loudly. She hoped it would drown her thoughts, but they seemed to grow louder with the band. She stumbled. Jeff reached out and held her steady as if he'd done it a hundred times before.

Amy glanced back to see Cord talking to Sibila. Her heart constricted in her chest, her mouth went dry. He hadn't wasted any time. Sibila was young, beautiful and his race. It would be better for everyone this way, she tried to convince herself. She glanced at the other woman. Very young.

Jeff stood back so the others could be seated. Sibila went first, followed by Cord. Amy stopped to let Jeff go in. He grinned. "Ladies first."

She moved to her seat. Now she would have to sit between her lover and her date. Her stomach knotted. Her lover, all right. One who had found another woman in record time. He'd probably brought her with him.

As she took her seat she could think of nothing but she and Cord alone, in bed, making love. He was too close. His cologne wafted over her. His body heat permeated her skin. She could hear his even breathing. She placed her arm on the arm rest. Cord's was there. Her fingers brushed over his skin. Their eyes met. His gaze traveled over her face and searched her eyes. Amy had the urge to scream out, "This is not what you think. I love you." Still, she pulled her arm in and sat mute.

The warm-up band was getting still louder, and the crowd was standing and dancing. Sibila stood on her seat and screamed for more. Amy watched her for a moment and then realized Cord was staring at her. She brought her gaze to his. Anger had been growing at how fast he had replaced her. She glared for a moment, then mouthed the words, "Young enough for you?"

Cord glared back, the storm in his eyes shooting lightning bolts in her direction. He glanced toward Jeff. "White enough for you?" he mouthed back.

Amy felt the blood drain from her face. He had never been mean to her before. But then she had never given him a reason before. Except when she asked him to be her, as he put it, "stud service." She was hurt. Still, this was what she had wanted. No, this is what she had to do. They couldn't be together. She shrunk in her seat as he turned his gaze to watch the dancing young woman.

"Jeff," Amy leaned into him.

He patted her hand and smiled at her. "Yes?"

"I'm going to get something to drink." Let me out. Her outside calm belied the scream inside.

He stood and leaned down to her. "Don't be silly. What kind of a man would let you go out for your own drinks. I'll get it."

She grabbed his hand, desperately trying to come up with something else. "You'll miss the opening of his act if you leave right now."

Jeff smiled patronizingly at her. "This is for you, not me."

Before she could protest he was gone.

Lionel Richie came on the stage to thunderous applause. He began to sing, "All Night Long." She chanced a sideways glance at Cord. He was watching the performance, seemingly lost in his own world.

The music went on. Amy couldn't imagine where Jeff had gone. Then she heard her favorite song, "Love Will

Find A Way." This time when she glanced at Cord he was looking at her. He shook his head regretfully. She dropped her lashes quickly to hide the hurt. All of her hopes were dashed with that one look. She sighed heavily, clasped her slender hands together and stared at them. Everything Lionel Richie sang was a love song. Inside she sobbed uncontrollably. On the outside she was calm and in control.

Jeff returned with the drinks when the performance was more than half over. Amy hadn't missed him but she asked, "Where have you been?"

He whispered in her ear. "Killing time with an old friend. Hope you don't mind. It's just that this isn't my kind of music." He let his gaze go to the stage and then back to her. "Are you enjoying it?" His face bore a hopeful grin.

She nodded and pushed a smile to her unwilling lips. It wasn't his fault she was in love with the man on the other side of her. She moved her gaze back to the stage and feigned complete interest. In reality she was trudging through her own personal hell.

The performance ended. Amy jumped up as if she had been on a hot seat. Jeff smiled. "Let's go somewhere where we can be alone."

Amy looked at Cord who was staring at her. It's over, rang in her head. The concert and our friendship. She shook her head and turned back to Jeff. "I have to be at work early tomorrow. I'd better go home."

Jeff led her up the aisle. When they were outside the theater in the main lobby, he shook hands with Cord. "It was good meeting you." Then he winked and continued, "I hope your date doesn't have to go to work in the morning." He shot Amy a meaningful gaze.

Cord politely grumbled something Amy couldn't make out. Then he turned and strolled away with the young woman.

When they were out of earshot of the other couple, Cord turned to Sibila, who was hanging on his arm. "This is where you and I part ways, young lady." He pulled his arm free.

"Sibby baby, where have you been?"

Cord looked up to see a couple about his age approaching them. He recognized worried parents when he saw them.

Before he could speak Sibila answered, "I went with Cord to the Lionel Richie concert."

The man who was about Cord's size gave him the once-over. "Little young for you, isn't she, man?"

Cord wanted to break the young woman's pretty little neck. He held out his hand, "Cord McCune, and you are?"

"Your date's father."

The angry words shot at Cord. He needed this like he needed to work with Amy for the next three months. "As lovely as your daughter is, she is not my date. We just sat next to each other."

The other man accepted Cord's hand. "Sorry." He rolled his eyes towards his daughter, who was in an animated conversation with her mother. "I should've known."

Cord glanced over his shoulder. Amy was watching as Jeff spoke with another man. He couldn't let her know there was a problem. He wanted to take his tired head back to his room but instead he said, "No harm done. Why don't you and your wife join me for a drink as soon as you tuck the little girl in?"

Sibila's parents laughed. "You sound like you have children."

Cord nodded. "A son." He offered the young woman a fatherly smile. "Just about your age."

Sibila giggled. "Could I have his phone number?"

The adults laughed with her. Together they strolled through the casino. Cord took one last look. Amy was gone. It's just as well, he thought. Let her think whatever she wants. He watched as the mother clucked after her wayward chick. He turned to Sibila's father. "Let's go have that drink."

He would deal with Amy tomorrow.

Five

Amy was late. She hadn't slept until the early hours of the morning. Every time she closed her eyes she could see Cord enjoying himself with that girl and the other couple. They all seemed to be so natural together. More than ever she was convinced her decision was the right one. Painful, but it was right.

When she woke she was already two hours late for work. Now here she was strolling in and it was almost lunchtime. Steve would have one more reason not to leave the job in her hands. If he wanted a reason. But she was sure he didn't.

Cord would have teased her. He would have told her she was always late. But that was in the past. Today he would probably think she was late because of Jeff. She cringed. Thank God she didn't have to see him today. She wanted him to think she and Jeff were an item but yet she didn't want him to think that. Her life was becoming too difficult.

She had feigned a headache and gotten rid of Jeff as quickly as possible last night. He had tried to kiss her, but she had pulled away. Amy rubbed her arms. The thought of him made her skin crawl. That was the last she would see of him and she was glad.

She passed the staff, who barely gave her notice as they pounded away on their keyboards. Steve would be leaving in a couple of days and she needed to concentrate on work. She hoped she hadn't taken on too much. After all, she would be doing both of their jobs.

She gave a sigh of relief when she finally reached her assistant's desk just outside of her office. She was greeted by a large bouquet of flowers that she had to lean around. "Morning, Shell." She inhaled the sweet essence of the spring blossoms. "Is it a special occasion or did Leo do something wrong?" She smiled at her friend.

"Neither." She handed the card from the flowers to Amy. "These are for you."

Amy's heart leaped. Maybe Cord wanted to make up. Maybe they could be friends. Her smile grew large as she pulled the card from its holder. Her heart fell as her hopes were dashed. She glanced at Shelley, who was obviously waiting to see who had sent them. "They're from Jeff." She moved the vase to the table beside Shelley's desk. "Why don't you put them in the break room for everyone to enjoy?"

"Okay?" Shelley's response was questioning.

Amy pulled a stack of papers from Shelley's out box. "All for me?" Her strained voice was going to give her away. Shelley nodded in response. She forced herself to settle down. "Any messages?"

Shelley shook her head. "No, but Steve has been meeting with Cord McCune for the last two hours. He says you are to join them when you come in."

"Cord? What's he doing here?" She could feel her breath coming harder and her palms felt damp. This was his assignment? What was he going to do? How long was she going to have to see his handsome face, hear his marvelous voice and smell his masculine aroma? Her knees grew weak. She couldn't be this close to him and remain sane.

Shelley shrugged her shoulders. "Too bad you didn't know he was coming. You could have given him the package."

Amy stared blankly at her assistant. "What package?"

"The one you had me send yesterday." Shelley's eyes riveted on her boss. "Are you all right?"

Amy knew her assistant was growing suspicious. She breathed deeply. She could do it. He wouldn't be here long. And then her life would return to normal.

"Of course I am. You mailed it then?" Hoping against hope that she hadn't.

"Yes. It went out in last night's mail. Isn't that what you wanted?"

"Yes. Good." God, how would she explain that? I'll worry about it later, she thought. She glanced at her watch and then at Shelley, with more control and confidence than she felt. "Would you buzz Steve and tell him I'll be right in?"

"Sure. Anything else?"

"No." She tried to offer a smile, and then entered her office.

She pulled open the bottom desk drawer where the chocolate box had been. The slight smell of candy filtered through to her muddled mind. She quickly dropped her purse in and closed the drawer on that memory. She grabbed her office makeup bag and freshened her face. Then she ran a brush through her hair and pulled it back, clasping it with a barrette. She needed to look all business and in control. This would have to be the performance of her life. She braced herself. She put on her best face, walked the few steps, or the longest mile, to her supervisor's office and entered.

"Amy?" Steve looked up waiting for an explanation.

"Car trouble," she lied and then looked into Cord's knowing eyes. Swift heat traveled her body as his gaze raked over her, assessing her frankly. It was quick but it was there. His disappointment in her, poured from his face.

She glanced in Steve's direction to help gain control. "Cord," she forced herself to look back at him, "What brings you here?" Her confidence grew. She had actually sounded normal. She was getting good at this. Maybe there would be an Oscar award in her future.

Cord looked to the other man. "I think Steve can explain." His voice was absolutely emotionless and it chilled her.

Steve gave Amy a wan smile. "Why don't you sit down and we'll get on with this."

Get on with what? Amy was rattled. She had no idea what was happening. Her weakened knees carried her to the only other seat in the room, next to Cord. "Have I done something wrong?" She shrugged to hide her confusion.

She didn't look at Cord. She didn't have to, she could feel his body heat and God, he smelled so good. She kept her fixed look on Steve, almost afraid of what she would do if she looked at the man she loved.

"Of course not." Steve inhaled deeply after what seemed like an eternal pause and then continued. "The state office thinks that Cord here," he paused as he nodded in Cord's direction, "should replace me for the next three months."

Amy felt screams of frustration at the back of her throat. Her head was spinning. She lowered her gaze in confusion. She'd been positive she would be appointed to take Steve's place, even if it was only temporary. She wanted to run, but pulled herself together with the last of her strength. Her bearing was stiff and proud but her spirit was in chaos. "I don't understand the need..."

"It's a practice the main office likes to enforce now and then. It has nothing to do with either of you." Cord's heart went out to Amy. He glanced in her direction and knew she was being held together by a thin thread of determination. He knew more than anyone what the temporary promotion meant to her. She was qualified and she wanted to prove it. He couldn't tell her that this office was suspected of embezzlement. His anger over last night began to shift to sympathy.

"It seems like a waste of manpower for the state to do that." Her questioning gaze searched Cord's face.

He turned his attention to Steve. It was important for him to remain detached but it wasn't going to be easy.

"She's probably right. But you know how the state office is. Sometimes they let everything ride and other times they go gung-ho. They are probably getting heat from someone above them." He wished this wasn't true but it was. He was the one getting the heat. He had no choice. Cord paused and then continued, "Besides, Steve, you might enjoy the change of pace working in the main office."

Cord could feel Amy glaring at him. She knew him too well. If he wasn't careful, this covert operation would blow wide open. "Whatever it is, you are stuck with me until Steve returns." He gave her a sideways glance and then returned his attention to the other man. Their personal relationship was already over, he told himself. He was glad it had all blown up last night. It would make his job much easier.

Steve stood and turned to Amy. "I have a few things to clear up before I leave. Would you show Cord the ropes and help him settle in?" He walked to the door and opened it.

It wasn't a request. Although it sounded like one, she knew he wanted them to leave his office. She had no idea what ropes to show him but she nodded. "Sure, if there's anything I can do to help..."

"My secretary will be giving Shelley my schedule. For a while you can attend the meetings with Cord." He stopped to think for a minute. Amy watched him. There was something strange in his demeanor but she couldn't put her finger on it. "There're a couple of fund raisers coming up. Please attend and do your best. Between the two of you, you should be able to answer any questions about our programs."

"Of course." It all sounded so final. She was sure she must be imagining things. Without looking, she spoke to Cord. "If you will follow me to my office, we can get started."

On their way to her office she put the pieces of her mind and body together, at least temporarily, and managed to bring out her professional self by shoving her personal feelings just under the surface. She introduced Cord to Shelley and explained he would be the acting executive director. Amy noted the surprise that registered on Shelley's face and gave her a we'll-talk-later-look.

Shelley looked from one to the other. "It's nice to meet you, Mr. McCune."

"Cord, call me Cord."

Shelley's still questioning face brightened. "Okay, Cord. Could I get you a cup of coffee?" Her cheeks grew red.

Amy smiled at her. Who wouldn't be taken in by Cord's charisma?

He shook his head. "If you'll direct me to the coffee pot, I'll get my own." After Shelley gave him directions he turned to Amy. "Would you like one too?"

She nodded. And watched his long muscular body stride off toward the break room. How was she going to get through this one? Cord was obviously in control of his emotions. It hurt that he didn't care as much as she did. She wondered how his evening had gone with the young beauty, but she wasn't going to ask. That would be too masochistic.

"Amy? Amy." Shelley spoke loudly and pulled her from her musing.

She stared at her assistant. "What?" Her voice was a hoarse whisper.

"I'm sorry they went over you again. I know you're quite capable of doing the job."

Amy shrugged her shoulders. "As long as I still get a paycheck it doesn't really matter." She knew Shelley could tell she was lying but she didn't have time to worry about that now.

The more immediate problem was Cord. He was going to be here for three months. How could she keep her composure that long? Visions of his naked body flashed through her mind, drawing heat to her more intimate parts. She suppressed images of him with the beautiful young woman he'd found so quickly last night. This would be no easy task.

"If there's anything you need to talk about—I'm here." Shelley spread her hands in an open gesture.

Amy stared at her friend. She would understand. Shelley was in an interracial marriage, but she wasn't ready to tell anyone. Besides, from Cord's action she could see there was nothing to tell. "Thanks. You're a good friend."

Cord rejoined them and handed Amy the cup. "It's hot."

Their fingers brushed lightly at the exchange. Amy could feel her stomach knotting. Even the lightest touch sent her reeling. She took a sip and glanced at him over the top of the cup. "You're right, it is hot." Heat traveled up her neck to her face. She turned from his questioning gaze and opened the door. "My office," she spoke, barely audible. Get control. He is simply a business associate. The knot pulled tighter. She would never be able to convince herself of that.

The door closed behind them with a loud snap. The noise frayed her already alerted nerves. They were alone, together. For a moment they stood in frozen tableau. They stared at each other across a sudden ringing silence, neither knowing what to say or how to say it. Amy pointed to a chair. "Have a seat." She stood by the window and stared out.

"Amy, this is business. I know how badly you wanted this position." He hesitated and then continued. "Whatever has happened between us, personally, we have to set aside."

She heard the chair creak as he dropped into it. With her back to him she pulled her arms tight around her middle. "I don't think we have anything personal. It was all a dream." Her mind was on the beautiful young woman he was with last night.

Cord stood and walked to the window. "Then I think we should get on with the job at hand." He showed no signs of the havoc that she was going through.

Amy fought the dynamic vitality he exuded. She drew herself away as if she'd been burned and moved to her desk. To safety. If she had turned, she would have thrown her arms around his neck and begged for forgiveness. But that wouldn't accomplish anything.

The decision she'd made was a good one. Just being with Jeff had let her know that. His bigoted attitude was exactly why she was protecting Cord. She couldn't let anyone know how she felt. It would cause them both pain.

"I'm sure you know everything about the financial matters of the agency but maybe I can fill you in about our programs." She spoke with quiet but desperate firmness as she explained the in house financial procedures. He knew the state portion of the process, so this was all she could think to show him.

It was a relief to have something to say that didn't cause her stomach to tighten more. "This one, for example, is the halfway house. We work in conjunction with the sheriff's department on this."

Cord slid his chair to her desk and studied the examples. Like a scientist with a microscope, he became totally involved in his work. Amy slid her chair back slightly to stop the onslaught of emotions. His very presence was more than she could take. Her hands shook as she handed him a folder. She was glad he didn't notice. Or maybe he just didn't care.

While he studied the papers, she studied him. He was completely engrossed. She was both excited and aggravated. How could he concentrate? Was their time together so meaningless? Four days ago we were in bed together, she thought. Her gaze slid over his full lips and square jaw. Her body ached to return to the ecstasy. Angry with her own weaknesses and his uncaring attitude, she tossed him the next file he'd requested.

He jerked his head up and glared at her. "Amy..."

She was staring at him. He didn't finish. She had started this war and she would have to be the one to end it. One way or the other.

He knew the best way to handle this was to stay strictly business. "Would you get me this year's budget for this program?" He pointed to a file.

"What? Now I'm your secretary?" she exclaimed in irritation as she pulled the file drawer open.

He glared at her. "This isn't going to achieve anything. We have a great deal of work to do..."

"I could have taken care of this on my own," she reflected with some bitterness.

"I know that. I didn't make this decision. Now, we can make this easy on each other, for old times' sake, or we can give each other hell." He waited for her reaction, watching as she bit down hard on her lower lip. "What will it be?"

"You're the boss," she retorted in sarcasm. "I guess we do it your way."

If only that were true, he thought. We'd be back at the hotel in the hot tub. If he had his way they would go to his hotel room and stay there for a month. He could feel the muscle along his jaw twitching. She was trying her damnedest to draw him out and he wasn't buying. He couldn't. Their personal life was just that, personal. "Thank you." He spoke aloud to stop thinking about them together. "Now if I could have the master budgets for the agency."

She tugged on a file drawer and pulled out a packet, laying it in front of him. "Is there anything else I can do for you, sir?" With that she stood and walked back to the window.

Her sarcasm was grinding on him but he wasn't going to let her know. Hell, he was investigating her and her boss. He didn't need all of this. Cord stood and walked to her. "When we parted you told me it wouldn't work between us. I'm just trying to make the best of a bad situation."

"I know." Her green eyes misted over. "But you also told me that we were meant to be together. What happened to that?" She bit even harder on her lower lip. "I was replaced like a blown-out light bulb."

Cord sighed in exasperation. "Amy, you told me I wouldn't be alone long." He weighed his next statement carefully. "You were right. Does that bother you?" He watched as a tear escaped and she brushed it away.

"You could have taken a little longer. Didn't anything we did mean something to you?" she choked out.

He turned her to him and brushed at the tear. "I obviously took longer than you did. I could ask you the same question."

"That didn't mean anything," she blurted.

Cord thought of the romantic scene he had happened onto last night. "And neither did my date." His date. He was truly happy when her parents showed up and sent her to her room. A small grin twitched his mouth as he thought of it.

"What's so damned funny?" Her voice had taken on an hysterical edge.

Cord placed his hand on her arm to calm her down. She jerked away. "Have you changed your mind?"

"Yes...I mean no." Tears streamed down her cheeks.

He handed her a tissue. "Then we're right back to where we started. What you do is none of my business and vice-versa." He sat down and picked up the file she had laid on the desk.

"No, we're not. Now you are my supervisor. How long have you known about that? When were you going to tell me?" She threw the tissue on the desk and grabbed another.

"None of that is important. This is business and the decision was out of my hands." In a way this was true. If he didn't love her so damned much he would have sent Mark, no matter what treasury wanted. He just couldn't let someone else in here, somebody who might think she was guilty. Their personal relationship was on the rocks but he could still help an old friend.

He glanced at her tear-stained face. The pain he saw matched his own and almost made him crumble. But he knew this was the best way. He reached for another folder. "Now let's get to work."

She stared at him. His face was closed, as if guarding a secret. Some sixth sense brought her fully aware. Something was amiss. It wasn't just their personal differences. No, something else passed in his stare before he closed down.

The intercom buzzer sounded. Amy welcomed the interruption as she never had before. "Yes," she spoke in a hoarse whisper.

"Are you coming down with a cold?" Shelley asked.

"No it's just stuffy in here." She glared at Cord, who was reading the program contracts. Why was he so damned interested in the programs? He got reports every month. What is he looking for that he thinks he hasn't already seen?

"Oh."

There was a long pause. Amy thought her assistant had hung up or taken another call. "Shell?"

"What? Oh, yes. Jeff Delaney is on line one. Can you be interrupted?"

Amy glanced at Cord. "Sure. Put him through." The last person she wanted to talk to was Jeff. After last night she had promised herself she would never go with him again. "Jeff, what a nice surprise."

Cord's head snapped up and Amy smiled in response to his frown. She wanted to hurt him, as she had been hurt. It wasn't just the other woman, although Amy thought of her as a girl, but he was now her boss. For some reason Amy's intuition was on overtime. She didn't know what it was, but she was sure there was something more to Cord's assignment.

She listened as Jeff's grinding voice asked her out. "Tonight? Let me check my calendar." She flipped through, noting that Shelley had written in all of Steve's appointments. Daily she would be at appointments with Cord and some evenings for the fundraisers. She would have to get sick or something. She glanced to see if the phone call was having its desired impact on Cord. It wasn't. His face was buried in the folders. "Sure, tonight would be fine."

She replaced the phone and avoided looking in Cord's direction. "I'll be back in a few minutes."

Cord glanced up and then back at the papers in front of him. "Hope tonight's outing doesn't make you late tomorrow."

She turned and smiled sweetly. "Well, if it does you can fire me." Sarcasm dripped from her lips as she went through the door and let it close loudly.

She quickly covered the few steps to Shelley's desk. "Shell, would you get me Jeff on the phone?"

Shelley looked at her curiously but dialed the number from memory. "Good afternoon. I am calling for Amy Summers. She would like to speak with Detective Delaney, please." Shelley tapped her fingernails while she waited, keeping her questioning gaze averted. "Do you know when he will return?" She glanced at Amy. "Tomorrow? She'll return the call then."

Amy plopped down in the chair beside Shelley. "Where is he?"

"He's working on an investigation and won't be in until tomorrow." Shelley hesitated and then jumped in. "Amy, maybe I could help. Just ask." She reached out and touched her friend's arm.

Amy dragged herself from the chair. "Believe me, if I thought anyone could help me, you'd be the first one I'd ask." She started to leave and then turned back to Shelley. "Buzz me in a minute and remind me of my meeting with the Mackinac program director."

Shelley glanced at the empty time slot on the calendar and then at her friend. "Sure. I'll give you about five minutes."

Amy felt more confident when she returned to Cord. "Now, let's see. What were we working on?"

Cord's eyebrows shot up. He looked at her as if she were up to something. "I don't believe we were working on anything. But I could use your help."

"Of course. What would you like?" When his face registered disbelief, she felt good.

Before he could answer, her buzzer rang out. "Yes?" She listened as Shelley gave her a weather report. "Oh my gosh. Thank you. I'd forgotten about it." She glanced at Cord's stern, handsome face, then returned to Shelley. "Mr. McCune, I mean, Cord," she smiled demurely at him, "will need your help with some files while I am gone. Would you see to his every need?"

"Okaaay?" Shelley's answer was a questioning, elongated word.

"Thanks Shell, I owe you one."

She gathered her briefcase, purse and sweater. "I have a luncheon meeting with the Mackinac program director.

Shelley will help you with anything you need." She pointed to a button. "Just push this one."

Cord smiled, his dimples flashing. "You have a good
meeting. Will I see you back here today or will this be an
all afternoon thing?"

She returned his smile. "I don't have any idea. But I
will try to be on time in the morning." She left, feeling the
heavy load lifting as she walked out the door.

The drive home helped her sort through her feelings.
Even if she wanted to turn back, it was too late. She shook
her head. It would cause too much pain for both of them.

"Mom," she called out as she entered the house. The
purr of the sewing machine took her to the back of the
house. Mrs. Summers was sitting at the sewing machine
studying a pattern. Amy marveled every time she saw her
mother doing normal things. It had taken her a long time
to recover from the stroke.

Her mother glanced up. "You're home early." She
studied her daughter's face. "Have you been crying?"

Amy shook her head. "I just have the worst headache."
She hated lying to her mother.

Mrs. Summers rose quickly and felt her daughter's
head. "You do feel warm," she clucked. She shoved Amy
back through the door. "You go to bed. I'll bring you
some tea."

Amy smiled at her mother. "You don't need to fuss
over me. Just a little rest and I'll be fine."

Her mother brushed a wisp of gray hair from her forehead. "I guess I can take care of my daughter." She smiled

warmly at the younger woman. "You've certainly taken care of me enough."

Amy followed instructions. When her mother returned with the tea, she felt guilty. There was nothing wrong with her that having Cord wouldn't solve. As she watched her mother flit around the room, she knew she couldn't ever do anything to hurt this dear woman. "Mom, I love you."

Mrs. Summers patted her on the arm. "I know you do, dear. Now you just get some rest."

She watched her mother move toward the door. "Mom." Her mother's concerned face turned toward her.

"Jeff Delaney is supposed to pick me up at seven." She hesitated. She hated to ask her mother to lie but she couldn't face him tonight. "Would you tell him that I'm sorry but I'm not feeling well?"

Her mother's eyes widened. "Two nights in a row." She moved closer to her daughter. "I could have sworn you were interested in that man you met at the conference."

"Mom, I told you I didn't meet any man at the conference." Her mother knew her too well but she wasn't going to share this with her.

Her mother smiled warmly at her and then opened the door. "Whatever you say, dear."

Amy watched as her mother carefully closed the door behind her. Then she turned her head toward the window. Her life had become one big lie and she hated it. Still, it was better than either Cord, her mother or Sara being hurt. Sara, she thought, thank God she is on her senior trip. Two weeks should be enough time to pull herself together. She closed her eyes. Maybe, just maybe, she could sleep and bring some peace to her mind and body.

Six

The sun from her office window rested on her shoulders. She leaned back and let her eyes slip closed. The headache she had feigned on Monday was real at the end of the week.

The whole week had been like the first day at the office with Cord. As much as she wanted to remain in a business mode, her body fought her all the way. At meetings she had become tongue-tied. He took over without missing a beat. Several times during the week, Cord had saved her. He had obviously put their personal relationship out of his mind. But she couldn't do the same.

Now she had to face tonight. The fund raiser. In a few hours they would be at a dinner dance together. As if he didn't look good enough, tonight he would be in a tuxedo. She groaned. Two months and three weeks to go.

She glanced at the clock. She needed to leave soon. Picking up her phone she buzzed Shelley and as soon as she answered, began talking. "I'll be leaving early to get ready for tonight. Is there anything you need from me before I go?"

"I have the letters you dictated this morning. Just a minute and I'll bring them in for your signature."

Amy signed the letters and glanced up to see Shelley staring at her with the same look of concern as her mother. She sought the words to nip it in the bud. Advice was something she didn't want. "Shell..."

Shelley cut her off. "I've watched both of you this week. I know what's going on."

Amy let out a long breath. "Oh."

"Amy, you can't pass up a chance for happiness because of race."

"How do you know it's me."

"Because he knew your race but it's obvious you didn't know his. Don't let that stop you."

"I don't want to deal with any more problems."

Shelley picked up the letters. "You're dealing with a problem anyway. Love is too important to turn your back on."

Amy stood to leave. "I thought you would understand."

"I do, that's why I'm sticking my nose in. I couldn't live without Leo. Our race difference is only important to others." She moved to the door. "Think about it."

"Sure," Amy answered just before the door closed. Think about it? That's all she thought about. Yet she kept returning to her original decision. How could she do this to everyone involved? Shelley was right! It did matter to others. That's why she couldn't do it. Wouldn't that be selfish?

She pulled on her light jacket and walked past Shelley. "See you on Monday."

"Amy?"

She turned slowly towards her assistant, struggling to keep her irritation from showing. "Yes."

"I only spoke out because I know what you are going through. For months Leo and I kept our relationship a secret. Now we laugh about it. Most of all, we begrudge the time wasted worrying about others." She smiled warmly. "Have a good evening."

Amy wanted to respond but she didn't have a rebuttal. "Thanks."

■ ■

With a few minutes to kill before her dry cleaning was ready, Amy paced the sidewalk of the mini-mall. If I'm late he will think it's because of him. No, he'll think it's because I'm always late. She stopped to admire the flowers for spring planting, continuing her self-conversation aloud. "I just don't care," she muttered to herself.

"Plants can be a real problem."

His deep chuckle washed over her. She couldn't turn around. Anything she might do or say would just be a continuation of her idiocy this week. "You're right, of course. I—I'm trying to select something for my mother." She wasn't, but now that she had said it, it sounded like a good idea. She moved around the plants, more to escape his nearness than to get a better view.

"My mother loves plants too. Maybe I should take her something tomorrow."

She whirled to gaze into his rich brown eyes. "You're leaving then?" She could hear her heart pounding in her chest. Maybe he'd had enough too. Maybe her life would return to normal. Still, if he was gone, it would be forever and she wasn't sure she wanted that either.

Cord stared at her, hurt registering in his gaze before he closed his expression. "For the weekend."

"Oh." She was becoming an expert at being a buffoon. "Of course. There's nothing to keep you here over the weekend." She wanted him to tell her she was wrong. That he couldn't stand a minute away from her. But she knew that wasn't going to happen. He had moved on.

She shrugged her shoulders as he stared at her, hoping to look like she didn't care. "I have to get going or I'll be late."

"Amy..." He paused.

She looked up. "Yes?"

"I think you are right. We can be friends. Why don't I pick you up for the fund raiser tonight?"

She shook her head and looked away. Yes. She wanted to say yes. But she couldn't be that near him, without...

She tried not to think about it. But her face grew bright red as her original offer pushed to the surface. Did he mean friends with an occasional sexual rendezvous? She glanced in his direction. Seeing that his face was offering friendship only, she felt an unreasonable disappointment.

He laid his hand lightly on her shoulder. "Come on. Let's put an end to all of this foolishness. I'll pick you up in an hour and a half. You can critique my presentation on the way."

His dimples flashed, melting her heart, and his light touch warmed her. What could she say? He was right, wasn't he? They could be friends, couldn't they? After all, he had been her best friend for two years. "Sure. And I'll try to be on time."

His smile grew wider. "Now don't go changing. I've grown accustomed to you this way."

She returned the smile. "I don't think I could if I tried." God, it felt good talking to him as if they were normal again. Even if part of it was a facade. At least it was a start.

He waved as he strode away. "See you in a little while."

She turned in his direction a couple of times as she walked to the dry cleaners. Relief flooded her. The anger that had been spawned between them was set aside. Now if she could only forget those three blissful days at the conference, she could function close to normal.

■ ■ ■

Cord took the steps to the sprawling porch of Amy's old Victorian home two at a time, relieved they had regained civility. It would make his job easier. When he finished, he would recommend Amy for the position. Maybe they could continue some kind of friendship, even if they'd both rather have more. He knew she did, and so did he. But never on her terms. Not as an occasional stud, although the idea had its appeal. But at what price?

He knocked with a renewed determination. Amy's mother came to the door, left standing open to let in the warm spring air. Mrs. Summers looked at him and then he noticed her hand go to the latch. It was locked. And she left it that way.

"Could I help you?" she asked in an uncertain voice.

Cord knew prejudice was a deep-seated thing, and the gesture spoke volumes. A black man at her door made her nervous. He braced himself and put on his most charming smile. "Mrs. Summers, my name is Cord McCune." He was going to continue but when he mentioned his name, her hand went freely to the latch and pushed the door open.

"Mr. McCune." Her face lit in a surprised but welcoming smile. "Come in."

"Thank you." Her changed attitude lifted his spirits. "Is Amy ready?"

Mrs. Summers shook her head. "Goodness no. That girl will be late for her own funeral."

He laughed with her, relieved at passing this hurdle. He stood by the door. "I'll wait here for her."

Mrs. Summers smiled warmly at him. "Nonsense. Come with me. I was just about to have a cup of coffee. Would you join me?"

Cord followed her as she led him into the large open kitchen. He waited as she poured their coffee, then asked, "How are you feeling?" Thinking that might be a little too intrusive, he added, "I mean Amy says you have been ill."

She waved her hand. "That was two years ago. I'm fine. Amy worries about me entirely too much."

He smiled, wondering what he could talk with her about. Flowers? He knew she loved them. Her yard was filled with nicely groomed spring blossoms. She sat across from him.

"Mr. McCune?"

"Cord," he offered as he listened carefully. Sometimes he could hear more from what people didn't say than from what they verbalized. She sounded as if she was going to be serious. Maybe this is where she tells me to keep my distance, for her daughter's sake, he thought. I mean, how would it look? He held his breath, waiting for the other shoe to drop.

"Cord. I like that name; it sounds strong." She waved her hand as if to clear away stray thoughts. "So, you and Amy attended the conference together, last week?"

He stared at her. She acted as if she knew. Still, Amy was adamant about not telling her. It must be his imagination. He chose his answer carefully. "We were both there."

She leaned closer to gaze into his face. "Ahhh." She paused as if assessing him. "I hope you both learned what you needed."

Jesus. What was the woman getting at? She sounded sincere but he couldn't tell. "I think we did."

"It must have been a tough course. Amy has had a headache almost every day—and night for that matter—since her return. In fact she had to cancel a date Monday night because of it."

He could feel her stare boring into his soul. Somehow she knew—or was she just fishing? She had let him know

Amy hadn't kept her date with the cop. What was she looking for?

Whatever it was, this was damned uncomfortable. He couldn't tell if she was okay with them being together or not. "I'm sorry to hear that. I'm sure the headaches will ease soon and she can make up for her lost time out."

Shrugging her shoulders, Mrs. Summers poured a dab more coffee. "Now that you mention it, she seems a great deal better this evening. Wonder what brought that on?" She smiled at him but still studied his reactions to her words.

Cord swallowed hard. She was definitely fishing, and he was going to be reeled in. "Maybe because it's the weekend and she can relax."

"Perhaps." She offered him a bright, knowing smile. "Now, if I understand this right, you will be working in Amy's office for awhile?"

"Yes." He shifted in his chair. Maybe she was upset because Amy didn't get the position. If she was, she was a great actress.

"How long will you be here?" She never dropped her investigative stare.

"Three months."

"Oh?"

He couldn't imagine what was concealed behind that one questioning word. He glanced at his watch. It was time for him to get off the hot seat.

Mrs. Summers rose and he followed suit. She waved her hand at him. "Please sit. If you'll excuse me, I'll hurry her along."

Cord took a deep breath and let it out as he watched her hustle out of the kitchen. Amy's mother wasn't as naive as Amy had thought. He wondered if she had any idea that her mother knew. What she knew, he wasn't quite sure, but she knew something.

He stood and took his cup to the sink. At least Amy had told her mother he was picking her up. Yet it was obvious she hadn't mentioned his race. Either it wasn't important enough to mention or she didn't want to get in a tussle with her mother. He hoped it was the first.

"Cord?"

He turned to see Amy and her mother standing in the door. Amy's pink, thin-strapped gown clung to her hips. Leaving well enough alone would take some doing. He didn't look any further. He knew what was under the dress and he didn't want to let himself go down that path. "You look very nice." There, that was non-committal.

His gaze went from Amy to her mother. Something in Mrs. Summer's soft gray eyes was sending him a message but he couldn't read it. He pulled his gaze back to Amy. "We'd better leave."

As they walked out the door, Mrs. Summers said, "You have a good time tonight."

Cord could hear it in her voice. She knew and she didn't seem to be disturbed. Still, Amy was positive it would send her mother back to the hospital.

He took her elbow and led her to the car, still pondering Mrs. Summer's conversation. He shook his head. No. I'm seeing what I want, not what really is.

Amy glanced up at Cord as he shook his head. His eyes were darker than usual. Something was troubling him, but she didn't know what.

Her mother would have been courteous, she was sure of that. Maybe she accidentally said something offensive. A week ago she would not have given a thought to what her mother might have said but Cord had made her aware of how insensitive people can be, including herself. It amazed her how little she'd thought of the plight of a minority race until she was directly involved.

After they were in the Navigator, she broached the question. "Did something happen? I mean, did my mother offend you?"

Briefly he glanced her way as he pulled the vehicle into traffic.

She could see him weighing his response. The silence between them grew louder, making her uncomfortable. "I'm sorry. I'd hoped she would meet you and like you instantly."

He regarded her quizzically for a moment. "Why?"

She shrugged her shoulders. "Well, if we are going to be friends..."

"Then I would have to get along with your mother?" He said the words tentatively, as if testing the idea.

Amy turned in her seat to look at his profile. How could anyone, including her mother, resist him? His body was perfect, every muscle carefully sculpted by bodybuilding. The charcoal tuxedo only added to his perfection. His profile was rugged yet gentle. In fact, his features were so perfect, so symmetrical, that any more panache would have made him too perfect. She gazed at his full mouth that always looked warm and ready. Most importantly, his charm overwhelmed her. He was so darned sincere, honest, honorable. What was wrong with her? He was the man of her dreams.

He glanced in her direction. "Amy?"

She jerked her guilty gaze away, surprised by the sudden interruption of her private musings. "Yes?"

His mouth twitched with amusement. "Do you need me to repeat the question?"

"What question?" Her mind scrambled until she stumbled onto what he had said. It was sandwiched between his perfect body and being her dream man. Her face prickled with heat. "Oh, that question." She paused. "Of course Mom wouldn't have to like you but it would be nice."

He shot her a sideways glance. "Oh." Amusement flickered in eyes that met hers.

She needed to change the subject. "Have you seen the Soo Locks yet?"

Again a flash of humor crossed his face. "No, would you like to show them to me?"

Would I? she thought. "I'm not sure our friendship is ready for a long test. Let's just see how we make it through this ride and tonight."

His eyes scanned from her face to her shoulders and then to her breasts. "I wasn't suggesting..."

"I know you weren't," she cut him off. His heated gaze was too tempting. If she allowed him to speak the words, she might not get the genie back in the bottle. And she probably wouldn't want to. She stared straight ahead.

He pulled the vehicle in front of the Objibway Hotel. A large banner read, 'Welcome to the 15th Annual Human Services Fund Raiser.'

As they walked up the steps, he turned to her. "I don't know why you are holding back. Your mother knows."

She jerked toward him. "Knows what?" Her breath caught in her throat. "What did you tell her?" Her strangled whisper was barely audible.

Cord's face looked as if she had struck him. He averted his gaze to the entrance. "You of all people should know me better than that." He stared straight ahead. "I think we should go in."

She glanced at him again. He had closed his expression. Her heart squeezed in her chest. "I didn't mean anything..." She dropped it because she knew she had. And so did he.

"Oh Amy, dear."

Amy looked around as they entered the lobby to see who was speaking to her. Her gaze fell on the waving hand of the fund raising chairperson. "Mrs. Delaney." She glanced at Cord, who had pasted a smile on his face.

The older woman covered the short distance between them and hugged her. "Amy, you look absolutely radiant tonight." She held her back. "There is something different about you. Have you changed your hair or something?"

Amy laughed politely. "You're not used to seeing me in a dress." She'd forgotten Jeff's mother was the chair. She hoped he hadn't told her about them dating. Or whatever it was.

"Don't be silly, dear. You always look lovely. My Jeff tells me you have been dating him." Mrs. Delaney's eyes glittered as her face broke into a broad smile. She looped her arm through Amy's, trying to lead her away.

Amy stopped and turned to Cord. His face was smiling but his eyes were stone cold. Mrs. Delaney had made it obvious that she didn't see him, or didn't want to. She had also made it clear that she was very happy with her son's choice.

Amy pulled in a long breath. "Mrs. Delaney, this is Cord McCune. He is taking Steve's place and will deliver the welcoming speech tonight."

Mrs. Delaney's eyes brushed over Cord. Her brow creased and her eyes narrowed. After a few seconds she returned her attention to Amy. "Do you think that's a good idea?" She kept her gaze averted from Cord. "I mean, most of the people know you and Steve. It just seems..."

"Mrs. Delaney."

Cord's rich voice boomed larger than life. "It's a pleasure to meet someone who is so generous with her time and efforts on behalf of those who are truly in need."

Amy watched as Cord's charisma worked its magic. The older woman's face lit in a brilliant smile. "Thank you." She blushed as if on cue. "I hope you didn't misunderstand what I was saying." She brushed at imaginary lint on her dress. "It's just that we are all so comfortable with the job Steve and our own little Amy are doing." She glanced at Amy and then back at Cord.

Amy's stomach rolled in nausea. The woman was as fake as a three-dollar-bill. Jeff didn't come by his bigoted attitude by accident. Still, she couldn't let this woman push Cord out. He had prepared a wonderful speech and he was going to deliver it.

She braced herself. "Mrs. Delaney." The woman looked in her direction, the smile still etched in her marble features. "Cord has prepared the speech and I haven't. He can do as good a job or better than I." She paused. The older woman seemed to be scrutinizing her every word. A cold chill ran through her. She was being appraised to see where she stood.

Mrs. Delaney's face finally broke into a smile. "Of course, dear. I understand."

Amy felt guilty at her relief. What did she understand? Did she think Amy agreed with her? Amy pushed her anger down even though she wanted to choke the woman. Yet, if she made a scene it would be worse for Cord and for her. Cord's stony glare was well concealed behind a mask, one she knew he had taken years to develop. "I think you will enjoy hearing the same old thing from a different perspective."

"Oh course, dear." Mrs. Delaney's voice was filled with a patronizing skepticism. Again, she hooked her arm in Amy's and led her toward the banquet hall.

Amy could feel Cord's stare burning into her back. She turned slightly in his direction. He hadn't moved. She glanced from the older woman to the man she loved. Even though this proved her theory even more, she couldn't do this to him. She politely removed her arm from Mrs. Delaney's and moved toward Cord. "If you will come with me, I'll show you where the speaker's stand is." She offered him a weak smile.

Cord hesitated and then joined the two women as they moved through the crowd and entered the banquet hall. Amy felt as if she were walking on hot rocks. How could this be? How could that woman treat another human as if he weren't there?

As they moved to the front of the hall, Mrs. Delaney was swept away by the manager of the hotel. Amy's body shuddered in relief. She wanted to kiss the hotel manager for the rescue. She turned an apologetic smile toward her friend, the man she loved, the man of her dreams, her heart breaking for him. "I am truly sorry." She felt herself wither under his glare. Her fears had come to fruition. It hurt more than she had imagined to see the man she loved treated as if he were a piece of furniture. "This is one time I wish I had been wrong." She held her hands tightly twisted in front of her. She wanted to take him in her arms and push away the hurt in his eyes, but that wasn't possible.

"I do too." She watched as his face relaxed.

"Is it always like this?"

A thin smile creased his face. "No. Sometimes it's worse."

"I'm sorry. You have to know not all are like that." She let her hands fall to her side.

"I do. There's you and..." He chuckled. "Don't worry about it. Black skin can be very tough."

She gazed into his smiling chocolate eyes. "I like your skin." Her cheeks tinged dark pink. "I don't remember it being tough at all." The color in her cheeks deepened as she thought of running her fingers over the smooth skin of his back.

"Maybe you should try it again. You know how the memory can play tricks on you." His chuckle came from deep in his throat.

She swallowed hard. An intense tingling grew in the pit of her stomach and she had to fight her overwhelming desire to be with him. In the end it would hurt both of them. "Maybe," her voice was a rasping whisper, "you should take your place at the podium." She followed his gaze as it traveled the room.

He looked back to her. "Maybe you're right."

Amy's heart went out to him as he began his welcoming address, his voice rich and confident. Obviously he was accustomed to speaking and if anyone could see past his color, he had a great message.

She glanced around at the faces turned in his direction. Surprise was etched on more than half of them. On a very few faces it was obvious they were listening to the message.

None of this was right. She gazed at the tall, handsome, confident man she loved. He was everything she wanted. She had loved him before she knew him and she still did. How could she let something so shallow as skin color come between them?

Her skin turned damp and clammy. Guilt crept over her, covering her in a murky haze. She was no different than Mrs. Delaney. Oh my God, she groaned inside. I am as bigoted as the people I am scorning.

If he was willing to fight the bigots, then she should be. She watched him, her heart filled with renewed joy and determination. They would get through this together. The rest of the world, or at least her community, didn't mean as much to her as he did.

Seven

"That was one fine dinner, for a fund raiser." Cord leaned back in his chair and smiled at Amy.

The music flowed in from the adjoining room. Amy returned his warm smile. "I hope you didn't eat too much to dance."

Cord quirked an inquisitive eyebrow. "Are you suggesting that we dance?" His eyes roved over the few people still eating and then out to the ballroom where most of the guests were. "In front of all of them?"

Her heart swelled as his liquid brown eyes gazed at her. She couldn't wait to tell him her decision. She nodded. "Cord, I..." Just then she was grabbed and pulled from her chair.

"I knew you were waiting for me to ask you to dance." Jeff peered into her face. "Saving the first and last for me? That's a good sign, a good sign indeed."

"Jeff,—uh—I didn't—I mean, Cord and I..." She fumbled for words as she glanced at Cord.

He stood. "I think while you two dance I'll take in some of that fresh northern air."

Jeff gave Cord a brisk pat on the back. "Thanks, old buddy. You two can discuss business anytime." He jerked on her arm. "Come on."

Amy glanced at Cord's face as she was whisked out onto the dance floor. He had closed the door to his emotions again. If she was going to stand up for him, no, for them, she had to begin soon.

"How's it working with that guy?" Jeff's voice carried a heavy dose of sarcasm.

"Cord? He's great!" She kept her voice light but her throat burned with unuttered protest.

Jeff held her at arm's length and studied her face. After what felt like an eternity, he laughed. "Amy, you are so sweet. It wouldn't matter who they sent to work with you, you'd be nice."

She clenched her teeth. How could she respond to this bigoted fool? Nothing would change the way he believed. She was at a loss for words.

She glanced toward the door. Cord stood watching her. She offered him a smile. When she smiled Jeff pulled her tightly into his arms and kissed her soundly as if he thought the smile was for him. She recoiled inwardly while pressing her hands on his chest. "Jeff, please."

He pulled her more tightly to him, his strength far greater than hers. "Why not? What did that come hither smile mean? It's time to quit playing kid games. We both know we want each other. Soon we'll announce our engagement and then they'll all know."

She pushed back as far as he would allow and looked to where Cord had been standing. He was gone. Her heart fell to her feet. She knew he had witnessed the scene and even if it wasn't real, he would have no way of knowing.

She felt an acute sense of loss wash over her. Dull icy talons gripped her heart with guilt. She had allowed this to happen. It was her fault. Her emotional whirlwind blew in a sharp anger. Pulling her hands free from Jeff, she pushed on his chest with newfound strength. He was forced to release his grip to maintain his balance.

Startled, his wide eyes stared at her. "Wh—What in the hell are you doing?" His nostrils flared and his lips grew thin.

Under his glower Amy grew apprehensive. She had never seen him like this. She was afraid to speak. She didn't want to make a scene in front of all of the other guests. Anything she said could be misconstrued. She bit her lower lip and pushed her hair back. Stay calm and reasonable, she told herself. She gave a little shrug of her shoulders and stared back.

Jeff came closer to her but didn't touch her. He stared for a minute and then a cynical smile grew on his thin lips. "Does my little gal prefer privacy?"

Privacy? Her mind screamed. The only privacy she wanted was from him. She wished this nightmare were over. She wanted to run from this place. Run to Cord for comfort and to explain, but she didn't even know if he would listen. She took a deep breath and stepped closer to Jeff. "I think we should talk." Her bearing was stiff but proud.

Jeff's shoulders relaxed a little. "I don't know if I can be alone with you and keep my hands off you," he snickered. "Let's go out onto the veranda."

She gave him a guarded glance. "Maybe I should mingle with the other guests then."

Jeff grabbed her arm and then pulled his hand back in response to her glare. "There are people out there, it's safe."

Amy shrugged her shoulders and nodded. She followed him into the warm night. The veranda was filled with dancers, lovers and people simply enjoying the first breath of summer. She leaned on the railing and breathed deeply. If only Cord was the one with her. Fresh summer evenings should be shared with the one she loved.

Jeff leaned beside her. "Maybe I've been moving too fast. It's just that we were so close when we were kids."

Amy's stomach churned. He had been her friend. Yet like now, he had read more into their relationship. Somehow he had turned the high school friendship into a lifelong love. She had to tell him without making an enemy.

She didn't look at him. "Jeff, we are friends."

"I know, that's what makes our relationship so good." He smiled and patted her hand.

Amy edged her hand away. How was she going to tell him? He had their life planned for the next fifty years. All based on his fantasy of a relationship.

She was startled by a pat on her back and she jerked around. She'd never been so glad to see the meddling old woman. "Mrs. Delaney, is there something you need?"

Mrs. Delaney shook her head, a knowing, yet apologetic smile on her face. "I'm afraid I have to borrow Jeff for a few minutes." She smiled broadly at Amy. "You'll forgive an old woman for wanting to show off her son?" Her lips grew pouty. "Won't you, dear?"

"Of course." She paused, thinking she'd answered too quickly. "My mother would do the same thing," she added to keep everyone happy. She turned to Jeff. "You go with your mom. We can finish our conversation some other time."

Jeff held back. "If you'll wait—I'll be back soon."

Amy shook her head lightly. "I really should be mingling with the guests. A quarter of our funding comes from our donors."

Mrs. Delaney took Jeff's arm. "How many times do I have to explain that these functions are business, not pleasure." She offered Amy a knowing smile.

Amy returned the smile and spoke again to Jeff. "Unfortunately your mom is right. Don't worry. We'll talk again. I'm sure of it." When she let them all know Cord was the man she loved she was sure they would talk.

"If you're sure." Jeff returned Amy's smiling nod and then walked away with his mother.

Amy exhaled the air she'd subconsciously drawn deep into her lungs. She leaned against the railing for support. This problem with Jeff couldn't have come at a more difficult time. How was she going to keep him at arm's length? He had built a fantasy world that she couldn't possibly be a part of. Even if she weren't in love with Cord, Jeff would not be someone she would eagerly pursue.

She pushed away from her support and surveyed the veranda. It wouldn't be difficult to find the tall handsome man she had come with. She walked among the guests, greeting and smiling, all the while searching for Cord.

A warm breeze washed over her. The smell of summer was definitely in the air. She smiled as she inhaled deeply. This time the deep breath was to soak in the summer, not to fight off the unwanted attentions of Jeff or his mother. She loved summer in northern Michigan.

Her gaze did a fast survey, landing on Cord's handsome face. There he was, smiling and talking with one of the community's leading women. He had obviously charmed her since she stared at him as if he were the last man on earth. Amy understood the feeling. To her he was.

Her breath caught in her throat as she watched him take the beautiful woman in his arms and twirl out onto the dance floor. Her long, raven hair hung straight down her back. Her ultra-slim body pressed against his. Amy turned her head. The last thing she wanted to see was another woman in his arms.

Amy walked through the gardens. The sweet smell of flowers mixed with the bitter taste of jealousy. She knew Cord wasn't doing anything wrong. He'd just met the woman. But it pained her to see another woman where she belonged. Still, it was her fault she wasn't the one in his arms. She'd been a stupid fool to let a small thing like skin color come between her and her best friend, her lover.

She felt heat pulsate in her lower body as she thought of him as her lover. A week was a short time, yet it seemed like an eternity. She wanted to return and cut in, but she didn't know what he was thinking now. And if he was going to leave with that woman, then she didn't want to see it.

She'd had enough of the emotional roller coaster for one day. She slipped back in through the side entrance and made her way to the concierge desk. The young man stood eagerly awaiting her request. She pulled a bill from her purse and placed it in his hand. "Would you call for a taxi, please?"

"Yes, Ms. Summers. You look tired. Why don't you take a seat in the lounge. I will come for you when the taxi arrives."

She stared at the young man. He had used her name. She must know him. It wasn't like she came here often. "Do I know you?"

He grinned widely. "I'm Shelley's younger brother."

"Chip?" She gazed into his face. What a pleasant surprise — a friendly face with no demands. "You've grown a great deal since I last saw you."

He nodded. "Shelley told me you would be here tonight. If you'd like, I can take you home."

"Thanks, Chip. I'll just take your suggestion and wait for the taxi."

"Sure thing. I'll get right on it."

Amy nodded and walked the few steps to the almost empty lounge. She guessed everyone was at the party. She fell onto the plush, deep-rose, soft cushioned divan and closed her eyes. What she needed was a life full of Chips and Shelleys. Quiet and unassuming people. Like that was going to happen, she thought.

She slid farther into the cushions. The dimly lit room was quiet. The soft strains of a ballad drifted in from the ballroom. She wondered what Cord was doing. His handsome face played through her mind. Tranquility and warmth enveloped her. God, she was tired. Her last thought was that she didn't want to leave this little bit of heaven.

"Amy?" she heard Cord call. His voice came from somewhere in the distance. Was she dreaming? If she was, she didn't want to wake. His smooth voice wrapped around her like a warm blanket. She curled into a ball.

A hand gently shook her shoulder. "Amy!" His voice was more insistent.

Her long lashes flew up. She pushed her hair away from her eyes. Her handsome knight crouched before her. She was confused. "Cord?" she questioned while she tried to wipe away the cobwebs. His warm gaze melted into hers. She wanted to reach out and touch him to make sure he was real. "How..." She stopped when she saw Chip standing behind him. Young guilty eyes stared at her.

Chip offered a sheepish grin and gave Amy a pleading gaze. "I called my sister. She told me to find Mr. McCune. She didn't want you taking a taxi home." He gave a slight shrug of his shoulders and raised his hands. "I hope I did the right thing."

Cord stood and placed a twenty in Chip's hand. "You did exactly right."

Chip glanced at Amy with a hopeful look.

"Of course you did. Your sister always knows what's right for me. Thank you." Her heart was dancing in her chest. Cord was here and she could plead her case. She didn't care how it had happened, he was there with her and that's what mattered.

Chip seemed to grow in stature with her praise. His smile was wider than his face as he backed out of the room.

Cord returned his liquid gaze to her questioning stare. He held out his hand. "Come on. You promised me a dance."

Amy went willingly into his arms. His warm body drew hers like a magnet. "Cord, I—we need to talk."

He placed a finger on her quivering lips. "Let's dance first."

The music was at a distance but they didn't really need any. It had only been a week but it might as well have been forever. She snuggled in. "I've missed you."

He held her back and gazed into her eyes. "Nothing has changed. I'm still black."

Amy could feel his gaze searching her soul. If he searched far enough he would see she had realized their relationship was right. "Maybe I'm not as white as I used to be."

His eyebrows knitted together in a question mark. "And that means?"

She stared into his face. His jaw had set and a muscle twitched along the strong, lower line. She ran her fingers over the tightened muscles. "It means I love you and I know color has nothing to do with it."

His piercing gaze studied her. "Your friend Jeff and his mother are very white."

Her dancing slowed as she pondered. He was offering her the chance to turn back before it was too late. But it was already too late. She had been a fool to let what others thought stand in her way. She only had one life to live and she wanted to live it with Cord. "I know, but they aren't my friends."

"Jeff thinks he is more. I saw the kiss." Amy saw pain flicker over his face.

Lightly she brushed her lips over his. "I don't think Jeff knows what he thinks. And you saw him kiss me, not the other way around."

He chuckled and then his face grew serious again. "I think you should take a little more time to think about this."

Amy's heart was singing as she brushed her lips over his cheek. "I don't need any more time. I've already stolen a week from us. If you will have me—my time will be yours."

He pulled her tightly against him and whispered into her ear. "Remember, I'm not willing to settle for a occasional tryst."

She locked her arms around his neck and pulled his mouth to hers. Hot lips brushed hot lips. "Nor am I."

His arms slid around her waist, and she felt the iron grip of his passion. It seemed to push the air from her lungs while pressing new life into her body. They glided to the music. Soul mates finally joined.

Their closeness was like a drug. His lithe body had captured hers and they moved as one. Amy purred. Somehow she found her distant vocal chords. "Don't ever let me go."

His hot breath moved over her cheek as he answered hoarsely, "I hope you know what you are doing."

She pulled back slightly. "I know."

He studied her face. "Babe, as you pointed out, this isn't just about you and me. It won't be an easy road."

His gaze sent warning shivers up her spine. "I don't expect it to be. But it's my life and I have only one to live."

Cord's face grew an easy smile. "My lady had better stick close." Gently he rocked her back and forth. "For awhile we'll be on a roller coaster." He brushed her hair back and slowly, thoughtfully, kissed her lips. "When the ride stops I want you to still be in the seat with me."

She drank in the sweetness of his kiss. It was a kiss for her weary mind to melt into. She never wanted another week like the one she had just lived. "I'll be there." She breathed the words through parted lips.

Cord gave a barely audible groan. "Let's leave."

Reluctantly, slowly, Amy moved from his firm embrace. "Just give me a few minutes to say goodbye." Her body was crying for release, but her mind knew she had responsibilities.

Their hands dangled together while they caught their breath.

"A few minutes will be too long but I'll wait." He dropped to the cushions he had pulled her from earlier.

"Will you come with me?" she asked faintly, drawing a step nearer to him.

He shook his head. "I don't think you are ready for the crowd's reaction."

Amy took his hand and tugged on it. "I don't think there's a better time."

He grinned and straightened his shoulders. "Whatever my lady wants, my lady gets."

"You remember that on our 50th anniversary." She grinned; he had unlocked her heart and soul and now she would tell the world. Amy felt full of strength, with a new sense of peace. She knew who she was and that person was in love with this man. Her friend.

Cord allowed himself to be pulled from the divan. He nudged her as they walked from the lounge. "Does that mean we are going to get married?" He chuckled. "Are you proposing to me?"

She felt her cheeks grow hot. He had never said he wanted to marry her, she had just assumed. She whirled to face him. His broad smile relieved her of her embarrassment. "And if I am?" her silky voice held a challenge.

Cord held up his hands in mock defense, "Then the answer is yes. I'm certainly not going to argue with my lady."

She tossed her hair to one shoulder. "Good."

"Amy?"

She held her breath as slowly and seductively his gaze slid downward. "Hmmm?" she whispered breathlessly.

Amusement flickered in the eyes that met hers. "Next time, could I be the one to propose?"

Seeing the amusement in his eyes, she laughed. "Next time, and as many times as it takes until we get to the altar." She grabbed his hand. "Come on, everyone will be gone before I get a chance to thank them."

Cord pulled his hand back and stared straight ahead. Amy followed his gaze. Jeff was coming toward them, his narrow carved face etched with anger. She felt Cord's presence as he moved beside her. She steeled herself. Somehow he had found out. She took a deep breath. "Jeff, I was just coming to find you and your mother."

Angry eyes glared from Amy to Cord and then back to Amy. "I thought I told you to wait on the veranda for me." He grabbed her hand. "We weren't finished."

Amy pulled her hand back as Cord moved between them. "That's no way to treat a lady." His fist clenched and unclenched at his side.

Jeff's face grew crimson. "I don't think this is any of your business. Why don't you leave Amy and me alone."

"Jeff." Amy moved around Cord and faced Jeff, fighting to sound firm. "This is Cord's business."

Jeff looked from one to the other and then at the lounge. His face flashed fire-engine red as his eyes wildly darted back and forth, growing wide as realization set in. Stepping backwards, he shook his head as if trying to clear away unwanted thoughts and sights. Finally he glowered at Amy. "You could have told me before I told everyone about you and me."

"Jeff."

Amy glanced around. So far no one was paying attention. She had to keep this private. "Why don't we go into the lounge and talk." Her voice was quiet and deceptively calm.

Fury carved its way into Jeff's features. "I think you've already spent too much time in the lounge." He shot a venomous glare in Cord's direction and then returned his anger to Amy.

"I don't need you to explain. I'm not an idiot. You're making a big mistake." His voice hardened ruthlessly. "You'll both be sorry. Very sorry." Without another word he abruptly turned and left them.

Amy turned to Cord. "I'm sorry." There was nothing else she could say. Jeff's anger wasn't unexpected but the fury of it was far more than she could have imagined.

Cord stood ramrod straight, his fist still clenching at his sides. His stare followed Jeff. "I am too." Slowly he brought his gaze back to Amy. "It's been a long time since I wanted to knock someone on their ass."

Amy laid her hand on his arm. "And I thank you for being the bigger man."

"That was part of it. The other part is that he's a cop and I'm a black man." His voice was cold and lashing and his eyes were filled with pain. "He's just aching to throw my butt in jail."

She rubbed his arm in an attempt to calm him. "I don't know what to say. I've never faced racism." She dropped her head. "I can't put you through this."

He lifted her chin with his finger. "Are you ready to give up already?" His voice was like an echo from an empty grave.

She stared into eyes that had been deliberately cleansed of all emotion. Slowly, she shook her head. "I don't want anything to happen to you. I'm scared." Hot tears spilled onto her cheeks. "I couldn't face it if something happened to you," a sob escaped her lips, "because of me."

Cord placed his arm around her shoulder and led her out the lobby door, in the opposite direction of the hall. "I'm going to take you home."

Amy rested her head on his shoulder. There was no sense staying and trying to make amends. She was sure Jeff had gone to mommy immediately.

She tried not to look as Cord led her through the crowd and out the door, but she could still feel the repugnant stares. She shuddered at the hate she felt from people who had thought she was wonderful a short while ago.

Amy sighed heavily as they pulled in front of her house. They hadn't talked much, but she had watched Cord's face. Every time he clenched his teeth the muscle along his jaw line rippled. She dropped her gaze to her lap. Her knuckles were white from her tightened fist. Taking a deep breath, she made an effort to put in order the bits and pieces bouncing around her mind.

Of course she had thought their relationship would cause problems. Still, she'd been totally unprepared for the degree of intolerance. How could she have known how painful it was to be black in a white world? She definitely lived in a white world. She was angry and embarrassed to have those people in the same race with her. Yet, she chided herself, had she been much better? It took love to wake her to her indifference.

Cord knew. Yet he'd been willing to face the recrimination. She glanced at him. His sculptured face had relaxed a little but he fixed his eyes straight ahead. He looked as if he were watching an old film. A film he'd found distasteful when he saw it the first time, yet one he was forced to watch over and over.

Her hand moved to his thigh and rested there. Cord moved his gaze to hers. "The roller coaster ride has just begun." His voice carried a heavy dose of resignation.

She ran her fingers over his thigh thoughtfully. "I don't have a weak stomach. If I'm on the ride with you, I'll be okay." As calmly as she could manage she asked, "Will you?"

A tentative grin played on his lips. "I have to admit it's been a long time since I've had to face racism of this magnitude, but I've had a lifetime of training."

His slight grin lifted her spirits. "Good. Then it's something we will face together." She glanced at the house. "Speaking of facing it, I have to go in and tell my mother." The light from the television flickered in the living room. Amy sighed heavily. "Before Mrs. Delaney and her little darling use their town crier techniques to let everyone know." She spat out the last words contemptuously.

"Now pull yourself together." He patted her hand. "It won't do your mother or our case any good if we go in there carrying a chip."

Her eyes stopped roving and fixed on his face. "We?"

"Yes, we. Amy, I told you your mother knows." He placed his hand on the side of her face. "I'm sure of it."

"Oh." She thought about their conversation when they entered the Objibway Hotel. "Is that what you were trying to tell me?"

His hand moved gently over her face. "Yes."

"How do you know?" She couldn't imagine how her mother could have figured it out.

He shrugged matter-of-factly.

"She was a mother asking questions of a potential suitor for her daughter." He leaned closer to her face and brushed her lips. "If I'm wrong you can shoot me."

Amy giggled. "Don't think you will escape my wrath that easily."

His hand moved to her neck and pulled her mouth to his. "I'll remember." His mouth closed over hers. Her lips parted in welcome. Promising shivers ran through her. Soon she would have all of him all of the time.

Eight

Amy led Cord from the entrance hall to the dining room. A large platter of cookies sat in the middle of the table. Next to it was a carafe of coffee and three of her mother's finest cups.

"Mom must be expecting company." Amy's baffled voice was full of questions.

Cord chuckled. "At eleven o'clock at night? Your mother keeps strange hours."

She glanced at him and then back at the table. Near the head she saw an old book. Slowly she moved around until she could read it. It was her mother's high school annual. Even more baffled, she stared at Cord. "Maybe—maybe she is expecting an old friend."

Cord reached out and took her hand. "Maybe she is expecting us."

Amy shook her head. "But how?"

"Cord is right, sweetheart."

Amy guiltily pulled her hand back and swung around to face her mother. "Mom, I..."

"I know, dear." Mrs. Summers quickly walked to the head of the table.

"Mom, I don't understand." Her gaze darted from her mother to Cord, trying to read their looks. Did something happen when he was alone with her mother? She didn't know what else to think or say. Fear of misinterpreting her mother's words kept her quiet.

Amy had been here before. When her mother wanted to discuss something serious, it was always at the dining room table. Still, she hadn't uttered a word about Cord.

Mrs. Summers calmly asked, "Won't you both sit and join me?" She poured the coffee. "Amy dear, why don't you offer Cord some of my maple cookies?" Her gaze was approving as Amy followed instructions.

Amy glanced at her mother's smiling face. Maybe she's ill again, she thought. Sometimes stroke victims have problems. But she knew that wasn't true because her mother had never looked better. She placed a couple of cookies on her own plate after Cord had accepted his. "They are still warm."

"I baked them after you left for the evening." She brushed at a wisp of grey hair on her cheek.

"Why are you upset?" Her mother baked in the evening when she was trying to solve a problem. Amy moved closer to her mother and placed her arm around her shoulder. "Mom, what is it?"

Her mother laughed softly. "Nothing, dear. I just wanted to have fresh goodies for when the two of you came home." She opened the album and picked up a packet of pictures and letters.

Amy watched as her mother's short, thin fingers lovingly pulled the old faded ribbon. She stared as her mother sorted through her memories and then settled on something.

The older woman's voice softened as she finally spoke. "These memories are an important part of my past. When I share them with you, I ask only that you remember I am a human being as both of you are." Misty grey eyes searched both of their faces and then returned to the objects in front of her.

Mrs. Summers selected a picture from the stack, stared at it for a moment and then handed it to them. "This is a picture of me with," she hesitated, "a man. I loved this man with all my heart and he loved me." Her voice grew softer, as if disappearing into a dream. And then wistfully, "But our parents would not allow such a union."

Amy and Cord sat close to each other and stared at the picture of a young Native American man. Their gazes met. A silent agreement passed between them. They wouldn't speak until she was finished.

"When we were young," the older woman spoke to them and to her own soul, "interracial relationships were not only forbidden by society but were illegal in some parts of the country. My parents quickly arranged for a marriage to your father, and that was the end of it." Amy started to move toward her mother but the older woman held up her hand. "Let me finish, please."

Mrs. Summer's eyes were misting heavily. "I was brokenhearted. It didn't matter to me who I married. The truth was if I couldn't have John, I didn't want anyone. So I was the good daughter and did as my parents wanted. I married your father. It wasn't fair to either of us but we agreed to make the marriage work. And we did."

Amy took Cord's hand under the table as they watched her mother sort through her mind for more.

She picked up her spoon and stirred her coffee. Slowly her gaze rose to Amy's. "You made our marriage worthwhile. Eventually I came to love your father, but it wasn't the same kind of love John and I shared. Your father was a warm, kind and generous man, but he deserved more." Her melancholy speech over, she folded her hands on the album and looked from one to the other.

Amy covered her mother's hand with hers. Tears slipped from her eyes. She understood what her mother was saying. Cord was right. Somehow her mother had known. Now she was sharing a part of her that had been held close to her heart. A secret shared for her daughter's happiness. Tears blinded her and choked her voice as she rose and hugged her mother. "Oh, Mom, I'm so sorry."

Her mother wiped the tears from her own eyes. Then she dabbed at her daughter's. She rose. "I think you two have something to discuss." They watched as she disappeared through the kitchen door.

Amy moved to follow her, but Cord pulled her back. "Let her have her time."

"But I should go to her. She's hurting." Amy stopped and stared at the door, uncertain who was right.

"We all deserve our private time. Your mother has laid a lot on the line for our happiness. Let's just give her a few minutes."

Amy nodded in agreement. "I can't believe what she just told us." She walked back and slumped in her chair.

"I mean, I knew she and Dad didn't have a marriage made in heaven but they seemed happy enough."

Cord knelt in front of her. "They were as happy as they could be under the circumstances. Your dad must have loved her very much to play second fiddle. And it's obvious your mother loved him for that." He took her hands in his. "Let's not make the same mistake."

Amy studied their hands. The two colors looked so beautiful together. They belonged together. Somehow they would make it. A soft smile lifted her lips as her gaze met Cord's. "Is this a proposal?"

Cord leapt to his feet. "Don't move — I'll be right back." He took two long, bounding strides to the kitchen door and returned before it stopped swinging. Attached to his hand was a smiling Mrs. Summers. He spoke to the older woman first. "Mrs. Summers, I would like your permission to ask Amy to marry me."

Mrs. Summers smiled warmly at him. "You don't need my permission. But I thank you for asking." She brushed at her hair with nervous fingers. "So ask her." She laughed lightly.

Amy laughed nervously with her mother. Cord made them both feel alive. She hadn't seen her mother this happy in years. It puzzled her because she had always thought her mother was upset over her divorcing Tom. Before this went any further she had to know. "Mom, I thought you were still set on me being with Tom."

"Oh honey, that was eighteen years ago. When Sara was a baby. Of course I was worried." She glanced at Cord. "But I never wanted you to be unhappy."

Cord brought Mrs. Summers with him to where her daughter sat. Amy looked up at the two of them standing smiling at her. Cord dropped to his knee and took her hand. "Amy, would you spend the rest of your life with me?"

Amy threw her arms around his neck. Cord lifted her to her feet and then pulled his future mother-in-law into his embrace too. Mother and daughter laughed as they were swept off the floor and then set back down. "Yes," they both answered.

Cord threw his head back and roared with laughter. It looks like I have two women now."

Amy held both of her loved ones. Joy filled her heart. How could she top this moment? Her gaze fell on the picture of her with Sara. A chill swept through her. "Mom," her voice was barely audible. "What about Sara?"

Cord loosened his grip some and gazed at her lovingly. "We will cross that bridge when we come to it."

Amy let out a sigh. "That bridge will be home in a little over a week."

Mrs. Summers patted her daughter's arm. "Sara will be fine. She isn't as naive as you think. When you were at the conference, Sara and I laughed at the preparations you had made and discussed how you were acting like a woman in love."

Amy's face flushed red, remembering the panties and bra she had bought especially for the conference when the three of them had been shopping. "But how?" she breathed out.

Mrs. Summers laughed. "Oh honey, we are women. We recognize the signs." She smiled at her daughter and then began fussing with the dishes on the table. "Well, I must get this cleaned up and go to bed. You two just run along."

Amy hesitated and then began to help her mother. Mrs. Summers removed her daughter's hand from the dishes, smiling broadly. "I think the two of you have some things to work out." She glanced at Cord, "There is the matter of your parents and family. I think the sooner you go to them the better. They may not be happy at first but remember, they are your parents and I'm sure they love you and want the best for you."

Cord nodded. "I was going to leave in the morning to see them."

Mrs. Summers smiled at the young couple. "Well, don't just spring it on them, Cord. You tell them first and then after the dust settles take Amy to them." She smiled at her daughter, "It would be impossible not to love her."

Amy's lashes fluttered, and her heart pounded. Things were happening so fast. Was she ready to be thrown into another culture? Would his parents like her? Accept her? Fear gripped her heart. Yet she smiled at the two people in the room. "Mom, I think Cord can handle it." Yes, but could she?

Cord slipped his arm around his best friend. "Why don't you go to Lansing with me in the morning? You can go shopping while I meet and tell my parents. If everything is okay, then we will go see them together." He squeezed her to him.

"That is a wonderful idea, Amy," her mother threw in as she finished clearing the table.

"Sure." Amy's heart was pounding heavily against her rib cage. She wasn't nearly as confident as Cord or her mother but it seemed to be settled.

Her mother scurried out of the room, making herself look too busy to stay with them. Amy turned to the man she loved.

"When are we leaving?" She wanted to hear in a month but knew that wouldn't be the answer.

"In the morning." He pulled her closer and whispered to her, "Why don't you pack a bag while I help your mom with the dishes. Then we can leave right from the hotel in the morning."

Amy's face felt as if it had burst into flames. The thought of being in his arms thrilled her, but her mother... She lifted her gaze to the man she loved. "What about Mom?" her voice barely a whisper.

Cord chuckled. "You pack, I'll take care of mom." He winked as a wide grin grew on his face. "Amy, she knows we are going to leave here together."

Amy nodded. "Guess she does. She is wiser than I ever imagined." She stood on tiptoes and brushed a light kiss on his lips. "I'll be back soon."

Amy and Cord walked hand in hand down the steps of the rambling Victorian porch. Cord opened the door of the Navigator and leaned in to kiss her as he buckled her belt. "Wouldn't want anything to happen to you now." A sensual grin spread from his mouth to his eyes.

Amy's heart was singing a sweet song. She was with the man she loved and her mother was happy about it. In fact encouraged it, she smiled to herself. Her mother was definitely wiser than she had ever given her credit for.

She settled herself into the rich leather of the bucket seat and turned her head to avoid headlights that had popped on. She looked at the car, shielding her eyes a bit. Yet she could see Jeff leering at them. She glanced at Cord. He had noticed too, and his back had gone ramrod straight.

"Cord?" she shivered the question. "Wh—what do you think he is doing?" Her heart thudded. Jeff and his mother were the pillars of the community. They could destroy Cord and her with a few well-placed comments.

Cord shook his head. "I have no idea. But I'm sure we will discover his plan very soon." He turned to Amy. "Baby, this is not going to be easy." He paused to take a deep breath. "The threat Jeff issued tonight wasn't idle." Gripping the wheel he looked straight ahead. "It isn't too late for you to get out." His eyes were filled with pain as he turned his gaze to her. "I mean, you don't have to go through with this."

Her heart melted for him and all in his race. How could a person go through life living with such hatred and fear of retaliation because of their skin color? She was beginning to understand more of what his life had been and love him more for his ability to rise above it.

She rubbed her hand on his thigh. "Let's forget it for now." She tightened her grip on his thigh. He started, as if to ward off an enemy. "Cord, I'm sorry, I was just trying to get your attention."

A slight smile pushed onto his lips. "You have it, baby." He glanced around as he turned the key in the ignition. "I think we should go to the hotel."

Amy nodded. She knew he wasn't with her mentally. His senses were sharpened and alert for signs of trouble. She glanced at Cord's handsome face and wondered if she would ever get used to always looking over her shoulder. Life would be different now. Still, she wanted him and she would try to be ready for whatever came her way.

The hotel room was huge and brightly decorated in various shades of blue. Mirrors lined the wall surrounding a big hot tub. She glanced around and saw the one king-size bed. Her breath caught in her throat as she realized she would soon be back in her lover's arms. Shyly, she looked at Cord. He stood staring out the window. "Cord?"

Slowly and thoughtfully he turned to her. "Yes?"

"What are you thinking about?" Amy could see the struggle in his eyes, new worry lines in his face. She felt a twinge of guilt: She had been only thinking of being in his arms and making love, while Cord had been worrying about them.

Cord smiled. "I was thinking having a reservation to go to would be all right. My Native American brothers and I have problems in common."

Amy went to him. She knew what he meant. The reservation was off limits to white justice or injustice. She laid her head on his chest just under his chin and listened to his heartbeat as it slowed. "We will make it together," she whispered. Her insides quivered as his arms came around her in an ironclad grip.

He kissed the top of her head. "Don't worry your pretty head about it. I've been here before." He thought for a moment. "And I will probably be here again." His lips brushed her forehead and sought her lips, reclaiming them and crushing her to him.

The hunger of his kiss shattered all thoughts. "Em...,"she moaned lightly. His tongue traced the soft fullness of her mouth. Though her lips felt hot and swollen they begged for more. Pressed against him, she could feel the physical evidence of his heated desire.

He lifted her and carried her to the bed, his eyes holding hers. "This is forever, baby." His voice was hoarse with passion.

Amy held his melting chocolate gaze. "I know." Simple words spoken quietly while two hearts matched rhythm.

Without speaking, he reached his hand behind her back and slowly drew down the zipper of her evening gown, then gently removed it and neatly laid it aside.

Amy's heart thudded in her chest. This felt so natural. She belonged to him and she knew it. He removed her nylons one at a time, then stood and stared at her as she lay in her lace bra and panties. When he looked into her eyes, she could see love and desire. But in the deep recesses, a storm was brewing.

In the dead silence of the room, she watched as he turned and walked to the window to peer through the drapes. "Damn," he cursed. Moving away from the window, he slowly, thoughtfully, removed the deep charcoal gray tie that fit so nicely around his neck. He folded it and laid it on the vanity. Next he slid the jacket off and hung it on a hanger, then his pants. Amy watched in fascination. Not only was he gorgeous but he was so darned neat. "Cord." The word was barely audible to her own ears. Still he turned to her, giving her his full attention.

"Yes?" His stilted voice ran a chill through her, but his attention didn't waiver as he slowly turned on the water faucet to fill the hot tub. His thoughts, though, were someplace else. She shivered, seeing a part of him she didn't know.

Slipping from the bed she stared thoughtfully at her overnight bag. Was there something wrong with her? Had he changed his mind? She shook her head to clear the ugly thoughts. Finally she reached down, unzipped the bag and retrieved her light robe. She couldn't explain the gnawing in her stomach. Because they had been friends before they were lovers, she instinctively knew something was wrong. She wanted desperately to be with him but... "Cord."

"Hmm?" he answered as he tested the water.

She fumbled to tie her robe. "I—I feel like something is wrong." Now that was an understatement if she'd ever made one. He looked at her. Though a smile pushed the corners of his mouth, it didn't get anywhere near his eyes.

"There's nothing wrong, Amy. I have a lot on my mind." The storm in his eyes eased a bit. "I did ask you to marry me tonight and I want everything to be right for us."

She moved to where he was. "I am with you so everything is right."

He pulled her into his arms, and his large hand pressed her head to his chest. "That's right. We are together and that makes it all right."

She could hear his heart thumping loudly beneath the thick muscles that supported her head. A big sigh escaped her lips. "I love you."

He kissed the top of her head. "I love my lady." His mouth moved to her ear. "I won't let anything happen to you." His steel grip pulled her in. "I won't lose you now." His mouth traversed her soft ivory cheek to find her mouth. Claiming her waiting lips, he crushed her to him.

Fully alert, waiting, wanting, Amy felt her knees weaken. He moved his mouth over hers, devouring it. Amy shivered from the top of her head to the tips of her toes.

No one, not even Cord, had kissed her like this. Forcing her lips open with his thrusting tongue, he explored the deep recesses of her inner warmth. Amy's body molded into his. She relinquished any thoughts of Cord's seeming distance.

Cord moved his lips to the hollow of her throat. Then he pulled at the loose tie of her robe and pushed the robe gently from her body. Amy shivered in delight. This was the man she loved. This was what she had expected. His hands glided to unhook her bra, freeing her. Caressingly, he moved his hands down her back and slipped her lace panties from her hips.

She searched his eyes and saw something primitive in their depths. Was it his feeling for her? She didn't know and at the moment didn't care. Her fingers traced the well-defined muscles of his back, feeling his body shudder. His response was all she needed. Her exploration continued down until she came to a barrier. She pushed his briefs to the floor and trickled her nails over his firm rear. "I love your body," she murmured into his chest.

"Mmm," he groaned, then swept her up into his arms and stepped into the bubbling hot tub. His mouth swooped down to capture hers as they sank into the water together. Her legs wrapped around him to ensnare his body. They mutually shuddered, but not from the water.

They were locked in a nuptial embrace, one that said forever. Amy dove into the depths of his ebony eyes. She saw love but she also saw pain. How could she help? She didn't even know what was wrong. They were almost as close as two people could be physically, yet he wasn't aroused. How could this be? He had been minutes before, or had she imagined it?

She held his face in her hands. "Tell me." Her voice was soft, yet demanding. "Are you worried about what your parents will think of me?"

Cord pulled away and laid his head back against the edge of the tub, closing his eyes. A disgruntled gasp escaped his lip. "No."

His one word answer took her aback. Suddenly she felt her nakedness. Her heart beating a drum roll in her throat, she reached for a towel. Sitting on the edge of the tub with the towel wrapped around her, Amy felt tears springing to her eyes and trickling down her cheeks. "Well, what then? What's wrong?" her voice cracked with sobs.

Cord stared at her, seeming to really see her for the first time in a while. His trance-like stare softened though he didn't reach for her. He just shook his head. "It's my problem, has nothing to do with you."

Hot, painful tears stung her eyes. "Wh—what do you mean? I thought we were one now."

Cord didn't want to tell her that he'd seen Jeff's car by his in the parking lot. His stomach knotted. Amy wasn't that white man's woman. She was going to be his wife. Damn, he thought.

Cord grabbed a towel and wrapped his lower half as he wrenched himself from the hot tub and from her. He couldn't make love tonight. "Damn it," he cursed to himself. His anger was for racism but he shot his remark at her. "You could never understand."

He quickly walked to the window and drew the drape back a little to look again. As he'd expected, Jeff was still there. He dropped the drape. "Your friend has set up a vigil tonight." He spoke as if to accuse her.

"My friend?"

"Jeff," he groused.

"But why?" Her voice was filled with confusion.

Shaking his head, he moved to the bed. "I have two choices." He glanced at Amy, who had gone to peek out the window. "I can stay here and do my job or let that asshole run me out of town." He didn't want to do either. Doing his job meant investigating Amy and now he had this nutty cop chasing him.

He just wanted his life back. He retrieved his briefs and pulled them on. "That racist redneck isn't going to win this one," he announced decisively. Amy's wide-eyed stare added to his dilemma. He met her stare and then looked away. How could he explain? This war had been going on for centuries and she knew little about it.

He paced the floor, his mind whirling, and very aware of Amy watching him. Outside was a man who wanted to do whatever it took to run him out of town. Besides that, he was investigating Amy, the woman he planned to marry. The stress was overwhelming. He swung around and almost knocked her off her feet. He caught her and pulled her into his arms, "Baby, we have to talk."

She nodded and looked up at him. "I want to."

He looked lovingly into her silvery green eyes, eyes that showed love and fear. The knot in his stomach grew tighter. The last thing he wanted was for Amy to fear him. He led her to the love seat by the corner fireplace, sat her down and then ignited the gas in the small fieldstone hearth.

He stared into the flames, searching for answers to give her. Finally, he broke the long drawn-out silence. "Amy, I..."

"Yes," her voice was soft and pensive, and her eyes were fixed on his face. Worry lines gathered on her brow.

"I love you." He had to tell her so much, and yet that was what came out.

"Thank you." She kept her eyes riveted on him.

Cord took one long step to the love seat and sat beside her. "Amy, there are some things I need to tell you." He could see the questions in her eyes. Her mouth opened and then closed again. There was nothing she could say. It was all up to him and he knew it.

"At first I thought we were just friends." She nodded agreement, her face composed. He took a deep breath. "The truth is, after a very short time I knew I was in love. Somehow, through a miracle, we connected and there it was." He stood and began pacing. His shoulders were squared and proud, but his fist clenched and unclenched. He stopped abruptly in front of her and drew a deep breath.

"Damn it, Amy, say something." He was staring into misty green eyes.

"Cord, whatever it is you want to say, I will listen. I don't know what's going on, but I will try to understand." She folded her hands and nervously twisted them in her lap.

"Amy, this assignment isn't what it seems. I am here to investigate the mishandling of state funds." Her eyes twitched and a flicker of incredulity momentarily crossed her face. Cord winced at her reaction, feeling as if he had hit her.

He wanted to pull her into his arms. Yet he wanted to finish, while he still had the nerve to tell her everything.

"I never believed it was you."

This time he hit home. Her face reddened and her eyes narrowed.

"If you never believed it, then why are you here?" Tears streamed down her face.

He took a step toward her, then stopped. "Baby, I didn't believe it. I was sure it couldn't be you, but if there had been any truth in it, I was ready to help you out." He stared at her for a moment and then walked to the window again. Jeff was still sitting there even though it was well after two in the morning. "That damned cracker," he spat. His anger overwhelmed him as he pounded one fist into the other.

Amy couldn't stay silent. Her life was on the line here. "You couldn't believe it but just in case it was true, you were going to help me? Help me what?" Her voice was shaking with hurt and anger.

Cord heaved a heavy sigh. "I knew your mom had been ill and that the cost of her rehabilitation had been prohibitive. With that and saving for Sara's college...you were under so much stress... He stopped and waited for the response he saw forming on her lips.

"You thought I had been so stressed that I took money that wasn't mine?" Her voice was growing in pitch.

"Christ, Amy, it was a fleeting thought. At the time I was presented with this...I acted impulsively, wanting to protect the woman I loved."

Amy's glare evaporated as she realized his sincerity, but she didn't understand how he could have had even a fleeting thought of her being dishonest. "Well, it isn't true."

"I know." They stared at each other, speaking volumes in the look. The silence stretched until Cord finally ended it with, "That's one for you and one for me. Now can we wipe the slate clean and begin over? I am in love with you. Nothing can change that."

"Okay," she said distractedly, still trying to digest the information, wondering if money had actually been taken or if there had been errors.

"Okay?" Cord parroted.

She looked up. He was waiting for an answer. His explanation had been from the heart, and she knew he had been thinking of her. "OK, the slate is clean."

"Thank you," he answered unsteadily.

So much to sort through, Amy thought. Nothing made sense. Then she remembered something else. Before he dropped the bomb he had called someone a cracker, whatever that was.

"Who?"

"Who what?"

"You called someone a cracker. Who?"

He stared at her, trying to shift gears. "Oh, that! I meant that idiot in the car out there."

Muscles tightened along his jaw as he was brought back full circle.

"Jeff is a cracker? What's a cracker? I—I don't understand." Her shaky voice sounded strange to her ears.

Cord came to her and pulled her into his arms. Brushing her hair back tenderly, he whispered, "Of course you don't." How could he explain without sounding racist? "I mean, he is someone who would beat a person of color, just because of his color."

Amy leaned back and looked into his dark stormy eyes. "Why that word?" She had so much to learn and didn't know where to begin.

Cord shrugged his shoulders, trying to look as if it didn't hurt. The pain and history were deeply embedded in his soul. "It comes from slavery times. That's what they called the white man with the whip. The one who left slaves bloody and tortured."

Amy sucked in air. There was so much for them to learn about each other. She wondered how they would survive the winds of change.

Nine

They talked most of the night. Finally, Amy had curled in his arms and fallen asleep, but he couldn't. Ordinarily the early morning sun peeping through the drapes would have made him feel good. But this morning he knew he was going to face a problem. He gazed down into her sweet face as she slept so trusting in his arms. Could she stand up under the pressure? Would their love take the beating?

Gently he pulled himself from around her and went to the window. Jeff had left, but another car with a different man had taken his place. Cord knew they were in for a traffic ticket at the least. "Damn it," he cursed.

"Cord?"

Amy's sleepy voice cut through his searching mind. He glanced at the vigilant car and then back at her. "So my lady awakes?" He watched as she stretched and tried to come fully awake. Her small hands pushed at the hair covering her soft face. His heart was filled with love. And fear for her. Still, he didn't want to turn back and he hoped she wouldn't either.

Her smile turned toward him. "Sorry, I must have dozed off. Did you get any sleep?"

He shook his head. "I'll be fine," he lied to her, trying to make himself believe it. He glanced at his watch. "If we're going to Lansing, we had better get on the road. It's at least a five-hour drive."

Amy slipped from the bed and came to the window. "I see we still have a guest. Hope he doesn't go to Lansing with us." She smiled at him but he could tell she was worried.

"Well, we'll find out soon enough." He studied the situation for a minute. "I wish there was another way out. I am not in the mood for dealing with a redneck this morning."

Amy stood on tiptoes and whisked a kiss over his lips. "I think I can take care of this."

Cord stared at her. Last night she had been filled with fear and trepidation and now she looked like she could take on the world. He chuckled. "Just what is it that you will take care of?" He brushed her loose hair away from her face. "I don't need my lady to take care of things."

Amy glanced at Cord's face. His narrowed eyes and set jaw were sure signs he wasn't going to like her taking charge. But their talking had cleared her mind. She might not understand being black, but she knew how to help. She would just have to be careful with his ego.

She glanced at the clock. Six o'clock. Shelley and Leo would still be sleeping but she knew Shelley stood ready to help. She punched in the phone number.

When Shelley's sleepy voice came on the line, Amy's face lifted in a smile. "Shelley?"

"Amy, what is it?" Her voice was fully awake. "Is something wrong?"

Amy could hear Shelley relating the story to Leo as they spoke. Soon Leo's quiet voice was on the phone. "Amy, we will be there in a few minutes. Don't worry about a thing."

"Thanks, Leo. You are good friends to have."

She turned to Cord. "You know Shelley?"

He nodded. "What does she have to do with this?" His graveled voice displayed his anxiety.

"She and her husband will be right over."

His brows furrowed and his dark eyes narrowed with an impending storm. "That's all we need .."

"No, Cord." She stopped his angry onslaught. "They are good people. Shelley's husband Leo said he would help us and I think in this case we need his help." She went to him and circled her arms around his waist. Pointedly looking into his eyes, she added, "It doesn't hurt to know someone on the tribal council." She brushed his lips. "Let's shower and be ready when they come."

Cord placed his hand at the back of her neck and pulled her mouth to his. "Guess I have to trust you on this one."

■■■

Shelley and Leo arrived in an hour with breakfast in tow. Leo pulled the cart into the room when Amy opened the door. Shelley, right behind him, giggled. "Leo likes to eat while he's making plans," she explained as she hugged Amy.

Amy held her friend tightly. "Thank you for coming." She turned and introduced Leo to Cord, watching as the two men shook hands. Though about the same height, Leo was slight in build. Cord looked extremely muscular against Leo's small frame. They laughed as they shook hands. Her heart did a little dance. They would like each other and together they would come up with something.

The women listened and watched as the men devoured their breakfast and each other's ideas. They got up at the same time and went to the window. Cord grumbled, "Persistent SOB, isn't he?"

Leo nodded and spoke in his deep, yet soft and lilting voice. "There is more than one way to do this."

"I know. You said." He shrugged his shoulders and looked out again.

A slow smile lifted Leo's face. "You have enough to worry about this weekend, without having a white tail on your butt. My plane's at the Hessel Airport, which is down the road a bit." Leo's arm indicated south. Cord's brow lifted in question.

Amy's lips curled into a smile. Hessel was 50 miles south but she and Leo knew that in northern Michigan nothing was far, unless it was well over 100 miles. Right now she and Leo, who were of different races, were just two northern folk, meeting on common ground. Race played no part in this understanding. Somehow this thought lifted her spirits. Maybe she and Cord weren't so far apart.

She spoke dubiously to Shelley, "Fly us there?"

"Whatever Leo thinks is fine with me. I could do some shopping, haven't been downstate in a long time." She shrugged her shoulders and smiled.

Cord and Leo turned toward the women. Their faces both registered surprise, as if they had forgotten they were in the room.

"They are all alike." Cord spoke to Leo and then glanced at Amy.

"Yep, get them near a city and they think they have to shop," Leo agreed.

All four laughed. The women went into the embrace of their men. Amy knew she and Cord were meant to be. She had never felt so sure about anything in her life.

Leo and Shelley led the way through the hotel to the back of the casino and their car. Forty-five minutes later they were at the airport and boarding the small aircraft.

"How long does it take?" Cord settled himself into the copilot's seat.

Leo taxied down the runway and then lifted off before answering. "With these skies," he checked the instrument panel, "two hours and forty-five minutes." Then he radioed his flight plan in.

"Didn't think it was required to file a flight plan in small planes," Cord remarked as he studied the panel.

"Don't have to. Can just use VFR—visual flight rules—but we fly over a lot of wilderness." He turned and smiled at his wife. "Then if you are late by a half an hour it's assumed you've gone down and the search begins. Right, honey?" He gave a soft laugh.

"Right." Shelley smiled. "As long as you follow the plan you file."

They all laughed at the inside joke that was easy to understand. Amy looked admiringly at her friends. They had worked out their problems and were obviously in love and at ease with their differences.

She looked at Cord who sat so proud and erect. He was everything she wanted in a husband. Her heart raced in her chest. After meeting his parents they were going to spend time together alone. She remembered the passion of his kiss and she could feel her face flush.

Shelley smiled and leaned over to her. "I know exactly how you feel."

Amy's face grew hotter. She turned to face her friend. "Cord proposed last night."

"And?" Shelley couldn't contain herself.

"And," Amy smiled brightly, "I accepted."

Cord turned and winked at Amy. "But she asked me first."

Amy blushed even deeper. "That isn't exactly the way it went." A small giggle escaped her lips.

"So when is the big day?" Leo tossed out.

Amy caught Cord's gaze and held it. "Not soon enough."

"Whenever my lady wants." His gaze dropped from her eyes, to her shoulders to her breasts. "Whatever she wants." His grin grew wide.

Amy felt hot lava rush through her body. The smoldering flame she saw in his eyes reminded her of their time together at the conference. Her fingers went to her lips as she recalled the burning flesh against flesh. That's what I want, she thought.

Shelley laughed. "Leo, I think we will have to change the flight plan. These two need a minister or a hotel room."

The laughter in the small plane reverberated. Amy took a deep breath. She was almost home free. She just had to convince his parents that she was the one for their son.

■ ■ ■

Cord hailed a taxi and gave directions to his apartment. He was relieved when the other three went off on their shopping expedition. Though he dreaded his parents' reaction, he anticipated his sister Leah would be his worst problem. He glanced at his watch, almost ten. If he hurried, Leah would still be asleep.

He drove his Lexus to his parents' two-story brick home. He sat and stared at it for a few minutes. They had worked so hard for this. Both had put themselves through college where they had met. They had given him and his sister a warm, loving environment and kept black history alive for them. Cord steeled himself and pushed the car door open.

He walked purposefully around the house and went in the back by the kitchen where he knew they would be. He drew in as much air as he could, filling his lungs to capacity, then blew it out through his mouth. He was as ready as he ever would be. He pulled the door open. Berating himself, he thought, that at his age it shouldn't matter what his parents thought. But it did.

"Good morning." He forced himself to sound cheerful. When his parents both looked up from their newspapers and smiled, his throat constricted. Their warm smiles gave him pause. Maybe he should forget this. Yet, Amy's face loomed in front of his. He had to proceed.

"Good morning, baby." His mother turned her cheek for a kiss. "What brings you here so early?" Her face broke into a wide grin. "And on a Saturday morning." Her voice was filled with a question more than a statement.

"Morning, Son." His dad turned the page of the newspaper.

"Dad." Cord knew his dad was listening even though he seemed totally absorbed in his reading. That came from years of teaching. "How are things at the university?" That wasn't what he wanted to say but it was all he could think of.

His dad slowly lowered the paper and stared at his son. His eyebrows lifted in question. "The same as last week." He smiled slightly. "Unless you've heard something I haven't."

Cord shook his head. "Have you had breakfast yet?" He looked down at his shoes, subconsciously checking to make sure they were polished. Years of schooling by his parents made him very aware of his appearance. He glanced from one loving face to the other. He wanted to take them to breakfast and away from Leah.

"No, we were just about to fix some. Would you like hot cakes this morning?" Mrs. McCune scurried around the kitchen. Cord held his hand out and stopped her.

"I would like to take you and dad," he glanced at his father, "to breakfast." He felt as he did when he was twelve and about to tell them he had broken their favorite piece of African art. "Just the three of us."

He had his parents' attention. His mother moved closer to him and looked pointedly into his face. Placing her hand on his arm she asked, "What's wrong?"

He could feel her love and concern. "Nothing, Mom. I just want to talk to both of you privately." He could feel the strain growing on his face.

Mrs. McCune moved closer and stared into his face. "As your attorney or your mother?" Her voice was creeping up the worried scale.

"As my mother." Again he glanced at his dad. "As my parents."

"Son, if there is something you need to discuss, we're here." Cord loved his father's voice, so deep, rich and clear. He had taken a class or two with him and he remembered how his voice carried so much authority. It bounced around the room and kept the attention of all of the students in the lecture hall.

"Dad, I would like to treat you to breakfast and I want to speak to you alone."

Mr. McCune surveyed the room. "We are alone."

His mother grabbed her purse. "Come on, Henry. It is obvious that Cordelle needs to speak with us alone. With no interruptions."

Henry laid the paper down. "I see." He pulled his long lean body from his chair and smiled at his wife. "Then we will go."

Cord smiled at the couple who had parented him. He knew he was lucky and that he was about to cause them some anguish. Still, he had made his decision and there was no turning back. He loved Amy and there was nothing that could change that. He scoffed at himself. He wouldn't if he could. Somehow he would convince them that this was right.

They were happily greeted by the maitre d' of the Pistachio Restaurant. "Good morning, Mrs. McCune, Mr. McCune, Cordelle." The maitre d' smiled broadly and motioned for them to follow.

The plush seats were filled with business and social friends of their family. They were greeted by everyone as they were led to their seats. Cord thought about the reception he had received at the fundraiser. What a different world. He shook his head. Very different. He had gone from invisible to complete acceptance.

He surveyed the posh surroundings. Live plants were hung in just the right lighting for their species. The area where they were seated was light and airy with bright spring sun bouncing off the crystal water goblets. He stared into the glittering light for a moment, mesmerizing himself with thoughts of Amy. He doubted if she had ever been in a place like this, where all races came together as one. Business and intellect separated people here. Not race.

When they were seated, they ordered breakfast. After the waiter left, Cord looked at his parents, who were both staring at him. He forced a grin to his unwilling lips. "Hey, I'm not going to die. You don't have to look like that."

Mrs. McCune uttered a sigh of relief. "Cordelle, you nearly scared the life out of me." Her beautiful light chocolate face had lost some of its color. Her dark eyes pierced into his soul. "What is it son?"

"Mom, I—could we wait until after breakfast?" He could do this for Amy—for himself. He swallowed the lump in his throat.

Henry McCune patted his wife on the arm. "Easter, Cordelle needs fortification first." He chuckled. "It is spring and a young man's fancy..."

"Cordelle, is that true?" Easter McCune's face brightened.

"Who is she? Where is she from?" The excitement bubbled from her.

"Mom..." He wanted to delay the inevitable.

"Of course, dear, after breakfast." Mrs. McCune pushed her chair back. "As long as we are having the brunch buffet, let's do it and then hear the news."

Cord and his father both stood to follow her. Cord was thankful for the reprieve. He loaded his plate without a thought as to what he was putting on it. When he consciously looked at it, he had to chuckle. He looked like he was eating for a dozen. Well, if he could eat that much he would hold off telling them for awhile.

Henry McCune glanced at his son's plate. "Guess you are hungry," he chuckled in his deep voice. Then only to Cord, "The little lady keeping you so busy you don't have time to eat?"

Cord smiled at the man he respected more than anyone. He felt his father would come around quickly. Yet, he'd heard his mother's negative comments on the subject many times.

The three ate, while Mrs. McCune beguiled them with stories of the recent courtroom battle she had won. She was a great attorney and an even better mother. Cord watched as her animated face told the other part of the story that her soft voice didn't. He was half-listening. His heart and mind were jumping ahead to his prepared speech. Finally she placed her knife across the top of her plate and looked up. "For a hungry man you haven't eaten much."

Cord swallowed hard. It was time and he knew it. His heart quivered with a mixture of the joy of sharing his love and the fear of hurting them. He glanced from one to the other. "Dad, you are right, it is spring." His heart pounded heavily in his chest as his parents' faces broke into bright smiles.

"Cordelle, that is wonderful. When are we going to meet her?" Hearing his mother's voice bubble with excitement, his heart thudded in his chest. She had wanted him to find someone for a long time. Still, he knew this wasn't what she had in mind.

"I was hoping you would invite us to dinner tomorrow." Way to skirt the issue, he thought.

"Of course, dear. I will invite the family. Is it that serious? I mean, you haven't brought anyone around in years." Her bright face filled with hope.

"I am going to marry her." Damn it, he cursed to himself. I was going to tell them about her first.

"Congratulations, Son. Henry McCune extended his hand and shook his son's.

"Thanks." He directed this to both parents. "There are some things I want to tell you about her." He took a deep breath. "I met her through work. She lives in the Upper Peninsula." He looked from one to the other. As a partial awareness set in, the smiles faded from their faces. He swallowed hard.

"Cordelle?" His mother questioned. "Where on earth did you meet a black girl way up there?" Her voice was filled with hope and foreboding.

He could feel the muscle flex along his jaw line. The stalling was over. "She isn't black." There it was out. He released the air he had been holding in his lungs. And waited for the inevitable.

He watched as they regained their composure. His mother looked as if she were about to enter the courtroom. His father looked as if he were entering a classroom filled with freshmen.

"Well, Son, it seems you have made your decision." His father's voice was very controlled.

"Henry." His mother gave her husband a sideways glance, and then returned her gaze to her son. "Is your decision final?"

Cord felt as if he were on the witness stand and chose his answer accordingly. "I love Amy. And we will be married as soon as possible."

Mrs. McCune glanced around her, as if afraid someone would overhear. "It would be better to let your love season." She took a drink of water. "Then if you still want to marry her, it was meant to be."

"We have been seasoning for two years, Mom. Nothing is going to change the fact that I love her." Cord glanced at his father. "Dad, I hope we will get your blessing." Then to his mother, "I hope you will understand."

His parents looked at each other with a mutual understanding, the way Cord had seen them do all his life. He always marveled at how they came to a meeting of the minds without speaking. He waited. One of them would tell him what they had decided. They turned to him at the same time. His father cleared his throat.

"Son, being African-American in this society is difficult enough without adding a mixed relationship to it." He held up his hand as Cord began to protest. "Let me finish. However, we do know the strength of love. If this is love, you must give it a chance." His parents exchanged brief looks.

His mother took over. "We only ask that you let your love season in both cultures. It can only last if you both are willing to try to understand the other's way of life." She patted Cord on the hand. "We support your decision and will be here for you." A warm smile grew on her face. "Tomorrow for dinner, then? You will bring Amy? That was her name, wasn't it?"

"Yes, Mom, Amy Summers." Cord had always felt blessed to have been born to his parents, yet until this moment he had never known the depth of their love. They were willing to accept possible condemnation of their community for his happiness. He walked around behind them and hugged them. "Thank you. I will heed your warnings." He spoke softly. "I love you."

He gave his mother a quick kiss on the cheek and gripped his father's shoulder. "I can't wait for you to meet Amy. I'm sure you will love her as I do." He pulled the keys to his car from his pocket. "You take my car home with you. I'll take a taxi back to my apartment." His father accepted the keys and both parents gave him a broad smile.

"Tomorrow, Son."

"Tomorrow," he said as he turned on his heel and strolled to the door. His heart was lighter. His next move was to tell his son Hank and invite him for dinner at his grandparents'. Then he could return to the one he loved, Amy. His heart sang as he hailed a cab and gave directions to his son's dorm at Michigan State University, a couple of miles away.

■■■

Unnoticed, Cord stood in the doorway as Hank packed to leave the dorm for the summer. He watched his tall, handsome son for a few minutes before he spoke. Hank was a liberal. Still, this was a little more than being open-minded. This would change all of their lives. He thought of Amy telling Sara. They both had to cross that bridge.

He cleared his throat. Hank looked up and an ear-to-ear grin grew on his face.

"Hey Dad, what's up?" He threw his clothes in the bag without folding them.

Cord cringed. He could have gotten a little of my neatness, he thought. He stepped over the boxes and hugged his son. "Just needed to talk to you."

Hank stared at his father. "You look serious. Is something wrong?" His voice was edged with anxiety.

Cord shook his head. "No, Son. For me everything is right and that is what I am here to tell you."

Hank let out a sigh of relief. "Go for it. You talk and I'll pack."

Cord grabbed some things and began folding. Not so much to be neat but to have something to do while he talked. "Son, I'm going to remarry."

Hank dropped his MSU jacket and stuck out his hand. "Congratulations, Dad. It is about time. Mom keeps saying you need someone."

Cord pulled his son in and gave him a big hug, then released him with a slap on the shoulder. "Your mother is a good woman. And damned clever." He did admire his former wife. She had been a friend throughout.

"So Dad, tell me about my new stepmom." He resumed his packing as if this were an everyday occurrence.

Cord thought of Amy and how to describe her. "Well, son, she is intelligent, warm, kind and has been my best friend for two years now."

Hank jerked a look at his father. "Seriously, Dad. What does she look like?" He gave his father a punch on the shoulder. "I am sure she is all that. But something turned your head in the first place."

Cord smiled, remembering her voice the first time he heard it. "Yes, Son, she has the sweetest, sexiest..."

"Ass?" Hank filled in and laughed.

"Voice." Cord laughed too. "I met her at work. Well, over the phone at work."

"And?" Hank was growing impatient.

"And she is beautiful. "Deep brown hair. Silvery green eyes and skin the color of pearls. With a touch of peach in her cheeks." He waited, holding his breath as he watched his son digest the description.

"You mean my new mom-to-be is white?" He slapped his knee. "Dad, that is the last thing I thought you would say." He chuckled to himself.

Cord's shoulders shifted down. "It doesn't bother you?"

"Hell, Dad, you have to live with her. I don't." He grinned widely. "But I am anxious to meet her. I want to know the woman who snared the untouchable."

Cord laughed with his son. "You'll get your chance. Grandma has asked us to dinner and I want you to be there."

"Sure, Dad. When?"

"Tomorrow."

"Can I bring my date?"

Cord hesitated. Amy would have so much to deal with, yet his son didn't ask much. "Sure. Be there at six, okay?"

"No problem, Dad." He punched him in the shoulder again. "Still got it, don't you?"

Cord smiled. "Got something, all right." He chuckled as he left his son's room. It felt good having it out in the open and he knew his parents would grow to love Amy. But Leah would be another subject altogether.

He hailed a cab. He had one more stop to make. When he had finished that, he reentered the waiting cab and was finally headed for the apartment and Amy. The battle was half over. And he needed to be with her.

Ten

Amy paced the highly polished oak floor of the dining area, counting each step. The clicking of her heels kept time with the mantle clock. Around the bottom of the sheer curtains hanging at the sliding doors, gentle breezes played. She stopped and looked thoughtfully through the glass panes. The balcony was filled with flowers, nicely arranged around rattan wicker furniture. His garden was perfectly manicured. Heck, she thought, everything about him was perfect.

She wrapped her arms around her waist and closed her eyes. She needed him. Wanted him. It seemed ages since she had held Cord. Amy squeezed herself as if she could bring him to her.

She wondered how it had gone with his parents. She twisted her hands together as she began counting off her paces again, anything to keep her mind occupied and off thinking. Yet she couldn't help wondering if she would be welcome at his parents'.

She surveyed the opulence of Cord's apartment, again trying to rid her mind of her troubling thoughts. Her survey roamed over the decor. It was masculine, yet there was something about the fine lines that made it appealing to the feminine eye. African art in all forms either stood or was neatly placed around the room and on the walls.

The rich, burgundy leather furniture sat on plush cream-colored carpeting in the sunken living room. Not an article out of place. She ran her finger over an end stand. Not even a hint of dust. It was a little uncomfortable being in this strange place with so much perfection, especially knowing she was not this neat. And she was going to marry him, this personification of perfection.

"Amy." Cord's voice startled her. She whirled around. Her heart turned over as their gazes met. Yes, she was going to marry him. He was everything she wanted, neat freak and all. She smiled inwardly.

"Yes?" she managed to say as her hormones mingled with feelings of trepidation raging through her like a hot summer storm.

"I told my parents and Hank. Mom wants you to come to dinner tomorrow." His voice was soft but filled with confidence.

"Were they okay with this?" Her voice faltered. "I mean, was it that easy? Are they going to be okay with this?"

Cord covered the distance between them and bundled her into his arms. He kissed the top of her head. "It will be when they get to know you."

She studied his dark eyes, searching for answers. Instead of answers she saw an eager affection. He radiated a vitality that drew her like a magnet. All other questions vanished as her body ached to be closer.

"Have you looked at the rest of the place?" he whispered hoarsely.

She shook her head against his chest. "No. But it's all so perfect, so neat." She gave a light laugh. "Don't you ever make a mess?"

"Hmmmmm. Only in the bedroom," he teased playfully.

The obvious invitation was more than she could resist. "This I have to see." She was accepting the invitation but couldn't believe he would ever have anything out of place.

He swept her into his arms and carried her down the long hall to the end. He shifted her to free a hand and opened the door. Without stopping he carried her to the bed and sat her down gently.

She glanced around her and couldn't help noting the huge room was perfect, nothing out of place. She'd been right. The bed looked as if it had been made by an Army drill sergeant. She had the urge to bounce a quarter on it. He was too neat. He tapped her chin with his finger. "Let me show you, baby."

She watched as in one fluid movement he stripped and threw his clothes on the floor, laughing at his comedic actions. "Now this is an improvement in more ways than one."

Cord's face grew bright with her obvious admiration. He came to her and tenderly but quickly stripped her and threw the clothes in another pile. "Now you see I can step out of my mold."

Amy held her arms to him. "Now come to my mold." The simple statement made his manhood jerk with awareness. She laughed lightly. "Some things are still in the right place."

Cord lowered himself beside her. "And we know where that is." He nuzzled her neck, planting hot kisses on her head her face and then her neck.

She slid her arms around him, bringing him close to her. She pulled his face to hers and lavished kisses over his forehead. "Yes, we do." Her breathless voice lingered in her ears. She had never heard herself this way. Embarrassed by her own overheated passion, she buried her face against the pulsing muscles of his chest.

Cord smoothed the wispy hair away from her face. "It's OK. We both feel like this." She felt the heat rush to her face. He even knew her thoughts. She looked at him and their gazes met in a flare of passion. As his lips covered hers hungrily, all thought of embarrassment vanished. This was where she belonged. She gave herself freely to the passion of his kiss.

Her hands traveled over his back, trickling over the muscles. She cherished him. Everything about him was perfect: his mind, body and soul. Her hands moved around his sides to his rear and lightly touched the taut muscles there. "You feel so good," she murmured.

Cord gave an involuntary shudder. "Baby," he hoarsely whispered in her ear, "if you keep that up this will be over before we get started."

Amy giggled softly. "We have all night. I'm sure you're good for more than once." She buried her face in his neck and nuzzled him. "You smell so good."

"I'm good for a lifetime." He smiled and looked at her thoughtfully. Then Cord gently moved her away, smiled down at her, rolled over and grabbed his pants.

Startled, Amy sat upright. "Wh—Where are you going?" Her heart screeched to a stop in her chest.

Cord shoved his hand in the pocket of his trousers and pulled out something. Then he lay back down beside her. "I'm not going anywhere, ever." He held out the tiny gift-wrapped box. "I made a stop on the way back here." His face was filled with passion, love, excitement and tenderness. He placed a hand on her bare hip. "This time, we have a right to do this." He watched as she untied the ribbons.

Amy's heart was thumping in her throat. His words were music to her ears. When the wrapping was gone, she carefully plucked a large, sparkling diamond wrapped in gold filigree from the velvet holder. Her eyelids fluttered up to meet Cord's waiting gaze. "Cord it's beautiful." Her voice a raspy whisper, she continued, "You didn't have to do this, it's been right from the beginning." Tears of joy popped from her eyelids to slowly trickle down her cheek.

Cord took the ring from her and slipped it on her finger. "I know it has. Now you are officially my lady. I know it, you know it and now everyone else will know it." He grazed her lips and tasted the tears. "Tears of happiness, I hope." He brushed at them. "I love you," he murmured.

Amy nodded. She looked at the warm, sensitive man she was going to marry. "Officially your lady." Her voice was filled with awe and amazement. She had been his since that predestined first phone call.

Cord drew her into his arms and kissed her forehead. "It won't be easy." He held her back to look into her face. "But it will be right."

As though his words released her, Amy slid her hand around his neck and pulled his mouth to hers. She was hungry for him. Hungry for his taste, his arms and his love-making. The touch of his lips was delicious. "You are better than a box of fine chocolates," she murmured against his lips.

"Mmmmm." He exhaled. She felt his body shudder. She curled in as tight as she could, feeling his strong desire for her press against her thigh. His arms grasped her and held her to him. She could barely breathe, but she didn't care.

His hand seared a path down her back to the soft flesh of her buttocks. The massaging sent waves of hot current through her. She could feel her nipples grow hard against his thick chest. Cord looked down at her. "Is that any way for a lady to act?" he chuckled.

"Your lady." She smiled teasingly while running a finger over his lips. "And she is waiting for her man." She held his look, almost offering a challenge.

Cord moved his hand to fondle one globe. The pink rosebud, now a deep rose, had grown marble hard. Tenderly he brushed it with his lips. Amy inhaled deeply. Her stomach fluttered in ecstasy, and her hands pressed against his firm butt, holding him in place as if forever.

Cord moved his hot lips over her knotted tummy and down to her arched womanhood. Amy jerked as the heat of his mouth found its way to her already heated flesh. She wanted him, all of him. Gently she tugged on his shoulders, bringing his lips to her waiting mouth, kissing him with a passion that was wanton and free.

Cord returned the drunken passion and sank his tongue into the depths of her mouth. Amy's mind swirled into an abyss of pure pleasure, lost to him forever. She wrapped her legs around him and urged him to take what was his. Her fingernails bit into his back as he plunged into her inner being.

■ ■ ■

They spent the next day alternating talking and making love. As time for the family dinner neared, they had settled the problem as not theirs but belonging to others. Together they could face the world. That world would begin with meeting his family.

Amy took careful pains to dress. As her fingers nervously buttoned the last button of her soft pink dress, she glanced up to see Cord staring at her. A smile lifted the corners of his mouth. Self-consciously she averted her eyes. "Is there something wrong?" Amy pressed the imaginary wrinkles from her lightweight summer dress.

Cord shook his head. His eyes glowed as he spoke. "No, everything is finally right." He moved quickly through the space that separated them and pulled her into his arms. "Stop worrying. They will love you, like I love you."

She rested her head on his chest and listened to his heart beat calmly. She released a sigh. He was confident. "I just don't want to come between you and your family," she uttered softly.

Cord held her back and looked into her eyes. "Amy, we are my family. We have a lifetime to put together. I am not going to let anyone come between us." He lightly kissed her forehead. "And if you don't want to meet them, you don't have to." He chuckled and glanced toward the neatly made bed. "We could practice making the bed after we make a mess of it."

Her gaze followed his to the bed. She laughed softly. "We have a lifetime to practice." Burying her face in his chest, she whispered, "I hate making beds." She could feel his arms as they reassuringly wrapped around her again.

"Then I will make the bed." He squeezed her tightly. "Now let's go before I have to do it again." He gently moved her away and took her hand. "Come on, let's get this over with." His eyes shifted to the bed again. "Then we can come back and get on with more important things. Like making beds."

Amy smiled as he tenderly tugged on her hand and pulled her through the apartment. Her heart was singing two songs. One was light and happy, the other a ballad of fear and darkness.

Studying the house as he led her to the door, she hoped the people inside the beautiful brick home were as welcoming as the house looked. Her stomach pulled into a full knot as Cord opened the door. Amy hesitated but felt his hand at the small of her back urging her forward.

The foyer, beautifully appointed with a large oval mirror hanging between gold candelabras, took her breath away. Two umbrellas hung on a coat tree across from the mirror and beside it was a deacon's bench. Her gaze shifted back to the umbrellas. One was green and white, which she recognized as MSU school colors and the other satiny black with a gold handle. It wasn't necessary to ask to whom each belonged. Neat, orderly, beautiful, yet warm and inviting. This was the home she had entered and this was Cord. The knot in her stomach grew tighter.

The aroma of dinner filtered through and mingled with the scent of highly polished wood. The knot pulled tighter and her heart began sinking. Cord was so accustomed to the finer things. She was so country. Not poor, but certainly not rich or of high social position. Her mind was tumbling, trying to put all of this in perspective. They were so far apart yet so close. How would this all work?

Cord's voice cut through her musings. "Well?"

She turned to him. "Maybe this isn't such a good idea." Her voice quivered under his intense study. "I mean..."

"I know what you mean," he spoke with quiet confidence. "It's your call. If you want we can leave. No one knows we are here yet."

She looked past the entrance into the even more richly appointed living room. She felt like Alice in Wonderland. It was so much more than she had expected. Amy looked into the face of the man she loved. She knew he was willing to leave, yet her heart knew he wanted her to meet his family. She forced a smile to unwilling lips. "Now that would be crazy of me to miss meeting the family of the man I love." Inside she wanted to run as fast as she could but she did love him and would try, for him.

Cord's face grew a large grin that reached the corners of his brightened eyes. "That's my girl." He placed his arm around her shoulder and tucked her neatly to him. "Let's go."

His protective arms made it easier to be led to her probable slaughter. She tried not to look at her surroundings as he led her through the house. Amy needed to focus on one thing: making a good impression on her future husband's family. As they neared the dining room the voices and laughter grew louder. She lifted her chin, straightened her shoulders and drew in a deep breath. She was as ready as she would ever be.

Cord's long hand settled on the large oak door. She held her breath. He started to push it but then leaned down and lightly kissed her lips. "My lady worries too much."

The kiss sent a warm shiver over her rigid spine. Looking into the depths of his dark eyes full of promise. She released a long sigh as her feeling of confidence grew. His look said it all. He was her man. She smiled. "Your lady is not worrying now." She stood on tiptoes and lightly kissed his cheek. "Let's go, I'm starving."

Cord's face visibly relaxed, and he chuckled. "If you're hungry for something else we can still leave."

Amy smiled softly as the heat of remembered passion filled her cheeks. She placed her hand over his on the door and pushed. "You are insatiable." The door swung open as Cord was about to respond.

Amy stared at the man, taller than Cord and about his age, who stood facing them as he held the door wide open. His grin grew from ear to ear. "Cordelle, good to see you, my man." Amy's cheeks grew hotter as the man's gaze lazily drifted over her and then shifted to Cord.

Cord laughed and accepted the other man's proffered hand. Amy smiled as she watched the handshake turn into a hug. Cord turned to her. "Amy, my cousin John." He glanced toward John, his eyes dancing with merriment. "John, my lady."

John turned his full attention to Amy. "And a damned fine looking lady, bro." She grew even hotter as John's gaze roved over her and then returned to her face. "Amy, the pleasure is mine."

She glimpsed Cord's brightly-lit face as she said, "Thank you, John. I'm very happy to meet you."

"Would you listen to that?" John guffawed and turned to the room of people who were watching. "The voice of an angel." John grabbed her hand and pulled her into the room. The people in the room laughed and soon she found herself in the middle of them, being introduced by this warm man. Cord laughed as she was led to first one and then the other and was greeted warmly by each.

Finally John led her toward an elderly woman in a rocking chair. Cord quickly moved to her side. Playfully hitting John on the shoulder, he said, "I will do this one." He grasped Amy's hand and then leaned down and kissed the woman on the cheek. "Grandma, this is Amy."

Amy could feel her face growing into a smile in response to the older woman's warm look. "I am so happy to meet you, Mrs.—" She glanced to Cord for a name.

"Grandma," the older woman stated as if she had already accepted Amy into the family.

"I am truly happy to meet you, Grandma." Amy's heart filled with joy as she looked into the fading dark eyes. She knew how Cord loved his grandmother and now she knew why.

Cord leaned down again, this time tightly embracing his grandmother. Then he stood and surveyed the room. "Where are Mom and Dad?"

"In the kitchen, baby." Grandma's loving gaze held her grandson's. "Why don't you take Amy to them?" She quickly looked around the room. "It would be nicer that way, baby." Her melodic voice had grown softer.

Cord nodded and kissed his grandmother on the cheek again. "As always, Grandma, you are right." He tugged on Amy's hand. "Come on. Let's go to my parents."

She looked back at Grandma's smiling face and then braced herself for the next introduction. Cord led her out of the dining room and down a short hallway to the kitchen. The aroma of food hit her churning stomach. It smelled good and made her nauseous all at the same time. Perspiration beads formed on her forehead, and she leaned against Cord for support as she felt herself fading.

Cord's concerned face was the next thing she saw as her mind cleared. She felt someone wiping her face with a cool cloth and knew it wasn't Cord because his hands were holding hers. She fought to clear her mind. Cord was talking to her. What had happened?

"Amy? Are you OK now?"

His dark eyes were clouded. She knew she had felt weak. Had she fainted? Although she wanted to look at the person who was wiping her forehead, she knew instinctively it was Cord's mother. Her stomach rolled again. Perfect, just perfect, she admonished herself. Now his parents would think she was a complete fool. Amy stared into Cord's face. "Yes," she answered her voice barely a whisper.

Cord pulled her into his arms. "You scared the hell out of me." Relief flooded his voice. She buried her head in his shoulder and whispered to him, "I feel like such a fool. I'm sorry."

"Nonsense," she heard a woman's voice scold her. "It is not easy meeting your future husband's family." The voice hesitated and then continued, "especially when you are in this condition."

Amy eased herself away from Cord and looked at the woman who had spoken to her. Mrs. McCune's face was as concerned as Cord's. But she had no idea what the woman was talking about. "Condition?"

Easter McCune's face broke into a welcoming smile. "I have waited a very long time for my second grandchild." Cord's mother looked behind her at the man who stood close to her. "Haven't we, Henry?"

Amy shook her head. "Oh no, Mrs. McCune, I'm not pregnant." She tried to think. They had been together the first time almost two months ago. Could it be? Her eyes grew wide as it dawned on her that she hadn't had her cycle since then. Her look shifted down as her hand went to her stomach. No. It couldn't be.

Mrs. McCune patted her hand. "Oh my, that was presumptuous of me. It's just that you have that certain glow about you and well..." She smiled through her embarrassment.

Cord's father slapped him on the back. "Well, Son, this is a bit more than we expected. Your mother almost always can spot a lady-in-waiting a mile away. I would bank on her word." The older man chuckled.

Cord glanced at his father and smiled and then looked back at Amy. "My lady is going to have our baby?" A smile played on his lips but his eyes were still dark and intense as he stared at her.

Amy felt heat stain her cheeks as she realized the possibility. "I—I don't know," she muttered. Her open stare darted from him to his parents and then back. "Maybe it's just all the excitement."

Cord picked her up and sat her on a chair. Then he knelt in front of her. "Are you feeling better now?"

"Yes." She answered without thinking about it, trying to focus, trying to remember what it had been like to be pregnant. Eighteen years was a long time. She was both excited and filled with anxiety. This had not been her plan. It was all too much.

"Let Grandma have a look here." Amy felt a gentle hand caress her shoulder, a touch that melted away the anxiety. She felt her shoulders relax and a calming warmth wash over her.

She looked into the time-worn face. Soft brown eyes were set deep in her aged countenance. Unruly gray hair framed the face of the wise and loving woman as she laid her hand on Amy's stomach and stared into her eyes. Amy waited, somehow knowing that Grandma had the definitive answer.

The five people in the kitchen were silent as the sagacious woman studied Amy. A smile crept into her fading eyes and her lips drew upward. The others were riveted on her every change of expression.

Grandma kissed Amy on the cheek. "In February." Her smile grew wider. The old woman looked at the others in the room. Her survey stopped on Cord. "Well Cordelle, I thought you were spent on this baby making."

Amy watched Cord's face as it froze in disbelief. She knew hers must look the same. As if someone had turned them on, the people around her began talking at once, hugging first her then Cord. Then as if by agreement they left the kitchen and the soon-to-be parents alone.

Cord grinned widely as the realization hit home. He dropped to his knees before her. Placing a hand on her tummy, he looked into her eyes. "My lady is carrying our child." He shook his head. "I never—I mean, I didn't think about it." He buried his head in her lap.

Amy placed her hand on his head and softly moved her fingers over him. "Nor did I." Her voice sounded as if it had come in from a distant storm. She wasn't sure she wanted to have a child. Not at this age. She shook her head lightly, trying to clear her thoughts.

Cord raised his head and looked at her, "What are you thinking?" His voice was filled with trepidation.

"I don't know what to think." Her eyelids shuttered down, avoiding his intense stare. She didn't want him to know that an abortion had entered her mind, if for only a fleeting moment. But it had been there.

Cord stood, bringing her up with him and into his arms. "My precious lady. We will get through this together."

Amy nodded her head into his chest. But she had no idea how she would get through this. All she knew was that she loved him and would do anything to make him happy. She released a long sigh and mumbled into his chest, "Think we should join the others? Dinner is waiting."

Cord shifted her and put his arm around her shoulder. "Yes. I think we should get this over with so we can talk." He lightly kissed her forehead. "Don't worry your pretty little head about it. Together we can do anything." He led her to the dining room.

The noisy room quieted as they took their seats. Grandma raised her hands and bowed her head. "Now it is time for thanksgiving." Amy watched as they all followed suit. She bowed her head but was not in a prayerful mood. Unless it was to pray that for once Mrs. McCune and Grandma had been wrong.

Eleven

When the amens were over the chatter resumed as if there
had not been a pause. Easter McCune raised her hand. An
automatic hush fell over the noisy group. She raised her
wine glass and said, "I would like to offer Amy a warm welcome into our family." She glanced over the group as their
glasses lifted. "Cordelle has asked Amy to be his wife and
has asked our blessing on this union." Again she surveyed
the group. Amy watched as Mrs. McCune's smile grew
wide with confidence. "I am sure you will all join me in
blessing them and welcoming Amy."

Amy released the air held captive in her lungs. They
were all smiling. Her eyes misted as she looked over this
happy family. Cousin John was laughing, deep, boisterous,
infectious laughter. She smiled to herself at how he held
the attention of the others. While he did that, she took the
opportunity to look at Cord's extended family and listen,
putting faces and words with names.

Amy marveled at the variety in skin tone, variations she
had just not before paid attention to. Tones ran from the
lightest of coffee shades to the black of onyx. She sighed
inwardly, acknowledging she had been more guilty of
stereotyping than she had thought. She was most struck by
their eye colors, variations of brown, gold, green and even
one with blue. Yet, she thought, they call themselves
black. Then she shrugged inwardly. Well, I call myself

white. Why hadn't she thought of any of this before she had met Cord? For sure, she would now. The door swung open with a loud swish, bringing Amy from her musings.

"Well, isn't this cozy?"

Amy's eyes were riveted on the statuesque beauty standing in the door. If her voice didn't command attention, her very presence did. She wore a fluorescent-pink t-shirt neatly tucked into snug-fitting jeans. Amy knew instinctively this must be Cord's younger sister Leah. She felt the cold glare as the young woman swept the group with her gaze. Amy shivered inside. It was evident Leah wasn't going to take this news pleasantly.

Amy noted the family seemed to take a collective deep breath, and she joined them. Her guarded look followed the beautiful young woman as she glided to her seat. Long, straight-flowing, ebony hair fell down her back and swayed as she moved. Her face was a perfect oval with lusciously full lips any woman would pay to have. Big round, light brown eyes were gilded with gold dust and sitting neatly between them was a straight nose that perfectly divided the symmetrical face.

"Welcome to the family dinner, Leah," Easter McCune spoke in a pleasant but authoritative tone.

"Mother, Father," Leah nodded in their direction. "Grandma," she offered a brilliant smile. "So we are all here to meet Snow White, I see." Leah's glare traveled over family members as if condemning them all for their actions.

"Leah!" Henry McCune shot a commanding stare along with his firm yet quiet voice. "We will have none of this at our table."

Amy felt Leah's gaze as it shifted to her and knew her face bore crimson blotches on each cheek. Though she wanted to look away, Leah was mesmerizing.

"Cordelle has chosen Amy to be his life's mate and we will respect his choice." Henry McCune's voice seemed to come from a distance. His words broke Amy's stare at the beautiful young woman. Amy shifted to look at him and saw that this darker, maturer version of Cord had his jaw set. She shot a quick glimpse to see Cord's reaction. He was half-standing with his mouth open, ready to speak. Then Grandma popped up as if she had been sprung from her seat.

"We are all God's children. We love one another as He loves us. He created us all in his image and placed us here this way." Her soft, loving face carried a stern overtone. Grandma surveyed each family member, stopping when she came to Leah. "And let not those among us tamper with God's plan." As quickly as she had sprung from her chair she was seated again.

Amy stared at Leah's contorted face. She obviously wanted to answer but knew she couldn't. Instead, she glared at Cord.

Cord offered his sister a big smile. "Nice to see you too, Sis." He paused, obviously waiting for a response that didn't come. "Leah, I would like you to meet Amy

Summers." He placed a protective arm around Amy. "Amy, this is my dear sister, Leah."

Amy's insides trembled but she tried to draw strength from Cord's arm, which held her even tighter now. She knew her voice was in there somewhere. She inwardly wrested herself together and braced herself against the anger she was feeling from Leah. With a half-smile on her quivering lips, she finally spoke. "Leah, I am very pleased to meet you." The words hung in the air, waiting for the recipient to acknowledge them. Amy moved closer to Cord, needing the reassurance of his body heat. Despite the warm summer day, she was chilled to the bone.

Leah gracefully lifted herself from her seat at the table and looked at no one in particular. "If you will all excuse me," she glared at all of them, "I seem to have lost my appetite."

As she moved toward the door it swung open and a young man with a girl in tow came in with a flourish. "Hello, my dear family."

Amy knew it had to be Hank. He was the only one missing and he was a young Cord. She watched as Cord stood and moved quickly to his son, embracing him. Her heart quieted at the sight. Leah was shoved to the side as father and son greeted each other.

Cord withdrew from the embrace and smiled at the girl who was with his son. Amy took a closer look. Her long, flowing black-pearl hair swung over her shoulder as she shifted her petite body to smile first at Hank and then his father. Amy could feel her eyes grow wide as she realized the girl was of Asian descent.

She glanced in Leah's direction. The hatred was there and about to spill over. Amy held her breath and waited for the onslaught.

Leah didn't disappoint her. "Well! I see, like father like son." The beautiful woman's arms folded over her chest as she eyed the young couple, waiting for them to wilt under her glare.

Amy switched her attention to Cord's face. The bright smile disappeared and then reappeared, brighter than before. From previous experiences, she knew he was steeling himself.

"It is a proud day when a parent sees his teaching of love for all people has been a lesson learned." Cord's voice rang like a deep, rich bell of truth. Amy's heart was bursting with pride. She had been given the gift of love from a man who was so good.

Leah stomped out of the dining area, letting the door slam behind her. John rose and smiled brilliantly at the family. "If you will excuse me," he cleared his throat loudly, "I think this is a job for 'Super John.'" The family came alive with the comic relief, the chatter and laughter resuming as the food was passed around the table.

Soon the clatter of silverware against serving dishes and china rang in harmony with the family song of love. But Amy felt her stomach churning. Her body was awakening to the new life growing within, one that would belong here. And at the moment, her tummy was not happy. She chanced a glance in Cord's direction. He was laughing with the rest but she could see the painful storm in his dark eyes. At that moment the food was passed to her. She had to grab her mouth and cover it.

Where had she seen the bathroom? Her mind whirled as she rose. Cord quickly swept her into his arms, and in several long strides had her in the bathroom. As she emptied the contents of her wrenching stomach, she felt a cool cloth bathe her forehead. Morning sickness, she had been morning sick all day with Sara. "Oh," she moaned. "I had forgotten."

"Forgotten?" Cord's rich, soothing voice filtered through her fog. He wiped her face again. "Baby, I'm sorry."

"Sorry?" Her head jerked toward him. "About the baby?" Her heart spun in her chest. Didn't he want the baby? Didn't he want her pregnant? What was he sorry about? Tears sprang to her eyes.

Cord gently drew her into his arms. "Baby, I'm sorry you're sick. I could never be sorry we have a gift from God on the way." He lightly swept the tears from her cheeks and kissed her eyelids. "We'll get through all of this together."

Amy buried her face in his shoulder and mumbled, "We have so much more than the baby to go through together." As sick as she was, she still knew that would be the easy part of their relationship.

Cord held her back and looked into her eyes. "Amy, we will face it all together. I am not blind to the discrimination you've felt today."

Her tension eased somewhat. He was worried about her when he had felt discrimination all his life. She moved her lips to his neck and tenderly kissed his warm skin. "I do love you, Cord McCune," she whispered.

Cord gazed deeper into her eyes. The look penetrated her heart and her soul. She held her breath, waiting for the results of his soul-searching.

A slow smile crept to his lips and then spread to his eyes. The bright twinkle she loved so much returned with a vibrancy she had not seen before. Amy circled his neck with her arms. "Hmmm, what is my lover thinking?"

Cord's chuckle came from deep in his throat. "Only good thoughts, my lady." As his grip tightened his attitude became more serious. She could see the bright twinkle fade as quickly as it had arrived and could feel his uneven breathing against her cheek. She knew he was going to say something serious, or at least was thinking about it. Yet, she wanted to soak in the moment. She loved the feel of her soft curves molding to the contours of his lean, hard body.

Cord buried his face in her hair. A big sigh softly lifted the wisps around her cheek and let them fall in disarray around her face. Amy braced herself for whatever he was going to say. His prolonged silence gripped her with anxiety. She leaned back to study his face. His brows pressed together over darkened eyes. Seeing a storm gathering, she held her breath and asked, "Honey, what's wrong?" She didn't want to ask and didn't want to know.

Cord shook his head. "I was just thinking of you and our child." He moved his hand to her stomach and rested it there.

"And?" She bit her lower lip as her nerves tingled. Even the comfort of his hand on her tummy didn't shake the growing apprehension.

He looked thoughtfully at her for a long moment. "The fact is, I have dealt with discrimination all of my life. And now I'm asking you and our child to do the same thing." He shook his head again. "How selfish is that?"

His arms dropped but he didn't move away. He stood staring at her. His fists clenched and unclenched. She watched his face as his mind sorted through his thoughts for the right words. Amy pushed back the hair that wasn't in her face and shifted from one foot to the other. She had to say something. "I don't think it is selfish to share your life with two people who love you."

He wrapped his arms around her and held her close to his chest. "This will be a real test of love for all three of us."

She curled into him, sighing deeply. "As a family we will pass the test." Her voice choked with tears of sadness and joy for the man she loved. Subconsciously she pushed her hand between them and placed it on her stomach. Knowing a new life grew within made her glow. She'd had this feeling only once before. Yet that once before had not been filled with the kind of love she had for Cord. This warmth surpassed anything she had ever experienced.

Cord placed his hand over hers. "Don't worry about Cordelle Jr. He will be fine and so will we."

Amy smiled gently. "Hmmm, you think Hank and Sara are going to have a little brother?" Her stomach turned a little. Sara had not met Cord yet and now she would have a sibling and a stepbrother to deal with. She shivered. This would not be easy.

Cord lifted her chin with his finger. "I know. I have to tell Hank too." He caressed her lips with his. "I think I will take you to the den where you can lie down." He lifted her easily and carried her down the hall.

She smiled as he gently placed her on the couch. "I am not an invalid." She reached up and ran her fingers down his cheek. "I'd like to be with you when you tell Hank about his brother."

Cord pulled the afghan to her chin and then tenderly kissed her. "Of course, darling. You just rest now." Her gaze followed him as he left the room. She had been sleepy but the closing of the door left her empty.

Her eyelids grew heavy as she surveyed her surroundings. The room was divided. She was in a lounging, reading area and behind the divider she could hear voices. She could hear John's voice but the tone lacked its usual rich sound, instead carrying a harsh, warning note. Amy strained to hear the conversation. She was positive it concerned her.

"If you are so ethnically pure, Leah, why are you wearing the hair fall?"

Amy held her breath, waiting for Leah's tirade. But what she heard was Leah's laugh, a laugh laced with sarcasm. "And do you think Snow White's hair is naturally curly?"

Amy brushed her hair away from her face. Her hair was wavy but not curly and it was natural. Damn, that woman was infuriating even if it was her fault for eavesdropping. She dragged herself from the couch and moved closer to the divider.

"I don't care what Amy does to her hair. She is obviously not worried about ethnicity like you are." John's voice returned the sarcasm.

"I suppose all I will hear for weeks is Amy this and Amy that. You all make me sick. Don't you have any feeling for your African-American heritage?" Leah's voice carried a caustic tone.

"My God, Leah. How can you say that? We all live it daily. I am proud to be black and to know we come from a strong and rich heritage. It is at the top of my list." Amy could hear the pride in his voice. She felt a pleasant connection with the man she had met and liked instantly.

Amy heard footsteps shuffle over the hardwood floor and then the light swish of an opening door. Her heart pounded heavily, fearing Leah would find her there. She glanced around. Thankfully the door on her side remained shut.

"Why don't you take your happy black ass back to the family dinner and leave me alone?" Leah's voice was calmer but still carried the angry, bitter resentment.

For a moment it was quiet and then John roared in laughter. "My dear, sweet cousin, you are the one who should take their sassy black ass back to the family and apologize." Amy could hear the laughter in his voice as he spoke calmly.

"Apologize?" came the shrieking answer-question.

John roared again. "Tough concept for you?"

"When hell freezes over." Leah's voice was firm.

"Or until Grandma gets hold of you." His laughter was infectious. Amy found herself smiling at his diplomacy.

"Grandma is an old woman. She takes this because her generation was programmed to think the whites were better and that mixing was a good thing for us. Well, I don't see it that way. Thank God they are past the childbearing years."

Amy's hand fell from the wall where she had braced herself and rested on her stomach. She had thought the same thing. Yet here she was with a new life within, and Leah would hate her even more. Perspiration beads popped out on her brow. Again, her stomach churned. She sat back on the couch, praying the nausea would pass and that she would not have to let them know she was there.

John's jovial laugh rang out again. "Amy doesn't look like she is past that to me." He paused. "And I sure as hell know Cord is still loaded."

"That is disgusting."

Amy could hear the disdain in Leah's voice. She laid her head down to stop the spinning. What would Leah do when she discovered the truth? Amy pulled the afghan back to her chin and closed her eyes. She didn't want to see or hear anything else today. She'd had enough of the roller coaster.

■■■

"Amy?" Cord's soft whisper filtered through her hazy mind. Her eyelids fluttered open. Through a sleepy haze she could see his face. His brows were furrowed, and his eyes were dark with worry.

"Yes?" She heard her mumbled answer that sounded like a question. Her stomach was still churning and her heart still shuddering from Leah's wrath.

Cord sat on the edge of the couch and smoothed her hair from her face. "Are you going to be all right?"

She leaned her head into his chest and nodded. "In seven more months," she whispered. Amy didn't want to tell him what she had overheard. Eventually they would have to deal with it, but not today.

Cord chuckled. "Guess I shouldn't have given you my room number." He hugged her tightly to him. "Sorry you are not well, baby. Still, us sharing a child is a great gift." He kissed her lightly on the forehead.

She smiled weakly. "This gift keeps giving." She felt his hand as it ran over her back reassuringly. Sighing, she spoke softly, "But it is a gift of love."

Cord moved her back and looked warmly at her. "We should be leaving soon. I want us to spend some time with Hank and tell him." His voice had a catch in it.

Amy gazed into his dark brown eyes and smiled. "Of course, darling." She sat upright. "Let me fix my makeup and comb my hair."

Cord assisted her in rising and said, "While you do that I'll go get Hank." He hesitated. "Unless you need me."

Amy gave a quick smile and wave of her hand as she made her way back to the bathroom. After she washed her face and reapplied makeup, she ran a brush through her hair. Glancing in the mirror she saw dark circles that told the tale of how she really felt. When she heard Cord call her name, she quickly dabbed on cover-up and blended it in, and then rejoined Cord in the den.

Cord and Hank were talking about college when she returned to stand by Cord's side. Both men turned to smile at her. Her heart melted. Hank's face was lit like a child's at Christmas.

Amy couldn't help returning the smile. She held out her hand. "I'm sorry I was unable to greet you properly in the dining room." His large hand wrapped around hers and then drew her into an embrace that felt like a bear hug.

"You have made Dad happy and that is all that matters to me." He squeezed her tightly and then added, "Dad says you have something to tell me."

Amy glimpsed Cord's handsome smiling face. Their eyes met with the fire and lightning of their first meeting. Amy felt her cheeks grow hot as she saw the remembrance in his face. She smiled and turned her attention back to her soon-to-be stepson. "We, your dad and I, have something to tell you."

She held her hand out to Cord, who took it willingly. The new family stood in a small circle. Amy's heart swelled. She could feel the warmth from each man's hand as they held hers. This was going to be a loving family even if they had to fight their way through the jungle of prejudice.

Cord cleared his throat. "Son," Cord's voice was full of love and a hint of fear. Amy squeezed his hand and felt the pressure as he returned the gesture.

"As I've told you, Amy and I are going to be married." He stared down in boyish fashion as he shuffled his feet. He cleared his throat again.

Amy gazed at this strong man's face. He was hesitating. "Hank, we do have news," Amy interjected.

Hank dropped their hands and stood back. His brow furrowed for an instant and then his lips flipped up in an easy grin. "Are you...? I mean, are we going to have an addition to our family?" He looked from his dad to Amy.

Cord squeezed her hand again and then let out a rich laugh. "Well, Son, as usual you have nailed it." Hank and Cord embraced.

Amy felt a momentary twinge as they left her out of their world. Don't be silly, she told herself. Would you want it any other way? She smiled to herself. If this were she and Sara it would hopefully be the same scene. Sara, she thought. They still had to tell her about their marriage and the new baby. Her heart fluttered at the thought. How would Sara take it? Sara? They had to tell Hank about Sara too. Her mind whirled. How would they make it through all of these emotional rides?

Amy lightly touched Cord's arm. His smiling face turned toward her as did Hank's. She glowed with pride and joy. How lucky she was to have the love of a man like Cord and the open admiration of his son.

"Honey?" His deep voice filled with concern as they looked at each other. His brow furrowed. "Is there something wrong?" He quickly moved to her side.

Amy shook her head and gave a weak smile. "It's just that we haven't told Sara any of this. We need to tell her before someone in town does it for us."

"Sara?" Hank's curious voice made them turn in his direction. His bright eyes were alive with expectancy.

"Sara is Amy's daughter." Cord smiled at his son and paused, waiting for him to digest this. "Sara was away the night we told Mrs. Summers, Amy's mother. We haven't had the chance since."

Hank smiled knowingly. "You think she won't be happy with this news?" He didn't wait for an answer. His eyes brightened with questions. "How old is she and does she look like her mom?" He threw his head back and laughed.

Amy smiled. His boyish cheer was infectious. "She is your age. And yes, she does." Somehow this young man had the knack of lifting heavy thoughts from her mind.

"Well then," Hank's brightly animated voice rang out, "once she gets over the shock of two old people falling in love, she will be fine with it." He patted Amy's arm. "We are the enlightened generation." His smile lit his whole face.

Amy released a long sigh. "I certainly hope you're right, hon." She moved closer, stood on tiptoes and kissed his cheek. "You are your father's son." She couldn't resist parroting Leah, but with an entirely different feeling.

Hank, beaming pride, bowed from the waist. "Well, thank you mom-to-be. I consider that a great compliment." He stood and winked at her. "And I didn't miss that you were quoting my aunt."

Amy's face grew hot. She hadn't meant to sound sarcastic. She needed to right that. "I'm sure your aunt meant it in the best way too." Of course she knew better but she wasn't going to have family members choosing sides or making her the center of a battle.

Cord and Hank roared in laughter. Amy's face grew even hotter. "Well, you know what I mean." She laid her hand on Cord's arm and squeezed it. "You two are not making this any easier," she said with a soft laugh.

She had never imagined this kind of closeness and so soon. Her throat constricted and tears tried to push through her eyes. This was love and she was part of it. She fought to keep the tears away but one popped out and rolled down her cheek. Both men stared at her question-ingly. She swiped at it and smiled at her new family. "We only have seven months of this."

Cord swept her into his arms and twirled her around. "It will be the best seven months you have ever spent." He held her tightly. "Hank and I will see to that." He turned them toward his son. "What do you think, oh son of mine?"

Hank's eyes were bright with pleasure as he smiled at both of them. Again, Amy was struck again by how much this young man was like his father. Hank lifted his hand in the air and snapped a salute.

"Sir, it is my duty to inform you that I am but a rank and file member of this family but I will do my best to help my mom-to-be." He smirked as he slapped his hand back to his side.

There it was. For the second time he had called her mom-to-be. Amy felt a rush of love for this young man who was everything she could ask for in a son. She knew his mother was important to him and that he loved her dearly, yet he was making room for her.

Cord looked from Hank to her. "Son, you will never be rank and file with us." He glanced back at Amy. She could feel the love between father and son and had the feeling Cord was going to ask Hank to be his best man. She nod-ded. He stood her beside him and gave his full attention to his son.

"Hank, I...," he glanced to Amy, "no, we would like you to be the best man at our wedding."

Hank's huge smile slipped from his face for a moment and then returned. "I would be honored." His voice choked with pride.

Cord continued, "And as your first act as my best man, I need you to do me a favor."

"This best man is ready and waiting for that opportunity." Hank returned to his playful nature.

Cord placed his hand on his best man's shoulder. "Please make our apologies to the family. We are going to slip out the back door." He smiled at Amy. "We have a plane to catch."

"No problem, Dad. I will give you a fifteen-minute head start so no one can cut you off at the pass." He chuckled and then hugged his dad. "You take care."

"You do the same, Son." Cord's voice was heavy.

Amy hugged Hank. "Thank you. You are the best man." She smiled at Cord. "Well, the best right after your dad."

Cord grasped her hand and led her through the house and out the back door into the warm, early summer air. Amy was filled with love from this family, a family who had been asked to accept an outsider and had done it, for the most part, willingly. She knew she had a long way to go but the door was open and she was ready to enter. Her heart was light as they sped down the highway and hurried to catch their flight.

Twelve

"Can you believe those jerks were still outside the hotel when we returned last night?" Shelley sat her coffee cup down with a thump. "It is so hard to believe those prejudices still exist in this century."

Amy could see the pain in Shelly's bright blue eyes. She patted her hand. "If it makes you feel any better I'm in the same boat now and I don't like it either." She pushed her hair away from her face.

"I know what you mean. Is that why Cord didn't come to lunch with us?" Shelley's voice grew concerned. "He isn't going to let these idiots chase him out of town," she hesitated and then added, "is he?"

Amy was only half-hearing Shelley. Her attention was drawn to a couple in the corner not far from them. She grabbed Shelley's arm and then placed a finger on her lip. Her wide stare met Shelley's and then moved back to the couple.

Shelley gasped. "What is Steve doing with Mrs. Delaney?" she whispered.

Amy shook her head. "Listen." It was a one word command.

Shelley fell silent. She grabbed her notepad and began writing quickly as she listened with Amy.

Amy glanced at the notes. They were in shorthand but she knew Shelley's accuracy was right on. Her heart pounded loudly in her ears as she tried to listen.

"Steve, you don't have to worry. It will be easy to pin this embezzlement on that black bastard." Mrs. Delaney spit the words in hate. Amy's hand flew over her mouth to keep from screaming in Cord's defense. She had to hear the plan.

Shelley touched her arm and whispered. "You go back to the office. I'll get the rest of this and bring it back." She smiled at Amy but didn't quit scribbling notes. She added, "You are in no condition to have this kind of upset."

Amy could feel her stomach rolling. She wasn't sure if it was the pregnancy or the bitter comments made at the corner table. Slowly and quietly she slid her chair back. Shelley glanced at her, gave her the okay sign, and then went back to taking notes. Amy slid her hand down to her tummy and then slipped out of the restaurant unnoticed.

■ ■ ■

Cord sat pouring over the books. He worked furiously. The sooner he had this out of the way, the sooner he and Amy could get on with their lives. He leaned back in the desk chair and smiled. His lady was carrying his child. This was too good to be true. His smile grew wider as he glanced at the door. "Hi baby, did you have a nice lunch with Shelley?" He looked at his watch. "Back early aren't you?"

She stood there mute. Her face was strained and she seemed to be staring through him. Cord leapt to his feet and crossed the room in one fluid movement. He wrapped her into his arms. "Not feeling well, baby?"

He tucked her head under his chin and inhaled the fresh aroma of her hair. He deposited a kiss on her hair and she snuggled into him. "Honey, should you go to the doctor?"

She shook her head on his chest. "I'm okay." she muttered, not moving her head back.

Cord felt his stomach twist. He recognized this pain. He had felt it all of his life and now she was dealing with it. He was sure of that. "What happened?" He said it with a fierceness directed at the perpetrator, but he felt her wince. She shook her head against his chest again. He could feel the muscles in his jaw as they clenched and then relaxed enough to talk calmly.

He led her to the lounge and sat down, bringing her onto his lap. "Now, you tell me all about it. Remember we are in this together." He inhaled deeply, taking in her vanilla musk. He moved his hand over her back trying to relax the tightened muscles under his fingers.

"Steve and Mrs. Delaney are plotting to blame the embezzlement on you." She blurted it out so fast it almost took his breath away.

He held her back to look at her. "How? I mean, what could they do to pin it on me?"

Tears streamed down her face. "I think they plan on saying I was part of whatever happened to the finances here." We were at a table near them and we could hear. Shelley took notes. They were so involved they had no idea we were there."

"Don't worry about it. I'm sure they were just talking to hear themselves talk." He wiped the tears from her cheeks. He knew they weren't just talking, but he didn't want to have her upset. This was the last thing she needed.

She shook her head again, tears splashing on his chest. "They were serious," she choked. "Mrs. Delaney got wind of the investigation the state office was doing from a senator friend of hers. She hired a private investigator and he found that Steve was guilty. Instead of turning Steve in, Mrs. Delaney joined forces with him. Between them they can make us look guilty."

He hugged her in tight reassurance. "Don't worry about it. I can handle it." His words were braver than he felt. He knew he was in a white world and the facts didn't really matter. He heard the outer door opening and footsteps thumping on the hardwood floor. He squeezed her, then slid her to the lounge and rose to see who had come in.

From the heavy footsteps he knew it wasn't Shelley. He opened the door and came face to face with Jeff Delaney. Cord stood ramrod still. He knew what was coming next and didn't want Amy to witness it. Cord stepped into the outer office and closed the door behind him.

Jeff looked down at his boots and moved his hand over his gun holster nervously. Finally he brought his gaze to meet Cord's. "Mr. McCune, I have an..."

Cord watched as Jeff struggled with something. The man seemed almost reticent to say what he had come to say. Cord stared him directly in the eyes. "What is it?" His voice sounded more demanding than he had intended.

Jeff shoved papers at him. "An arrest warrant." Cord held the papers loosely in his hand. "For what and for whom?" He knew, but he still wanted Jeff to say it.

Jeff locked his palms together and twisted them. He stared at his locked hands as if he wondered how they got that way. "For you...and Miss Summers. I mean Amy." Jeff kicked at the carpet. His voice was almost apologetic.

Cord's heart sank. He had a feeling they would name not only him, but Amy as his accomplice. He could see it all now. He and Amy had worked closely and both had access. Making a case would be easy.

He sucked in a deep breath as he read the charges of embezzlement and fraudulent use of state facilities. The list was short but from what he could see an easy fifteen years. "Crackers," he cursed under his breath.

Jeff's head snapped up when he cursed. Cord glared at the policeman and watched him wilt under his glare. Somehow he felt Jeff, who truly hated him, didn't believe the charge.

Cord heard movement behind him. Ever wary, he half swung around, keeping Jeff in his view. Amy stepped cautiously from the shadows of the door and stood staring for a moment. Cord held out his arms and drew her in, as if he were a magnet.

He looked down at her as she bit her lip and brushed her hair back, fighting back tears. He embraced her tightly. "It will be ok." His voice sounded strangely forlorn, even to him.

"Jeff." A sob strangled her voice. Cord shook his head at her, but that didn't stop her. He watched as she prepared herself.

"Jeff," she began in a more controlled voice, "you know this is not true." She breathed deeply. "You know me too well for this." Her open stare shifted to Cord and then back to Jeff. "Knowing me is knowing Cord."

Cord's heart overflowed with love for this woman. The woman carrying his child. "Honey, I'm sorry this has happened." He glared at Jeff. "We all know why it's happened but I don't think you believe in what you are doing either." Cord couldn't help wondering why Jeff was hesitant.

Jeff looked from them to the floor. "I'm doing my duty. Sometimes as policemen we're faced with situations we don't believe. However the district attorney has issued this warrant and has the supporting evidence." Slowly he reached behind him and pulled his handcuffs from his belt.

Cord felt his back stiffen. His fists clenched until he felt them begin to grow numb. He knew to fight this would only bring him more trouble. His mind whirled. He needed to get a message to his mother and wasn't sure of the one phone call at jail.

Finally he decided to take the high road. "Jeff, Officer Delaney," he waited until the police officer looked at him, "could we wait until Shelley returns? We need someone at the office."

Jeff nodded. "Can't see any harm in that."

Cord knew his next request would draw suspicion. "Officer, I need to close the computer system. It can't be left open to others. All of the ports are open and it's not safe." He glanced at Jeff and added as if Jeff would know. "Hackers, you know." Jeff nodded in agreement. Cord smiled to himself. If Delaney knew anything about computers he would know the state systems all had sniffers and firewalls. Cord smiled and looked to the police officer for his approval.

Jeff stared at them warily. Finally his shoulders dropped in resignation. "I see no harm in that but I have to watch."

Cord smothered a smile. Like Jeff would know what he was watching. "Sure, come into my office."

Cord sat down and began clicking buttons. The first one was his e-mail. He glanced at Jeff. His face was composed and Cord could tell he had no idea what he was doing. He quickly shot a note to his mother. Jeff was reading over his shoulder so Cord had to be careful. He wrote: "Cracker taking this one to one port. Port opened by E. McCune. Port closed." He pushed send and was hopeful his mother would understand the gibberish. If she didn't, he knew her curiosity would get the better of her and she would have to call. For once he was happy that his mother had an inquiring mind.

He glanced at Jeff who was obviously none the wiser. He glimpsed Amy's stoic face. She knew, but no one else would from her face. Cord smiled inwardly. She was his partner in this, and would be for a lifetime.

■ ■ ■

Amy called her mother from jail. She tried to explain everything but couldn't with the others around. Afterward, she paced the floor, counting the tiles as she did. What was keeping her mom? It was only a 10-minute drive and it had been an hour.

The officer in charge handed Amy some papers. "Ma'am, you have been released on your own recognizance." Amy accepted the papers and glared at the man. "What about Mr. McCune? Where is he? And how was I released?" She could hear her voice becoming hysterical. It was all so plain: She was white and he was black.

The policeman shook his head. "Have no idea. Looks like you have a high powered-attorney."

"I don't have an attorney!" Amy almost shouted. She whirled sharply as she felt a hand on her arm. "Mom?"

Mrs. Summers put her arms around her daughter and whispered to her. "Mrs. McCune got the strangest message from Cord so she called me."

Amy whispered back. "Why am I free and he isn't?"

Mrs. Summers released her daughter without answering and glared at the officer in charge. "Is everything all set then? I will take my daughter now." Her voice was firm and cool.

Amy was taken aback. Never had she seen or heard her mother in this role. Mrs. Summers was never direct. She watched her mother while signing some papers and accepting her personal belongings. Something was happening but she didn't know what. She needed to get her mom alone and discover what it was.

As soon as they were in the car she turned to her mother. "What's happening?"

Mrs. Summers smiled, "Now dear, I think that is the question I should be asking you."

"Mom, it's a set up," she blurted and then thought how much she sounded like others who protested their innocence. Leaning her head against the seat she stared out the window. "You will never believe the story I have to tell."

Mrs. Summers turned the car into the driveway and faced her daughter. "We have to make up the guest room for company." She didn't give Amy a chance to answer as she was out of the car and in the house by the time Amy caught up to her.

"What do you mean, we are having company?" She threw her arms in the air. "Mom?" Her voice grew plaintive.

"Mrs. McCune phoned." Mrs. Summers paused and looked at her daughter. "It seems she received the strangest e-mail from her son and wanted to know if I had any idea what it was all about." The older woman walked to the linen closet as if having a guest was an everyday event. Amy followed her.

"What did you tell her?" Sometimes she felt as if she was pulling nails out of cement trying to get her mother to finish a thought.

Stacking the linen in her arms, her mother moved quickly to the guestroom. "When she phoned I had just received your call from jail. I told her what I had been able to glean from you and then from Shelley." She busied herself making the bed.

"You've spoken with Shelley?" Again, Amy was surprised. Her mother never took an aggressive role. Yet here she was, completely in charge.

Mrs. Summers motioned for Amy to help with the lace spread. Amy pulled on her side and then, totally exasperated, she plunked down on the freshly made bed. "Mom, who is coming and how did you get me out of jail and not Cord?" Amy's mind tumbled with confused thoughts. She knew Mrs. Delaney was at the bottom of this. Yet, a feeling told her Jeff was not. Maybe if she could break him down she could discover what was behind all of the accusations. No, that wasn't a good idea either.

"Mrs. McCune, Easter, that is, is coming and she arranged for your release. She tried to do the same for her son but they would not allow it." She patted the pillows as she placed them in fresh linen. "Easter is flying in this afternoon."

Amy jumped from the bed. "Mrs. McCune is our guest?" Amy's head pounded. The McCunes were accustomed to the finer things. She glanced around the guest room which was, as always, spotlessly clean. The four poster bed was covered in lavender lace and the night stand had matching lace that brought out the lilacs in the wallpaper. Amy sighed. She had always loved this room. Yet it paled beside the McCunes' home.

How could she think of this when the man she loved was in jail? In jail because he dared to be with her. Tears poured down her face. Everything was such a mess. Somehow she would stop all of the madness.

■■■

Mrs. McCune and Amy's mother sat in the living room talking as if they had known each other a lifetime. Amy contributed little to the conversation. She had made up her mind that the best thing for all concerned was to break it off with Cord. If she were out of the picture, then he would stand a chance of beating this horrible accusation. Tears welled up as she thought of losing the love of her life. How could society and circumstances dictate who she would spend her life with?

Mrs. McCune's voice cut through Amy's painful thinking. "Don't you worry, child. I have as many connections as Mrs. Delaney." She stood and asked to use the phone.

In a zombie-like state Amy brought the phone to Cord's mother. She listened as Easter McCune called a senator's office and then a private investigator. She prayed his moth-

er would clear him but she thought she had a way that
would be faster.

■ ■ ■

For two days Amy watched her future mother-in-law as she
pulled strings to get her son a quick hearing and out of jail.
All of the time she knew the only reason Mrs. McCune's
son was there was because of her.

Amy rose as the judge at the hearing made his pro-
nouncement. She held her breath, but she knew what he
would say. There was no doubt in any of this for her or any
one else. Cord turned and looked into her eyes. Her heart
was being wrenched from her chest. She knew what she
had to do. Amy drew in a deep breath and stayed the tears
that wanted to flow.

"It is the decision of this court that there is enough evidence to bring this to trial..." Her shoulders dropped. She
knew it. Amy quit listening to the judge and watched as
mother and son hugged. The pain in their eyes was
unbearable. She would break it off with the love of her life
— for the love of her life.

"The defendant will be released on one hundred thou-
sand dollars bail." Amy heard the judge's voice boom over
the silent courtroom. The highly polished oak furniture,
walls and floors reverberated with his majestic voice. She
shuddered. In a few short minutes she would hold her
wonderful soul mate in her arms for the last time. "God
give me strength," she whispered.

Mrs. McCune and Cord walked toward her, arms around each other. Cord was bent, listening to his mother and his other attorney. Though Mrs. McCune was his main attorney, she had recruited a high-powered attorney friend of hers, a white male in his 50s, who could deal with the white establishment in this court. But Amy knew all she had to do was step aside and all of this would be over.

When they got to her, Mrs. McCune smiled and released her son. "I think the two of you need some time alone." Without another word, she returned to her table in the courtroom and began scribbling notes on her legal pad.

Amy turned her fixed look from the woman to the warm chocolate eyes of her fiancé. They were dark with worry yet warm with love for her. Her heart twisted and she couldn't speak.

Cord pulled her into his arms. She went willingly, knowing this would be the last time. He turned her and led her through the thick wooden doors and out into the sunlight. She wanted to soak up the warmth of his arms around her, his body close to hers. She needed this before she told him what she had to say.

"Baby, I am sorry about all of this," Cord began as he led her to a bench in the courtyard park. Amy shook her head and held her hand against his strong chest. She could hear the birds singing as a light warm breeze floated over her.

Everything around her was a lie. The weather, society and her being able to be with the man she loved. It was all a lie. Nothing would ever be the same again. She let her hand drop as they sat down in unison, then folded both hands in her lap and stared down.

"Cord," she began with a tremor in her voice. His eyes met hers and almost stole her resolve. She averted her gaze to her hands that were twisting in her lap.

Cord took her by the shoulders and turned her to him. "What? What are you trying to say?"

His voice was filled with anguish.

She wanted to throw her arms around his neck and make his pain go away but there was no turning back. Knowing she had to save him from this destruction, Amy drew in a deep breath. "Cord, I can't marry you." She didn't look at him because she knew her eyes would tell the real story.

"Amy." His voice was firm but filled with pain. "We are going to have a child. I know you love me and I love you." He paused to inhale. "Tell me what is happening."

Amy shook her head. "We aren't going to have a baby." Tears rolled down her face as she began the lie. "I miscarried the baby the other day." She closed her eyes. Hot tears burned down her cheeks. She swiped at them.

Cord turned her to him. He tried to lift her chin but she wouldn't let him. She couldn't bear to look in his face, his eyes. She knew what she would see.

His voice grew soft and filled with pain. "Oh my God, baby, I'm so sorry." He wrapped his arms around her rigid body.

Although his touch was almost more than she could take, Amy didn't let her defenses down. She couldn't. She had to save him. She detached and stood. "It isn't only the baby." She glimpsed his face. Worry lines grew over his brow and his eyes had grown wide with surprise.

"What do you mean, it's not only the baby?" With this he put his hand under her chin and forced her to look at him. She held her stance, but the touch of his hand on her face came close to shattering her resolve. She wanted those marvelous arms wrapped around her. She wanted to breathe in his essence and lay her head on his chest. Yet her resolve was still there. She had to save the love of her life from the fate she'd caused him.

Her lips trembled. "It was a mistake. I...I thought I loved you." The tears were falling to her soft pink shirt. "I don't want to hurt you. It's just...it's just that we weren't meant to be after all."

Cord stepped back. "That's it? We weren't meant to be?" His eyes narrowed as he studied her. "I don't believe you. You tell me what this is all about." His deep voice was quiet but demanding.

Amy knew she had to pull off the best acting job she had ever done. She shrugged her shoulders. "I've explained it the best I can. If that's not good enough for you, then so be it." She stepped back to put space between them. She didn't want him to feel her trembling body.

Cord stared blankly at her face. His mouth opened as if to speak and then closed again. She stood mute, staring back as her heart broke into pieces which fell at his feet.

Cord shoved his hands in his pockets, his stormy face turned to stone. "The baby...our love child...and you."

The stony face began to crumble. Although Amy wanted to draw him into her arms, she forced them to stay at her side.

"I'm sorry." Her trembling lips uttered the words her heart truly felt.

"Sorry?" he shot out at her. "You have no idea how sorry I am that I ever met you." Without another word he whirled on his heel and quickly left her alone.

Amy watched as his long, determined stride sought to put distance between them. Her heart yearned to run after him, but her legs were fixed in place. She had done it. The most unselfish act she had ever done. And also the most painful.

She stared after him as he met his mother by the fountain in the park. In the haze of the morning sun on the water, they looked like shadow figures. Still, Amy knew when Mrs. McCune turned to look in her direction.

Before there was a confrontation Amy quickly walked in the other direction, leaving an aching heart behind. She knew her heart would stay with him forever. Her hand drifted to her tummy. But she would always have part of him.

Thirteen

"Gram, I just don't know how this will all turn out." Cord lowered himself to the couch in his grandmother's room.

The old woman's rocking chair halted and the knitting needles ceased their endless clicking. She eyed her grandson. "Baby, you know what I always tell you. All things work together for good for those who love the Lord. For those who are called according to His purpose." She smiled brightly and set her chair rocking again. The needles clicked in rhythm with the chair and she hummed a hymn very familiar to Cord's ears.

"Guess I wasn't called." he grumbled.

"You certainly were. It just takes time to see His plan." She wrapped the threads around her fingers and began knitting again.

"Gram?" He edged to the side of the couch. "What are you knitting there. It looks like something for a baby."

"It is, child." Grandma smiled at him.

"Someone we know?" She was always knitting for family, friends and strangers."

"This one I know very well." Her eyes glowed.

"Well who?" Cord tried to keep the impatience out of his voice.

"Oh ye of little faith," she admonished. "For your child." Her face gathered a warm smile.

"But Gram," he thought she knew, "Amy lost the baby."

The chair stopped rocking abruptly. "Nonsense. That child has not lost your baby. She is still carrying it and is still in love with you."

Cord sat back on the couch and studied the old woman's face. Was she becoming senile? Or was this wishful thinking? "Gram," he began in a soft voice, "she did lose the baby."

"Cordelle," her tone was gentle but firm. "Has Grandma ever been wrong about something like this?"

"No," he shook his head slowly. Was there some possibility that she was right? They had always counted on her sagacity to get them through life's rough waters. He stood as if he had been washed ashore from life's storms, his mind searching to find the right answers. He knelt in front of the smiling old woman. "If this is true, then why did she say it? Why did she break up with me?"

He felt the warmth of a lifetime as his grandmother's arms enveloped him. His heart pounded heavily in his chest. Amy was not a liar. He knew her well. He was hurt and had not been able to see past the enormous pain.

"Amy is a good woman, Cordelle," she sighed softly. "She did it because she does love you." She ruffled his hair. "Child, don't you see? It was an unselfish act. Amy knows because you and she love each other, you are the target of those who have hate in their hearts."

Cord studied his grandmother's face. In her misted eyes he saw the pain caused by centuries of hate. He also saw the knowledge of human beings and her love for all. He was stunned for a moment. She was right. What she was saying was more like Amy.

"Gram, I love you." He held her in his arms and kissed her on the cheek.

"I love you too, baby. Now that you know the truth, don't you think you should do something about it?" Her soft laugh was youthful sounding.

Cord kissed her again. "I have no idea what this family would do with out the matriarch we have been given by the angels." He rose slowly. "What should I do?"

"You should follow your heart." She smiled broadly. "Oh, child, you have two weeks until the trial begins." She thought for a moment. "A trial I know your mother will not let take place." The smile returned to her thinning lips. "I would think you would go home and pack." She pushed him playfully. "Now git with you."

With one last kiss and a big hug Cord left his grandmother. But on his drive back to his apartment he began having doubts. What if Gram was wrong? What if Amy truly did lose the baby? What if she really did think it wasn't meant to be? He shook his head. His grandmother was never wrong about these things.

He ran up the five flights of stairs to his apartment and walked with a new life feeling. Once inside, he grabbed his luggage and began throwing things in the bags. His fetish to be neat was nowhere in his thinking. He was going to the woman he loved and he was praying she did love him.

Grasping his bags he headed for the door. As he reached for the knob, he noticed his unopened mail neatly stacked in a basket by the phone. Cord had not opened a single item of mail since first going to Sault Saint Marie to meet with Amy. He made a mental note to have his secretary from his accounting firm pick it up and take care of anything urgent.

Leaning against the mail stand was a box. He picked it up and read the return address. It was from Amy. He checked the mail-dated stamp. It was sent after their first meeting. His heart pounded as he opened the box. Why hadn't he noticed this before?

When the wrapping was recklessly discarded on the floor he was holding the box of chocolates he had sent her at Valentine's. Why had she returned it at that time? His heart sank. This was the real truth. She had never really wanted him. He dropped the box on the floor and stared as it flipped open. It was empty.

"What the hell!" He spoke so loudly it startled him. What kind of game had she been playing with him? When he kicked the box, it rolled over and he stared down at a note taped in the bottom of the box. 'This is how my life would be without you.'

His mind drifted back to their separation after the conference. There in the rain, in the parking lot, he had told her he was better than a box of chocolates. He stared at the note. She knew then, as he did, that they were destined to be together. Their lives would be empty without each other. "Gram was right."

He called his accounting firm where he had been working since suspension from his position from the state, a position he had kept only to be near Amy. He left instructions with his secretary to have his assistant take over because he would be gone for awhile. When he ended his call he told her to make him reservations at the Kewadin Inn and forward his calls there. With that out of the way, he had one stop to make. His mother.

This was not going to be easy. She had been as hurt as he was with Amy losing the baby, and then the breakup. He entered her office with the fear of a child who had to tell his parent he had a bad report card. Easter McCune looked up at him as he walked in and stood in front of her desk.

"I knew you would be here soon." She smiled broadly.

Cord stared at her for a moment and then realized his grandmother had covered all bases. "Mom, I want to go to her. I should have pressed her when she broke up with me." He sighed heavily and dropped in the chair in front of her desk. "It's been four weeks. Next week will be the Fourth of July. If she is still carrying our child, she should be showing. Shouldn't she?" He looked to his mother for the answer that he knew would be based in reality.

Mrs. McCune rose and walked to where he sat. She placed her hand on his shoulder and squeezed it tightly before releasing it. "Son, all women are different in the way they carry their babies." She patted his shoulder lightly. "If it is not evident, then you will have to ask her." She paused briefly. "I would place my bets on Grandma." His mother smiled at him knowingly.

Cord stood thoughtfully. "Then I will ask." He said it with a great deal more confidence than he felt. He placed his arm around her shoulders and they walked to the door together. "Thanks, Mom."

Easter McCune kissed her son on the cheek. "No thanks needed, baby. I will always be your mother." Mother and son embraced tightly.

Cord planted a kiss on top of her head as he reached for the doorknob. "And the best Mom anyone could have." He tossed her a smile. "How many guys have one of the best attorneys in the state as their mother and chief defender?" He chuckled as he leaned back in to tweak her nose.

His mother gave him a playful shove. "Get on with you."

He heard her laugh as he closed the door to the outer office. If only he could be as sure of Amy as he was the other women in his life. He picked up his stride. The only way to find out was to go to her and that was exactly what he was going to do.

■ ■ ■

Amy felt his presence before she saw him. Her heart skipped a beat. She stared at the computer screen and tried not to glance at the door when a shadow fell over it. She had just spent four of the longest weeks of her life. Just when she thought she could control her feelings he was here.

She pushed her hair back and bit her lower lip as she slowly moved her eyes to look up from the monitor and see the love of her life. His large frame filled the doorway. His dark eyes were guarded but a light grin touched his lips.

He held out the empty box of chocolates. "So you want to talk about this?"

Amy stared at the box. She didn't have to think. The moment she saw it she remembered having sent it. "But that was a couple of months ago." She tried to keep her voice controlled and without emotion, but she could hear crack as she spoke.

"Mind telling me what made the change?" He plunked the box on her desk and stood ramrod straight. His look dared her to give him the answer.

"I...I," she stuttered softly.

He dropped the empty box on her desk. "That's what I thought."

Amy drew in a deep breath. She had an idea where this was going and knew she could not stop it. Her heart had ached for him. She wanted to fly into his arms. Yet, the trial was soon and she didn't want their relationship to be responsible for him going to prison. She stared at the box.

"Amy?" Cord spoke her name softly. She dragged her fixed look from the box and met his eyes.

"Yes?" Her voice was being strangled by her heart. The storm in his eyes was subdued. He moved around the desk and sat on the edge, his lithe body within inches of her. She watched as he stretched his long legs out in front of him and laid a hand on each thigh. The aroma of his cologne filled her senses with a longing desire. She looked from his hands to his face.

He tilted his brows, looking at her uncertainly. She admired his marvelously perfect face as he drew his lips in thoughtfully. He was waiting for her to speak, but she couldn't. If she opened her mouth she would reveal her true feelings. She moistened her dry lips and then bit her lower one to keep from speaking.

His searching survey traveled over her face and down her body, stopping to stare at the slight pouch of her belly. Subconsciously, her hand rested protectively on her stomach as she underwent his close scrutiny. His eyebrows lifted in an unspoken question.

Amy couldn't stand the silence. "What?" Her voice was a strangled whisper.

The beginnings of a smile tipped the corners of his mouth. "We are still having our baby in February?" It was half statement and half question.

Amy felt her lips part in surprise. How could he know? She averted her gaze. She didn't want him reading the true answer. She had to recover before all was lost. "What would make you ask that?" Her voice trembled.

Cord released a long-held sigh. "Because it's true."

His simple statement brought her full attention back to him. Warmth flooded from his face as he broke into a soft loving smile. His scrutiny was sharp and assessing still, but love shone from his eyes. She had no place to go but to the truth. She nodded slowly.

Cord tenderly lifted a wayward tendril of hair from her cheek and tucked it behind her ear. Then he bent to kiss her cheek. "You don't have to protect me. I don't want to be shut out of your life because you think it's best for me."

Amy's resolve shattered. Tears flooded her face. Sobs caught in her throat as she spoke. "I have to. I love you."

Cord drew her into his arms and cradled her. "God, baby." His voice filled with anguish. He rocked them back and forth as he hugged her tightly to him. "Together. That's how we will get through this."

She nodded her head against his chest. She didn't know how it would all turn out, but for now she was safe in his arms. A sob shivered through her body. Relief and fear settled over her. His gentle rocking enveloped her in a peace she had not felt since the day that she sent him away. Yet, in the back of her mind she feared they would pay for this in the end.

Cord's mouth came down on her lips tenderly. Then with a fierce hunger, he reclaimed what was his. Amy felt the passionate heat grow as they fed on each other's love. He scooped her up in his arms and held her possessively. She curled into him, forgetting all of the sound reasons she'd had for setting him free.

"Oh, excuse me." Cord swung them around so they could see a smiling but red-faced Shelley. "Now this is more like it," Shelley laughed.

Amy felt Cord squeeze her tightly and then place her gently on the floor beside him, his arms still wrapped in a tight embrace. She didn't know how this would all work but somehow she knew it would. She returned Shelley's smile. "Yes, this is more like it." Her voice was filled with love and awe as she turned to look at the man she loved. "We will get through this together," she said in a hoarse whisper.

Cord's face grew a wider grin. "I think I have heard that before." He tapped his forehead. "Now where was that? I'm sure it wasn't long ago."

Amy laughed and lightly pushed on his arm. "That's where I get my best ideas." The anguish of the last four weeks was evaporating. He was here. They were together and this was the way it would be. She leaned into him as he snugged her tightly to him.

"Well, it's about time you two got it together." Shelley's face was beaming as if she had created the couple.

"Sometimes I'm just a little slow." Amy smiled and patted her tummy. "I think I'll blame it on my condition."

Cord threw his head back and laughed. "Somehow I knew it would come back to this." He shook his head. "Women can find the darnedest things to blame for their ability to be unreasonable. The office filled with their laughter. Amy felt the fears of her lifetime being lifted. Somehow she and Cord would do this together.

"Which one should I wear? She held two dresses just under her chin.

Cord shrugged. "The pink one?"

"Is that a question or an answer?"

"Both, I didn't want to be wrong." He stepped beside her. "Honey, whatever you wear is perfect with me."

Her heart turned over with love for him. "Now that was the right answer." She tried to hold back the laugh. "You sir, will go a long way with me."

Cord placed his hands on her shoulders and turned her toward him. "I will go the rest of my life with you." He paused. She could see a myriad of feelings crossing his handsome face. When he spoke, his voice was filled with trepidation. "I sure hope everything goes well tonight and that Sara at least halfway accepts me."

Amy slid her arms around his neck and stood on tiptoe to kiss him. She dropped back down and studied his face. Worry lines had gathered on his brow. His eyes were narrowed and darker. Sara had returned during their separation and tonight they would meet for the first time. She knew this was really worrying him. "I hope she does too." She paused to gather her thoughts. "I love my daughter but she has her own life. This is our life and we are going to live it."

He drew her close to his chest. "I know, baby. I just don't want you to have any more problems." He rubbed her back as he held her and rocked. He buried his face in her hair close to her ear. "You and the baby mean everything to me. We are starting a new life together in more ways than one."

Hot lava shot through her as he tenderly caressed her and spoke words of love. Her body reacted to his every word and move. She hoped Sara would accept him too, but whether she did or not, he was here to stay.

Slowly, unwillingly, she disengaged herself from his embrace. She smiled at him. "Now finish getting ready. We have to meet Mom and Sara at the restaurant." She had been at Cord's hotel for most of the week. She had told Sara she was getting married and had told her of the race difference. Sara had said very little. Amy knew she wasn't pleased but she hoped she had raised her well enough to be at least cordial to Cord.

Cord held out the chair for Amy. She sat and let him slide her in as she felt all eyes in the restaurant on her. She shuddered inwardly. Sara was going to get this reception too. Her heart went out to her daughter who wasn't there yet but would be soon.

Cord took the seat across from her and held her hand. He rolled the ring he had placed on her finger, the ring that had not been removed even when they were separated for that short time. The short time that had been an eternity.

They sat quietly, both thinking of the evening ahead and what it might bring. Amy gazed into loving eyes. Her heart swelled with pride. This man loved her and she loved him. She knew others were staring but none of that was important. The only thing that mattered was that they were together.

"Mom?" Amy was so mesmerized she wasn't sure if she heard Sara or if her mind was playing tricks on her. She glanced up to see her mother and her daughter standing by their table. She watched as Cord rose and pulled their chairs out for them. Her heart pounded heavily in her chest. This was what she had been waiting for, to bring the three people she loved the most together. Still, now that they were all here, her stomach bound itself into a knot. She drew in a deep breath and waited until they were seated.

"Mom." Amy leaned over and hugged Mrs. Summers. "Sara." Amy took her daughter's hand. Sara's large blue eyes darted from Amy to Cord. Amy released a long-held breath and studied her daughter's face. The large blue eyes were narrowed and dark. The perfectly arched eyebrows were drawn together over her small nose. Amy's heart jumped to her throat. Sara's stare reminded her of Leah's. She tried to swallow but the hard throbbing of her heart blocked the way.

She glanced at her mom, whose eyes were misted with anguish for her and for her granddaughter. Amy wanted this evening over right now, but it had only begun. She knew only seconds had passed, but it felt like hours. Looking at Cord, she could see him steeling himself for what was coming. His mask was on. In the depths of his eyes she could see the years of prejudice swirling. For the man she loved, this was just another cultural clash in a very long line. Though her mind raced for just the right words, still nothing came from her lips.

"Sara, I am very happy to meet you." Cord's marvelously calm, rich voice relieved Amy. The silence had been broken.

"Thank you." Sara's stare traveled over Cord and then returned to her mother.

"Mom," she spoke as if she hadn't just met her mother's fiancé, "after dinner I think we should talk." Sara's stare moved quickly over Cord and her grandmother and then back to her mother. "There are some issues we need to deal with privately."

Amy's head shook no automatically. "Honey, whatever you want to discuss..."

"I think a mother and daughter do have private issues and they should be discussed privately." Cord's smooth, even voice stopped Amy from finishing her statement. She glanced at him and saw the warning in his gaze. He knew the nuances of dealing with this. She would let him take the lead.

"Dad." Hank slammed his hand on his father's shoulder and chuckled when Cord lurched forward. "Good evening, ladies." He gave a half bow and then straightened. "How are we this evening?"

Amy could feel the smile growing in her heart and reaching her lips. "I'm fine, Hank." She gestured to the empty chair between Cord and Sara. "Please have a seat."

"Good evening, son." Cord's voice was lighter. His son's presence was a lift to him as well as to the others at the table.

As Cord made the introductions, Amy glimpsed first the smiling face of her mother and then the non-smiling face of her daughter. Sara's face was like porcelain except for two bright rose blotches on her cheeks.

"To what do we owe this honor?" Amy kept her voice light.

"Oh, I see," Sara spoke curtly. "Then I am the last to meet everyone?"

Hank laughed his boyish, playful laugh. "I knew it!" He glanced around the table. "They always save the best for last. It's kind of like desert. Who would eat that first?" He patted Sara on the shoulder. "Now this lets me know who they think is the best."

Sara's face had turned scarlet. Her glare was turning to an open-eyed stare of astonishment. "I...I don't think that was what they had in mind," she sputtered.

"Then you explain why they kept someone as fine as you hidden?" He winked at Amy. "So how is my new mom? Anything new to report?"

Amy shook her head as her breath caught in her throat. They were going to tell Sara about the baby when the dust settled. If she didn't think fast, the dust would be blown in all their faces. Her mother's hand on her arm brought her around. "Yes, Mom," she spoke in a barely audible voice.

"If you wouldn't mind I would like to go home." Her mother spoke quietly.

Amy's heart lurched. "Mom, are you ill?"

Mrs. Summers laughed. "Oh no, nothing that dramatic. We've been shopping all day and I think it has caught up with me."

Amy shot a meaningful look in Cord's direction. He rose. "Of course, Mrs. Summers, we will do that, and then rejoin our children here." He picked her wrap up from the back of the chair and placed it on her shoulders.

Amy saw Sara scoot to the edge of her chair. The red blotches had spread over her cheeks. Her heart went out to her daughter. She turned to Cord, "Maybe the children would like to go with us."

Cord offered a knowing smile. "Of course." He looked at the two young people at the table. "Come on." He gave a motion with his hand. "We could all use the ride."

"Dad, if you don't mind, I would like to stay here and get to know my new sister." Hank smiled broadly at Sara and then added, "Unless of course you want to go."

Sara eased back into her chair and her face took on a normal color. "No, I think I'd like to get to know you too." She spoke to Hank but caught her mother's eye.

Amy had no idea what that was all about. Maybe Sara wanted her to urge her to go along, yet maybe she wanted to stay. Amy stood frozen in place. What if Hank mentioned the baby? Before she had time to think about much more, Cord was tugging on her hand.

"Let's take your mom home and then we can return quickly." She nodded. It was as if he had been reading her mind. She didn't want to leave, still she had no choice. It was her mother, after all.

Hank stood as Amy and her mother rose to leave. He caught Amy's eye and winked. "Don't worry about a thing, Mom. Sara and I will flip coins for the best room in the house and draw straws for who gets what on college breaks." His laugh was marvelously contagious. Sara giggled as she watched him. Amy sighed relief and laughed too.

She looked to Sara. "Is this OK with you, honey?" Her daughter had turned toward Hank and was about to speak to him.

"Sure, Mom." She glanced at her mother and then returned her attention to Hank. "We will be fine. In fact, we'll order for you and it should be here when you get back."

Hank laughed. "Now there is an idea whose time has come. I am starving."

"Me too." Sara's giggle was light.

Mrs. Summers hugged her granddaughter. "I will see you in the morning, dumplin'." Then she hugged Hank. "I am so happy to meet you, young man. Amy has told me so much about you and I think I know why now." She smiled at the young people. "Have a good time."

"We will, Gram," they both said at the same time and then laughed.

"Dumplin'?" Amy heard Hank ask. Then she could hear their laughter as she and Cord left the restaurant with her mom. She prayed silently that it would stay that way until they returned.

■■■

They returned to the restaurant within the hour. Amy fully expected to find them at odds. Instead, she saw Hank holding Sara's hand palm up and both of them laughing. She felt her body release the tightly-held tension she'd had since leaving the restaurant and she could feel her shoulders drop from their hunched position. Her footsteps slowed as they neared the table.

What on earth were they doing?

"Mom, look." Sara's bright voice had returned. Amy couldn't believe the transformation.

"Yeah, Mom, look," Hank chimed in, and then chuckled. "Dad, have a seat I'll show you guys what I've learned about palmistry too."

Amy and Cord laughed with him as they took their seats. "And how did we get to this?" Cord eyed his son knowingly.

The waiter brought their dinners. "Ms. Summers, good to see you again." Amy looked up and realized Chip was their waiter.

"Hi Chip. I thought you worked in the concierge's office." Amy smiled warmly at Shelley's brother.

"Oh, I do that too. Starting college this fall, you know." He smiled at her and then turned to Hank. "OK, it's a deal. You show me around the MSU campus and I will show you how to navigate in the forest here."

All eyes turned to Hank as they waited for his answer. Amy couldn't believe this young man had turned so many heads in less than an hour. Yet he had, and everyone loved him. She smiled at Cord and whispered, "Our son the politician."

"Or con man," Cord whispered back to her as the three young people engaged in a lively conversation about what there was to do.

Cord covered Amy's hand with his and leaned close to her so no one else could hear. "See, it was meant to be."

Amy nodded. "I think Hank was meant to be a diplomat from the day he was born." She laughed lightly.

"I hope Sara is like her mother. When she decides to like someone, it sticks." He squeezed her hand.

"Me too." Sara was like her in many ways. She could only hope this was one of them. Amy watched Cord's handsome face as he beamed his pride in his son. Her heart swelled with love.

One more hurdle for them tonight. Amy felt some of the panic return. They had discussed telling Sara about the baby on the way back from taking her mother home and it was decided to see how the evening went and tell her after dinner. Amy looked at her daughter's smiling face as the two young men entertained her. She hated to tell Sara. She seemed so happy at the moment. Yet, if I wait, she may discover it and that would hurt our chances of becoming a family.

The dinner had gone better than Amy could have dared dream. Her heart was aglow with the warmth of a new family growing and learning to love and accept. She hated to break the spell. Yet it had to be soon. She pushed back her chair and smiled at Cord. "Why don't you and Hank go to the guest sitting area. Sara and I will be along when we have freshened up."

Cord leaned over and kissed her cheek. "That sounds like a capital idea to me."

Sara stood and moved to her mother's side. She smiled at Hank. "We won't be long and then we can do something."

Again Amy marveled at the seeming transformation in her daughter as they made their way to the women's lounge. Once inside, Amy and Sara both checked under the stalls to make sure they were alone. Amy giggled. "You would think I would get over that. It has been a long time since I was in high school."

Sara pulled a brush through her long, sandy blond hair. "I think most women do that. If not for privacy, then to see if a stall is open." She laughed lightly and then turned to her mother. "Look, Mom, I have no right to interfere with your life."

Amy held her hand up and shook her head. "Honey, this is our life. I am going to marry Cord. I love him." She paused to pull her thoughts together. "Still, I will listen to you and will do whatever I can to make this easier for you."

"Mom, this will be harder on you than on me. I'll be attending college and away from the everyday strife." She sighed heavily. "We live in a white world, Mom, and some of the people we call friends will not take this lightly. I am worried about you, that's all."

Amy's heart grew lighter. "Oh, thank God. I thought somehow you were going to be one of those who don't like mixed marriages."

Sara shoved her brush into her purse. "To be honest with you, I have never given it much thought. Now that I'm faced with it, I think of little else." She flipped her hair to fluff it and pulled her purse strap to her shoulder.

Amy wasn't sure what Sara was telling her or how to respond. Her mind tripped over bundled nerves and highly charged emotions. "And" she asked thoughtfully, "what is it you think?"

Sara leaned her rear against the counter and folded her arms over her stomach. "I am happy you have found someone to love." She averted her gaze from her mother's. "I like Cord and his son Hank. I just wish they were white."

She moved closer to Sara and took her hands in hers. "Honey, I love you. You are my pride and joy." She lightly kissed her daughter on the cheek and then continued. "I fell in love with Cord before I knew what he looked like." She explained how they had met and how they had helped each other over the past two years. Then she finished with, "You see, I fell in love with a man. Another human being. A man with a golden heart and soul. I don't wish he was white. I love the color of his skin."

Sara looked into her mother's eyes. Tears sat on the brims of her eyelids waiting to spill her fear of the unknown. "I know, Mom." Her voice quivered. "I feel awful about what I've been thinking. I've never met two people who are more likeable." The tears pushed out and streamed down her face. "It's just that...that..."

"I know." Amy put her arm around her and led her to the soft leather lounge. Mother and daughter held each other as the tears of frustration and fear flowed. Amy let her daughter finish and then held her back to look into her eyes. "I remember being eighteen. I know now that our friends accept in us what we accept in ourselves." She offered Sara a weak smile.

Amy lifted a wet tendril that was stuck to Sara's cheek and tucked it behind her ears. "If it will help you out any, I was just as shocked as you are that I had fallen in love with an African American. I, like you, had never given it much thought. I even tried not to love him. But that would be like trying not to love you. I don't love you for the way you look. I love you because you are you."

Amy sighed thoughtfully. This was the time to tell Sara the whole truth. Not later but now. "Sara?" Amy lifted her daughter's chin. "There is one more thing you need to know."

Sara's eyes grew wide. Her brows lifted her tear-streaked face in a question. "Wh—what?" Her voice trembled softly.

Amy straightened her shoulders and drew in a deep breath. It was now or never. She touched Sara's cheek with her fingertips. "Honey, we...Hank, you, Cord and I are going to be welcoming another life into our family in February."

Sara's eyes grew wider as the realization of her mother's words sank in. She drew back and stared at Amy. Amy's heart pounded heavily in her chest as she waited for her daughter to say something, anything. The silence grew and so did Amy's fear. This could be the last straw for Sara.

Sara's mouth formed an "O" but nothing came out. Her tearful face began to change and soon a smile gradually lifted her lips. She sniffed. "You mean Hank and I are going to have a sister or a brother?" Her voice was soft and filled with wonderment.

"Yes," Amy nodded. There was no need to say any more. She could see Sara working through her emotions and knew it was best to let it happen. She waited.

Sara's smile grew wider. "I have always wanted a sibling." She giggled. "And tonight I thought Hank was going to be it." She thought for a moment. "Does Hank know?"

Amy nodded again. "We were having dinner at Cord's parents a few weeks ago and I was having morning sickness. His family knew before I did." She laughed softly, remembering.

Sara giggled. "I hope the baby acts like Hank. No one will ever get in his way."

Amy pulled Sara into her embrace. "I hope the baby is a good combination of you and Hank. What a lucky child to have you two as siblings." Her heart was filled with joy at Sara's reaction. Now she could face anything. Together they would become a family.

Fourteen

"Did you ask Sara to be your maid of honor?" Cord embraced Amy as they sat on the deck of his hotel room. July had brought with it the hot winds that caressed Lake Superior and gave a freshness to the evening.

"Emmmm," she purred. "Uh-huh and she will." She yawned. "Can you believe what has happened in the past two weeks?"

Cord shook his head thoughtfully. "One more hurdle before we can walk down that aisle."

Amy knew he was thinking of the trial tomorrow. His mother had assured them that she had enough evidence to get the case thrown out. Still, he was a black man in a white world. She shivered involuntarily.

Cord held her closer, and buried his face in her hair. "As long as we have each other it will be OK." His hand moved over her side and settled on her growing middle. "We have too much going for us now."

Amy felt the heat of his hand on her tummy as it traveled throughout her body, making her very aware of his undeniable magnetism. She couldn't help feeling the tingle of passion growing inside her. She curled around to face him and placed her hands on his cheeks. "Mmm, I love you, Cordelle McCune." She kissed him.

"I love you so very much." His voice grew heavy with passion. His large hand took her face and held it gently.

"When this is all over we're going to an island and hide for a month." He kissed the pulsing hollow at the base of her throat and then hungrily reclaimed her lips.

Amy felt the heady sensation of his lips against her neck. She returned his kiss with a craving of her own, giving herself freely to passion. All thoughts were abandoned except that of their bodies entwined.

Cord gently scooped his lady from the seat on the deck and carried her to their bed. His mind wanted to go over the trial plan with his mother. Yet his heart and body needed to be with the woman he loved. He laid her gently on the pillow and pushed her hair from her face.

Her soft trusting gaze melted his heart. "My lady, my soul mate, my best friend, I'll love you forever." He lightly whispered a kiss over her brow, her cheeks her nose and then passionately reclaimed her lips.

"Mmmm," he moaned and then gave a shiver as her tongue slipped tenderly between his lips. He could taste the mint of her toothpaste, the heat of her passion. Slowly he let himself down beside her, never letting their mouths part, and snuggled her close to him. Tomorrow he might not have the chance to do this. Reality set in. He might not be here again for fifteen years. His lips moved over hers, his mind memorizing every detail.

Amy pushed lightly on his chest. She looked up into his face. He could feel her searching deep in his soul. "We have tonight, darling." Her soft, tender, understanding words engulfed him like a warm summer breeze.

He nodded, his throat too tight to speak. She knew without a word where he was and what he was thinking. He held her as close as two bodies could be without being one. He inhaled deeply, memorizing her essence. He thought he heard knocking. He lifted his head and perked his ears.

"Oh," his hoarse voice whispered as he dragged himself from the bed. "There is someone at the door." He chuckled and then gazed at Amy. "I thought it was my heart."

Amy smiled and playfully punched at him. "Answer the door," came her breathless command. She kissed him and whispering with lips together she said, "Honey, answer the door. And get rid of whoever it is."

"Mmm, this had better be important," he growled. Cord didn't want to move. He never wanted to be separated from her again. "Maybe they will go away if we ignore it." His tongue flicked and tasted her lips. He could feel her body arch and shudder under his.

The knocking became more urgent. Cord flopped to his back and threw his arm over his eyes. "Someone has perfect timing." Grudgingly, he drew himself from the bed and trudged to the door.

He looked through the peephole. "Crap," he cursed and leaned against the door.

"Who is it?" Amy sat bolt upright.

"That damned Jeff Delaney." He slid out the dead bolt and then turned the lock on the door as he peered again and saw Jeff pacing outside their door.

"What do you suppose he wants?" She straightened her clothing and slid off the bed.

"Probably wants to gloat about tomorrow," Cord growled in a low voice. "The vulture can't wait."

Amy moved to Cord's side and peeped through the hole. "He doesn't look like he is in a gloating mood."

Cord yanked the door open with a swish, startling Jeff. "Well?" Cord growled at him.

Jeff looked down at his shoes. "Sorry to bother you," he mumbled. "If I may, I would like to have a few minutes of your time."

Cord noted the time on his watch, glanced at Amy and then back at Delaney. He gave a quick nod and then stepped back. "You can have a few minutes." His voice was cold and uninviting but he didn't care. He watched as Jeff slowly entered. Now here was a man with something on his mind.

Cord pulled in a deep fortifying breath. He could feel his back grow stiff. He leveled his shoulders, ready to take this character on. "Have a seat." Cord pointed through a door to the living area of the suite.

Jeff entered the living area but didn't sit. He rubbed his palms together as if in July he had cold hands and began pacing again.

Cord and Amy followed him in and watched as he treaded back and forth. Cord's patience was wearing thin. "What is it, man?"

Jeff jerked around. "I need your help."

Cord stared at him. "My help?" Had this man lost his mind? "Who do you want to frame now? Are you offering me an out if I help you?" Sarcasm wrapped every word he said.

Jeff's chin dropped to his chest. "I don't blame you for not trusting me. And I know you won't believe me when I tell you I had nothing to do with the frame." He scuffed his foot into the carpeting. "But I do know who did."

Cord glared at him. "Then why don't you tell the district attorney so we can call this whole thing off?"

"I will." Jeff's face grew red and lines formed around his eyes and on his brow. "I just have to figure a way out for my mother."

"Oh, so that's it." Cord could hear his voice grow loud with incredulity. "Let's save the white woman who did this and maybe we can pull the nigger out too." His anger of many years spilled over into his words. He stepped back, feeling his fists clenching. He needed to get control. He could lose more if he didn't.

He glanced at Amy whose face had gone ashen, then back at Jeff whose eyes had grown wide with the outburst. He released his tightly held fists. "So what do you want me to do?" He wasn't going to give an inch if he didn't have to.

Jeff took in a long deep breath. "Tomorrow this will all come out in court." He paused and then went on as if he were on fire. "I have confronted my mother with this and she is contrite. She thought she was doing something for me. You know how that is. It was your mother who hired the detective who left a trail for me. Mothers are like that."

"My mother was trying to keep her son out or prison for life. Yours was trying to put me in." Cord was calmer but the rage he felt at the injustice would always be there.

Jeff nodded slowly. "Cord, she was wrong. We were wrong. We let society dictate a norm to us that shouldn't be a norm." His eyes were filled with the anguish of a man who had been wrong and was now asking his victim for help. He glanced in Amy's direction.

When Cord saw the look he gave Amy, his heart softened a little. He knew the feeling of loving her and losing her. He shrugged his shoulders. Taking Amy's hand, he urged her to move to the couch and sit with him. Amy offered him a warm smile, a smile that said I love you and I'm proud of you. He had the woman he loved, and he had the woman Jeff loved. Amy sat close to Cord, laying her hand on his. When they were seated, Cord looked at Jeff again. "All right, Jeff, sit down and tell us what it is you think we can do."

Jeff followed the directions and sat in a chair across from them. Cord watched as the stiffness left Jeff and he began to relax. In a way he could understand. Jeff had lost the woman he loved and because of it was going to lose his mother. Not that he could forget any of this but he knew he could forgive the bigoted attitudes. Gram had taught him not to harbor anger. It would destroy him quicker than his enemy. He waited for Jeff to gather his thoughts and tell them what he wanted.

"It's just that..." Jeff cleared his throat and began again. "I know you don't owe me or my mother." He fidgeted crossing and uncrossing his legs. "I am asking as one human to another. If you can find it in your heart, I would be grateful if you would ask the judge to consider the circumstances and be lenient." He stopped and looked at the couple in front of him. The pain lines were etched in his face and dark clouds covered his eyes.

Cord felt for the man but his feelings for Mrs. Delaney were not so nice. Forgiving was one thing, forgetting quite another. She had targeted him for destruction. His thoughts tossed and tumbled. Anger and pain mixed with sympathy for this man who'd had to swallow his pride and come begging for help. "And your mother? Does she know you are here?"

Jeff nodded. "She is downstairs in the lobby. We just had a...a discussion. She wants to come and speak with you."

Cord's face slowly slid into a grin. "I bet she does." He was sure Jeff would have had to drag his mother here. He couldn't help feeling sorry for the man. Jeff had been honest about his feelings for him, and it wasn't as much race as it had been a jealous lover.

Jeff's face turned a deep red. "She knows she was wrong. Yet, she does believe our races shouldn't mix." He looked from Amy to Cord and then back at Amy. "I know Amy well enough to know she's in love or she wouldn't be here." He swallowed hard and his eyes grew misty. Jeff looked down at his knees.

"Cord?" Amy's softly spoken question added to the thawing of his heart. He wrapped his arm around her, pulling her possessively close. He looked into green orbs that were pleading for him to help.

Silence settled over them. They were all measuring their wins and losses. Cord knew he was the winner here. He knew there was nothing he could do except help Jeff. He had been taught to be the bigger man. In this case it would take a real personal struggle, but he could do it. He would do it for Amy. He glanced at Jeff. And he would do it for this man who would lose all if he didn't.

"Jeff," Cord stood and the other man followed suit, "I'll do my best."

Jeff offered him his hand. "Thank you. That's all I can ask." He glanced at Amy and then back at Cord. "Your best is more than I deserve."

Cord wanted to agree with him but what would that prove? He hesitated. His hand, imprisoned by his side, felt as if weighed down by a rock. The rock of prejudice and hatred. He stiffly moved it up and accepted the other man's proffered hand. "I can't see where a retaliation against you and your mother would change what's happened."

"I..." Jeff stopped and turned toward the door.

Cord jerked around as the door swung open, his senses were at full alert. If this joker had planned another surprise, he and his mother would go down in court. Cord stared as his sister burst through the door. "Leah, what the hell?"

Her face was pinched with anger. Leah looked at her brother and then glared at Jeff. "I don't know what you think you're doing, whitey, but I heard you and the old bitch downstairs."

Cord's eyebrows shot up. He was accustomed to Leah's anger, but this time, she looked ready to kill. He moved to stand between Jeff and Leah. Whatever had happened, she was not going to be easy to handle.

"Get the hell out of my way," she shot out at Cord and tried to shove him.

"Leah?" Cord's voice took on a quiet but commanding tone. "Whatever is bothering you we will discuss it." He turned to Jeff. "You were just leaving?"

Jeff nodded and moved toward the door, edging past Leah. "Cord, Amy, thank you." He reached for the door.

"Not so fast, white boy," Leah hissed as she grabbed his arm. Her long red fingernails dug into his arm, making him wince.

Jeff looked to Cord for help. Then his gaze was brought back to Leah.

Cord noted the look Jeff gave his sister and he chuckled to himself. She was gorgeous. Jeff's quick cursory glance obviously pleased him. His eyes tried to take on the I-don't-want-to-look-at-this-beautiful-woman look but his gaze swallowed her whole. His eyes grew smokey, his lower jaw twitched and his face took on a reddish hue. Cord knew what he was thinking. Yet he knew the man didn't stand a chance.

"Leah," Cord placed his hand on her arm, "we know what Jeff was up to."

Leah jerked her arm away. "And you are still talking to him? I don't believe you know what I know." She flipped her raven hair and slapped her hands on her hips.

Cord chuckled aloud. All she needed was to start tapping her toe now. "Leah, we do know." He turned to Jeff. "This is my sister Leah." And then to Leah, "This is Jeff, the chief detective here."

"Nice to meet you." Jeff used the introduction as an excuse to let his smokey gaze take in more of the beautiful woman. He did this quickly, then looked away, fear of being caught written all over his face.

Cord chuckled as the two combatants squared off. There was no match here. Leah was in command. He smiled at his sister and waited for the next outburst he could see coming just under her darkened glare.

"You know this man and the old bitch he calls mother are the ones who planned framing you?" She acted as if she'd not heard the introduction. Her voice reached a fever pitch.

"That's not exactly it, but close." Cord shook his head and smiled. Leah hadn't disappointed him. "Why don't we all sit down and work this out?" He motioned to the table. Jeff sat almost immediately, then remembering his manners, stood and waited for the ladies. Leah took her sweet time, swaying as if she were hearing a rap song.

"Honey, I'll call room service and order coffee." Amy turned to the others. "Would you like something besides coffee?"

"Thanks baby, would you order some sandwiches? I'm starved." He winked at her. He saw the heat seep into her cheeks as they both remembered where they had been before the interruptions. She hesitated as their gazes met. He could feel the passionate glow within her. She emanated love with her look. He released a sigh and winked with a big smile. "Later," he mouthed. Her eyes sparkled as she blushed and then turned to the telephone.

When the snacks were delivered, the relatively silent group became animated. Leah fired the first shot. "I overheard you and your mother plotting against my brother."

Jeff's face burned red. "First of all, young lady, you didn't hear my mother and me plotting. You heard me talking to her about the plot. And next, as much as I hate what my mother has done, she is not an old bitch." His lower jaw flexed with anger.

"Well, what would you call her?" Leah hissed.

Jeff's eyes narrowed and his brows grew together over stormy eyes. "I would say she is a woman who loves her son. A woman who is bigoted and doesn't know any different." He drew in a long breath. "I, on the other hand, was bigoted and now I do know the difference. I might have been raised that way but life has taught me otherwise. I'm ashamed of what I've done in the past and ashamed of my mother too." He paused as he searched for the right words. "I would say, like it or not, she is my mother. I might not like what she has done but I love her."

Leah's mouth dropped open and then closed as if she thought better of it. Her tented fingers flexed like a spider on a mirror. Her long pause gave Cord a real chuckle. She was cunning and he knew she was putting the pieces of the puzzle together. She dropped her hands to her lap and looked at Jeff. "I understand the mother thing. My mother and I don't always agree."

Cord threw his head back and laughed. "Now that is an understatement if I've ever heard one." Then he added, "See, you do have something in common."

Leah shot her brother a withering glare. "We don't all try to please our parents for the sake of peace. There are times when a child must lead a parent."

Cord suppressed his laughter. He knew better than to get into this with Leah. "Oh, of course, Sis, you are right." He wasn't sure if he'd sounded serious enough or not.

Leah turned her attention to Jeff again. "And you are right. You should know better. We live in an informed society. All you have to do is get off your white ass and look around. Your color has not made you better. In fact, it might have made you worse." She let her gaze travel the length of him and then slowly lifted it back to his face. "You aren't bad for a white boy."

Jeff's face flashed crimson. Cord knew she had said what Jeff was thinking about her. He felt as if he were watching a weird comedy. "Look, Amy and I have to be up early in the morn. Could you two finish this in the lounge?" He stood, bringing Amy with him. "We are going to bed."

Leah glanced at her brother and then spoke to Amy. "I hope you are feeling well. Gram was the only one who had the guts to tell me about my niece or nephew."

Amy's eyes grew wide. She fidgeted nervously with Cord's hand. He squeezed her fingers, keeping her close to him. "Leah..."

"No, Cord," Amy stopped him. "I'm feeling fine thank you. I'm pleased that Gram told you. We had planned on telling everyone when this court thing was over." She smiled at Cord. "It looks like it will be over sooner than we thought." She paused for a second. "There is nothing we would like more than to tell the world we've been given a great gift of love." She laid her head on Cord's shoulder. "Now, if you don't mind, I'm very tired."

Cord smiled at Amy as he held her closer. His wonderful lady had handled Leah. His sister seemed stunned into silence. "You are right, baby. We need our rest. He patted her tummy. And he needs to grow."

Leah gave a half smile and then turned to Jeff. "Well, whitey, have you been liberated enough to be seen in a lounge with a black woman?"

Jeff stared openly for a moment. Then he reached for the door. "I don't know if I'm that liberated." His eyes raked over the tall gorgeous woman. "But I can tell you this. I'm ready to be seen with a stunning woman like you." He chuckled. "It certainly couldn't hurt my image."

Leah stood and offered her arm to him. "You are absolutely right. You show me a white girl...," she glanced at Amy, "other than my sister-in-law to be, who could hold a candle to me."

The room roared with laughter. Cord opened the door for them. "Well, you two, settle the whole thing in the lounge." He smiled at Amy's glowing face. "We have other things to do."

"I bet you do." Leah's sensuous laugh left no doubt what she was referring to. She grabbed Jeff's arm. "Come on, white boy, it's about time you had some real fun. We are gonna shake our booty."

"Whatever that is, lead the way." Jeff's laugh could be heard from the hallway.

Cord lifted Amy into his arms and carried her to their bed. "My sister the enchantress. Now that she has taken care of our intruder, I think we should resume our prior activities."

Amy's heart felt light. For the first time in weeks she felt that there would be a rainbow with a pot of gold at the end. She felt the heat of Cord's body as he lay down beside her and she curled into his long frame, burying her face in his neck. She whispered softly, "I'm so in love with you, Cord."

Cord lifted himself onto his elbow and looked lovingly into her eyes. Her heart took flight as she saw the heart-rending tenderness of his gaze. "You are my best friend, my soul mate, my lover, the mother of my child and soon-to-be life's partner. I love you more than this humble heart can say."

She lightly ran her fingers over his face, outlining his brow, his eyes, his cheeks and his lips. He held her fingers on his lips, kissing them sweetly. She felt her soft curves molding to the contours of his body. Cord smothered her lips and crushed her to him. His kiss was long, slow and thoughtful. Parting her lips, she raised herself to meet his mouth with a hunger of her own. "Mmmm," she moaned.

His tongue slipped through her sweetly parted lips and explored the depths of her mouth. She could feel his heart pounding against her breast. Shivers of desire raced through her as he caught her tongue and sucked on it tenderly. She arched to meet the hardened heat of his passion.

"Mmmmm," Cord groaned. Whispering against her lips he asked, "Baby, is this ok? I mean, with the baby and all."

"I don't think the baby cares." She pressed her lips into his neck and breathed a kiss there. She felt his whole body shudder against her.

"We have a very smart baby," he declared hoarsely.

"Uh-huh, we do." Her arms wrapped around him as his body covered hers.

His mouth traveled to her growing breast. He suckled, feeding hungrily from her body. Amy was lost to his passion. Hot lava poured through her, washing away the events of the evening and the day to come. A peace they hadn't had for a long time enveloped the lovers and they became one. They were whole.

■ ■ ■

Amy slid out of bed early the next morning, anxious to have the day behind her and nervous that something would go wrong. She slipped on her robe and quietly crept to the living area of the suite. She picked up the phone with room service on her mind. She needed something to settle her churning stomach. Then she noted the red light flashing messages and instead dialed the voice mail.

"When you are up and around, please call me. I would like to go over some things with you before we go to court." Amy heard Easter McCune's confident voice and felt a surge of relief. She dialed her room.

"Easter, this is Amy. How are you this morning?"

"I'm just great, baby. How are you and my new grandchild?" Easter's voice was filled with love and assurance.

Amy's spirits immediately lifted. She had known this woman such a short time but loved her dearly. She was a pure-hearted woman. A rare find. Amy smiled to herself, much like her own mother. "We are all well, thank you."

"That is good news. Is my son awake yet?" Her cheery voice showed no concern for the day ahead.

"No, I thought I would order breakfast and then wake him. He was very tired last night." Amy's cheeks grew hot as she thought of why he was so tired.

"If you don't mind, I will order breakfast for all of us and have it sent to your room. I do need to speak with my son this morning."

"Of course, Easter, we would love to have you and Leah too." They were family and she wanted her future mother-in-law to know she felt that way.

"Amy?" Easter's voice took on a serious note.

"Yes?" Amy's heart thudded. What was this serious? Oh my God, she thought, something bad is going to happen to Cord. Her knees grew weak. She sat down on the chair by the phone and picked up a pencil. Turning it from end to end she waited for the answer.

"Oh," she laughed, "it's not serious."

"Easter, you scared me." The pencil fell to the floor as she released a big sigh.

"Oh, baby, that was not my intention," she cooed. "I was just wondering if you would like to call me Mom. We are family now."

Amy's heart swelled with love for the mother of her future husband. "Oh, Easter, I mean, Mom. I'm honored you've asked me." Her life was finally coming together. "Mom," her voice trembled as she spoke the word, "we will see you in a few minutes for breakfast."

"I will be there soon. Give my son a good shake and tell him his attorney needs to speak with him before court this morning." She gave a soft laugh. "Bye now."

Amy replaced the receiver in its cradle and stared at the phone. So many things had happened since she and Cord had finally met but this was one of the nicest. If they could just get through today, together they could handle anything.

"Your mother is coming here for breakfast?"

Amy was startled from her reverie. She jumped at the sound of Cord's voice. "My mother?" she questioned.

Cord pulled her into his arms. "I heard you tell her we would see her for breakfast." He pressed her head to his shoulder and stroked her hair gently. "Still tired, baby?"

"No." She shook her head against his shoulder. "I wasn't talking to my mom." She smiled into his warm brown eyes. "I was talking to yours."

She watched his face as a boyish grin spread from his lips to his eyes. His face erupted with love. "You called my mother Mom?" His voice was a soft incredulous whisper.

"Uh-huh." She felt the love from him penetrating to her soul. "She asked me to and I was more than willing." Her heart jolted with his approval. How had she lived without love? How had she lived without this man? She hadn't lived. She had existed.

"My lady," his eyes grew misty, "you've stolen my mother's heart as you've stolen mine." He enveloped her in his arms, kissing her lightly on the head.

"Stolen?" she spoke softly against his chest. "I should've been a thief years ago."

Cord chuckled. "Then our child would have both parents in jail." He leaned back and tweaked her nose. "I love you, Amy Summers," he paused, "Amy McCune."

"Amy McCune?" Amy sighed. "I thought I would stay Amy Summers." She squeezed him tightly. "This we will have to discuss." Her voice was light, revealing the happiness in her heart.

"As long as you become my wife, I don't care what you are called." He pulled her closer. "I will always call you my lady."

Amy heard a knock and then, "Room service!" Cord gave her a tight squeeze and walked to the door.

"I sure will be happy when all of this is over and we can finish what we begin." He jerked the door open.

"Good morning." His mother pushed the cart past him and into the room.

"Good morning," Amy and Cord answered in unison. Amy watched as Mrs. McCune took over the day. What a powerful confident woman. With another knock Gram came dragging a sleepy Hank, and right behind them came Amy's mother and daughter.

"I see my mother has decided the family should have breakfast." Cord hugged his mom playfully yet lovingly.

"Cordelle, you know family is the only way to accomplish anything." She hugged him and then pulled a notepad from her briefcase. They sat on the chairs by the window, their heads together as they talked.

The small dining area of the suite was a flurry of action. Amy smiled as Gram and her mother laid out the breakfast and chatted about the new baby. Her heart grew warmer as she saw Hank and Sara flopped on the couch discussing the classes they would be taking in the fall. They had a long day ahead, yet they were all here and they were her family.

"Come along now." Gram clapped her hands twice. "Gather around and we will give thanks to our Creator." Her loving look roamed over each member of this unique yet loving family. She stretched out her arms and grasped the hands of the people on either side of her. She waited until everyone had followed suit, then bowed her head. She spoke in rich full tones filled with love. "Dear Heavenly Father, we come to You today praising Your holy name. We ask You to guide this family today as we seek the truth of Your love. Let others see us as You do. We thank You for the gift of each and every one of Your children gathered here to replenish their bodies with the gifts of nourishment. We thank You for the opportunity to serve Your plan as individuals and as the earthly family You have brought together. We ask You to bless us and stay with us throughout the gift of this glorious day. We do rejoice in the day You have made. In Your Son's name, we ask. Amen."

"Amen," was said in a hushed unison. Amy watched as each member took the words of the loving prayer to their hearts and digested the goodness for their souls. Today, she thought, is the first day of the rest of my life. There could be no better way to begin that life than surrounded by the people she loved and who returned that love.

Cord squeezed her hand tightly. She looked up into his caring, loving eyes. "I love you," she said more loudly than she had intended.

"We love you too," they all chimed in and the gathering was once again filled with the family laughter and chatter Amy had grown to love. Her cheeks grew hot as she took her seat. She was embarrassed but the heat was from the warmth in her heart for the family gathered together to support one of the members in a time of need.

Fifteen

"Sit here, my lady." Cord smiled at Amy. "This will be over before you know it," he whispered in her ear. In his mind he knew they had all of the evidence needed to throw it out of court. Yet he also knew prejudice. He filled his lungs with a deep fortifying breath. Amy slid onto the freshly polished oak bench in the courtroom, directly behind the defendant's table, only separated by the bar. Then he sat beside her for the few minutes they had before the judge would enter.

Mrs. McCune squeezed Cord's shoulder as she walked toward the defendant's table. He glanced up and saw her smiling down at him. "Mom." He didn't have to say any more. She reached over and patted Amy's twisting hands. Then Mrs. McCune gently motioned for her son to follow her.

He felt Amy stiffen as he rose. Cord turned toward her and saw misty, silvery-green eyes. She was experiencing so many new things in life and not all of them good. He watched as her trembling hand pushed her hair away from her cheek. His fingers lightly touched hers. "Don't fret, my lady. We have this one in the bag." He forced a grin to spread over his face until it felt natural. "It is your job to stay calm for our child. I will do any worrying that needs to be done." He gently tweaked her nose. A warm, loving smile lit her face as she nodded. He could tell the thought of their child calmed her. He dropped her hand and then joined his mother.

Cord began reading the papers and notes spread in front of his mother. "Where is the report from the private detective?" he whispered.

Mrs. McCune picked up a thick folder and handed it to him. "We have it all." She offered him a confident smile.

Cord turned to Amy, who leaned forward and placed her hand on the bar that separated them. Cord covered her small hand with his large one and pressed it. "We are OK, baby. Don't worry," he said in a hushed yet confident voice. He wanted her to rest easy until this was over.

The courtroom was buzzing. He could hear the low whispers of the people in the room and the papers shuffling at both their table and that of the prosecutors. Out of the corner of his eye he could see Mrs. Delaney and Steve sitting behind the prosecutor. She looked as if she was about to score the big one. He shrugged his shoulders. She must have changed her mind about wanting to talk with him and being contrite. He should have known that was too good to be true. Still, he believed Jeff and had given his word to aid in any way he could.

"Hear ye, hear ye!" Cord's attention was brought to the front of the room where the bailiff was announcing the beginning of the court session. A hush fell over the courtroom. He watched as his mother quickly poised herself and organized her papers. The whole scene seemed surreal. His life could be changed dramatically if this didn't go as planned. Then he heard, "Please rise."

The silence was broken by the scraping of chairs and the rustling of clothes as people stood. Cord's heart sank as the judge entered the courtroom. A stern look held the judge's face frozen in time. Cord was afraid that time was before his race had been liberated. He stared as the old, white-haired man adjusted his black robe and took his seat. He might as well have on a white robe with a white hood over his face, Cord thought. His stomach knotted. He knew no matter how much evidence they had, he was still black in a white world.

The bailiff stood stiff, watching the judge. Then he turned toward the room. "You may be seated."

On the oak-paneled wall behind the judge hung the state and county seals. On a pedestal next to the seals was a statue of blind justice. Cord hoped it wasn't just for show.

After a short speech the judge asked, "Are you ready with opening statements?"

"Yes, Your Honor." The prosecution spoke with firm assuredness.

"Yes, Your Honor." His mother's velvety, confident voice carried like that of a great orator. He looked at her face. Age only enhanced her beauty. Her gracious stance was that of a queen. He smiled to himself. If ever there was an attorney who would fight for him, it was his mother. Standing next to her was one of the best defense attorneys in the state. Who just happened to be white and a dear friend of hers. Cord drew in a deep breath and released it slowly. Yes, Your Honor, he thought, we are ready.

"What?" A loud screeching voice echoed in the court-room. Everyone's attention shifted to the seats behind the prosecutor. A red-faced Jeff abruptly stood from where he had been leaning to speak with his mother. He glanced around and then tried to calm her.

The judge slammed his gavel twice. "There will be order in my courtroom." He glared at Jeff. "Detective Delaney, you know the rules of this court."

"Yes, Your Honor." Jeff's face grew crimson. "If it pleases the court, Your Honor, I would ask to speak."

"It does not please the court, Detective Delaney. You are out of order. Now take a seat or leave this courtroom." Cord could see the court was not only displeased but downright pissed off. He watched as Jeff nodded his head and took the seat next to his mother. He handed her a manila envelope.

When Mrs. Delaney pulled the contents from the enve-lope and began reading, her face grew pale. Deep lines creased her forehead. Her mouth drew down and tears sprang to her eyes. She turned and stared at her son. "You have betrayed your own mother?" The shock in her voice was evident. She stood and threw the envelope at her son. "You would betray your mother for those black bastards?" Once again she was hysterical as she waved her hand in Cord's direction.

Cord's body tensed. He could feel the muscle in his jaw gripping to keep his mouth shut. His fists were tight

balls. His mother's hand covered one of his fists and
pressed it tightly. He glanced at her. Mrs. McCune shook
her head and gave him a loving yet a warning look.

The gavel slammed again and again. "Madam, you are
in contempt of this court. One more outburst and you will
be fined and/or imprisoned." He turned gruffly to the officer standing beside the bench. "Bailiff, if there are any
more such incidences you will remove the party from the
courtroom and hold them in the jail until this trial is over."

"Howard!!!!" Mrs. Delaney screeched. "Don't you try
to pull that court stuff on me." She pushed her way out
from her seat and quickly threw open the small gate that
kept spectators in their place. She trounced the short distance and was quickly standing in front of the judge. The
bailiff moved to stand beside her. It was evident that he
was reticent to grab her.

Mrs. Delaney shot the bailiff a withering glare. "Bill,
keep your hands off me." She pointed her finger and glared
at the judge. "How dare you speak to me like this?" She
screeched like chalk on a blackboard.

Howard, Cord thought. This woman who hated him
because of his color was a friend of the judge. This was
going to be tough. All the white guns were loaded and
pointing at him. He whispered to his mother, "Isn't this a
good reason to request another judge or another venue?"

She smiled and whispered back, "After that outburst
and the judge's obvious familiarity with the woman, not to
mention all of the evidence against Steve for the embezzlement and Mrs. Delaney in the conspiracy, the judge

wouldn't dare take this trial any farther." She patted his hand. "I am waiting to see how Howard gets out of this." She gave a mischievous smile.

He turned to look at Amy. With all the commotion going on no one would notice. Amy's face was ashen. She returned the look, her eyes misting heavily. He smiled at her and mouthed, "Don't worry." She returned a weak smile and nodded. Cord turned to look as the judge slammed his gavel again. The wooden block that had been used over the years gave a splintering sound and broke in two. The judge stared at it for a moment, his face grim.

"Mrs. Delaney." His voice was commanding but had taken on a conciliatory tone. "This is a court of law." He glanced at the bailiff and nodded. Then returning his scrutiny to the outraged woman he said, "You leave me no choice but to place you under arrest."

The bailiff moved swiftly, as did a female officer who quickly grabbed and secured Mrs. Delaney's wrists.

Mrs. Delaney's eyes grew wide as the handcuffs snapped. Red splashed her pale face. She stared at the young female officer. "Julie?" Her voice was filled with shock and horror. "How could you do this to me?" Tears of frustration sprang to her eyes. She quickly surveyed the faces of her captors. Sobs burst from her throat as she screamed, "Don't you people have any idea what this intruder has done?" She shot a hateful glare at Cord.

Cord was beginning to think this woman knew everyone in the courtroom except him. He glanced over his shoulder and saw Jeff frozen in place, his face grey.

Distress lines filled his forehead and his narrowed eyes were moist and dark. Cord felt for the other man. To have your mother a raging maniac was bad enough, but to have her arrested was the ultimate humiliation for an officer of the court.

Jeff, shame-faced, watched as his mother was led kicking and screaming from the courtroom. He picked up the manila envelope, carried it to Amy, dropped it in her lap and then whirled on his heel and left. Wide-eyed, she watched Jeff leave the courtroom. She held the envelope loosely in her hands as if she had no idea what to do or where to go.

Cord tapped on the bar to gain her attention. He held out his hand and she automatically handed him the envelope. "It will be okay," he whispered to her.

She shook her head and whispered, "I...I had no idea. I didn't know she had mental problems."

"Shhhh," he whispered, "it's OK." Cord gently rubbed her hand that lay on the bar between them. He studied her pain-filled eyes and wondered if this incident would make a difference in her decision to marry him. The pounding of the gavel on the broken block brought his attention back to the front of the courtroom.

"Will the prosecutor and the defendant's attorney approach the bench?" The judge's stern, deep voice resonated over the courtroom.

"Yes, Your Honor." The attorneys spoke in unison.

Cord watched as his mother approached the bench with great confidence. The judge covered the microphone and they talked at length. Cord could see his mother offering the judge the new evidence. The prosecutor's face grew astonished and the judge simply nodded and then released them from their conversation.

When the attorneys returned to their places, the judge spoke to the courtroom as a whole. "This session will be in recess while the attorneys for the State and the defendant meet in my chambers. "Court will resume in one hour." He pounded his gavel, picked up the two halves of the wooden block and left the room.

Cord waited until the door closed behind the judge then he quickly turned to his mother. "What's happening?"

"We are going to meet with the judge. He feels there is enough evidence to set this aside and arrest the proper people." His mother's face was confident, yet a sadness filled her rich golden-brown eyes.

He hugged her. "Mom, I'm sorry you have to go through this."

When he released her, she gathered her papers and neatly placed them in her briefcase. She looked at her son as she moved to follow the judge into chambers. "Cordelle, it breaks my heart to see prejudice and hatred tear a family apart." She brushed imaginary lint from her grey suit. "This judge is fair and this will be over soon."

"I know, Mom." She was sincere in her grief for Jeff and his mother. He loved and admired her more at this moment than at any other time in his life. "Do I need to go with you?" There was so much he wanted to say, yet he knew there was nothing to say. Hundreds of years had brought them here and it would take hundreds more to change.

"No." She shook her head. "This won't take long." Mrs. McCune looked past her son at Amy, offered her a reassuring smile and then looked back to her son. "Use this time to help the newest member of our family. I think she has had a rough morning and needs you."

Cord rose and nodded. "Thanks, Mom. Give 'em hell and we'll be here waiting when you return."

When the door closed behind his mother, Cord turned to his fiancée and held out his hand. "Come on, let's get some fresh air and something to drink." Amy accepted his hand and held on for dear life. Together they left the court-room.

The hot July sun drenched Amy with warmth as she sat on the park bench waiting for Cord to return with cold drinks. Her mind was whirling. She'd never been in a situation like this and couldn't imagine how Cord and his whole race had survived as well as they had. She watched as her mother and Gram strolled the park, stopping to admire the flowers and bushes. They seemed not to have seen what had just happened or were just accepting it as part of life. She hoped she too would be able to witness this horrid prejudice and move on to smell the flowers.

Cord's long frame came into view. Her heart skipped a beat as he strolled confidently over the path carrying cold drinks for them. His smile was bright. He, too, was acting as if he hadn't been attacked. She wasn't sure she would ever reach that point but she wouldn't give up her chance at love and happiness because others didn't like her choices.

"Mom." Amy started as a hand softly touched her shoulder, then relaxed as Sara sat down beside her. "Mom, I'm sorry this is happening. I feel so guilty that I almost bought into the same feelings Mrs. Delaney displayed."

"Oh, honey, you weren't buying that. I know my daughter." She hugged her. "You were concerned for me." She held her back and looked at her. "And of course you were having to accept that your mother had fallen in love."

Sara hugged her mother tightly. "And I know my mother is in love." She spoke softly. "I'm very happy for you."

"So what are the women of our family planning now, Dad?" Hank's jovial voice brought the women's attention to the men standing in front of them.

"We aren't planning anything." Sara smiled brightly. "But I am starving and the judge says we have an hour, so let's grab something to eat."

Hank offered Sara his arm. "I think that is a fine idea, dear sister." He chuckled. "For a little thing you do eat a lot." He turned to his dad. "This may be a consideration for you, Dad. Sara might be expensive to feed."

Cord and Amy laughed. Amy could feel the relief as Hank bantered with Sara. She knew in her heart that this young man, so loving and giving, would bring many joyful hours to their lives. She prayed she could help the new life inside her to be like him.

"Hank, you eat more than I do. Maybe Mom should consider that." Sara punched him playfully as they strolled off together, their laughter filling the park.

"A cold drink for my lady." Cord held out the soft drink and sat beside her.

Amy accepted the drink. "Thank you."

Shivers ran through her as his arm slid around her. "We have an hour. They will never miss us." His rich voice carried a hoarse tone.

"I want more than an hour." She blushed.

"We take what we can get," he laughed.

"Well, it seems the lovebirds are planning an escape." Shelley's voice rang through to Amy's consciousness. She looked from Cord's warm eyes to those of her friends. Shelley and Leo stood in front of them, arms around each other's waist.

"We thought we would come and lend our support but it seems Mrs. Delaney has given you all you need," Leo chuckled.

Amy slid over and patted the bench. "Sit with us for awhile. Court will be in session again soon and we do appreciate your support."

Cord stood and offered his hand to Leo. "We owe you, man, and we never forget a favor."

Leo shook his head. "Your friendship is payment enough." His face broke into a bright smile. "And of course an invitation to the wedding."

Amy's heart grew lighter as the people she loved surrounded them. "Invitation?" she smiled at the couple.
"We would like you to be in the wedding party. Sara and
Hank will be standing with us, but we would like to have
you standing with us too."

Amy felt the pressure of Cord's arm gently snug her
closer. His soft gaze told her he approved.

Shelley and Leo smiled. "We would be honored," Leo
answered for both of them. Shelley's face glowed with
love for her husband as she looked to him in agreement
and nodded.

Amy could feel the events of the day being lifted.
Somehow, the courtroom scenes diminished in light of all
this love. They would have a rough time, but that was
what love was all about. Together, with family and friends,
they would have a wonderful life. She hugged Shelley.
"We could never thank you enough for all you have done."

Again the two men were off in a conversation of their
own. They stood tall and handsome in the July sun. Amy
looked at them and then turned to Shelley. "You know, if
I hadn't made that reporting error two years ago, I would
not be here now." Her voice softened with the memory.

"I told you perfection wasn't all it's cracked up to be."
Shelley gave a quiet laugh. Then she nudged Amy as she
looked at the fountain in the park. "Who is that talking
with Jeff? She is gorgeous."

Amy faced the direction Shelley indicated. She could
see Jeff sitting on the edge of the fountain with the water
misting over him. His head hung low as he stared at his

feet. Standing in front of him, talking with her whole body, was Leah. "Oh, God." Jeff was already humiliated beyond words; the last thing he needed was one of Leah's tirades. "Cord..." Her worried voice choked the rest of her thought.

Cord turned to look at her and then followed her gaze. "I'll take care of it, baby." He looked at Shelley. "Will you stay for a few minutes while I go talk with my sister?" He didn't wait for an answer, but instead turned quickly and jogged across the park.

"His sister?" Shelley looked at Amy and then back at the gorgeous woman who was talking to Jeff. "Are they? I mean ... well, you know what I mean."

Amy had to laugh. "Leah is dead set against biracial relationships." Now that was an understatement if she'd ever made one. She thought about Jeff for a moment. "And I don't think Jeff would lean that way either. His mother would kill him." She thought for a moment. "That is, if the judge lets her out of jail."

Shelly laughed fully. "From what I hear, she deserves jail time, but I'm sure she won't get it." Her voice filled with curiosity. "Cord's sister seems to know Jeff."

"They met last night. Leah gave Jeff a real emotional and mental beating. Knowing her, she is going in for the kill right now." She sighed relief as she watched Cord join the couple at the fountain. Though not thrilled with Jeff, she knew he was just about at the end of his rope.

Leo dropped down beside them on the bench. "All of this over the color of someone's skin." He sighed heavily.

A lifetime of prejudice filled his reddish, sun-creased face. He shook his head. "When will we ever learn?"

Shelley patted his leg. "I think we are all learning and this is just one of the many lessons."

They sat quietly and watched as Cord talked with the couple at the fountain. Amy was dying to know what was being said, but she was also fearful of it. Cord's body language did not look as if he was on guard. In fact it looked quite the opposite. But then, Amy thought, he was good at hiding his true feelings.

Cord put his arm around his sister and began walking away from Jeff. Jeff stood, said something, and Cord whirled around. The three spectators all rose at once. Leo sprinted across the park toward the fountain.

"Oh my God," Amy breathed in disbelief. "Not now."

Shelley put her arm around her friend. "Wait, it may not be what it seems." Her voice had no conviction at all.

Amy watched as Leo arrived and seemed to place himself between Cord and Jeff. She could see words being exchanged but she couldn't see anger. Soon the four at the fountain were walking in her direction. Their conversation seemed amiable. Her mind spun and she held her breath until her lungs heaved. She couldn't imagine what was happening, and wouldn't have to imagine in a minute. They were almost to her.

Cord sprinted the last few steps to Amy and placed his arm around her shoulder. "Everything is fine."

"Fine?" She couldn't see how this was all fine. Or even what he meant by fine.

Cord smiled. "It seems Jeff and Leah have declared a temporary truce in the war of the races."

She looked at him with suspicion. A merry twinkle filled his eyes. Amy wanted to ask but the others had arrived.

"Leah, Jeff." Amy spoke the names softly, yet both looked to her. She didn't know what else to say. She looked to Cord for help.

"Amy, you have nothing to worry about." Leah took over, as usual. "I am not going to hurt your red-neck friend here."

Jeff smiled at Leah. "You don't let up, do you?"

Amy couldn't decide if they were joking or serious. Again she looked to Cord for help. His face was lit in a bright smile.

"Jeff, old man," Cord slapped him on the shoulder, "you will find my sister a tenacious zealot." He glanced at Leah and then added, "Still, somewhere under that gorgeous exterior lurks a heart."

Leah shot her brother a half smile. "Don't get carried away. I only told him I'd talked with Mom about her taking his mother's case."

Amy could feel her mouth drop open. "Leah? You did this?" She tried to hide her incredulous thoughts but they were there in the tone of her voice. She wanted to kick herself for not being discreet. She was going to have enough trouble with Leah without adding fuel to the fire.

"Look, almost sister-in-law." Leah drawled the last words. "I am not changing my stance on biracial relationships. I am just offering help to another human whose mother has made an ass of herself. Mrs. Delaney thought she could use your boss' embezzlement to get rid of my brother. The woman is cagey. If you think about it, she discovered the thief before the State did and put it to use." She turned to Jeff. "And don't get all uppity about this. She did make an ass of herself."

"Leah," Amy pleaded.

"No Amy, it's okay." Jeff's face seemed to have new lines cut in around the corners of his eyes and mouth. It was hard enough having your mother act like that. It seemed cruel to grind it in.

"Yes, it is OK," Leah continued. "Jeff and I'll work this out between us." Her voice was gentler but still determined.

Cord laughed. Amy looked at him. She saw nothing funny. "Honey?"

Cord snugged her into him. "For my sister, this is nice." He laughed heartily. Others joined in — even Leah.

Amy shrugged her shoulders. "If it works for all of you, then it works for me." Somehow this was working but she wasn't quite sure how.

Cord glanced at his watch. "I think it's time for us to return to the courtroom." He glanced at the small group. "No matter how this turns out...," he paused studying each of them, "I know we've all reached a new level of understanding and for this I'm happy." He didn't wait for an answer. He took Amy into his arms and hugged her tightly as he turned them toward the courthouse.

Amy seated herself right behind Cord. The bench was filled with family and friends, including Jeff and Leah. Gram and Mrs. Summers had been sitting there waiting when she arrived. She took a deep breath and listened as again the bailiff called the session to order.

The judge sat quietly for a moment as if contemplating how to explain what he had to say. Finally his deep voice boomed into the silent courtroom. "New evidence has been brought to my attention." He paused and briefly looked in Cord's direction.

Refocusing his gaze on the back of the courtroom, he continued. "It seems a great injustice has been perpetrated by bringing charges against the defendant and bringing those charges to this court." He glanced at the prosecutor's table. "In this court's opinion there was not enough searching prior to bringing charges."

He turned his head toward Cord and looked right at him. "This court apologizes for the injustice." His jaw set with the firmness of his conviction. "Justice should be blind." He laid his hand on the blindfolded statue. "Yet, as I'm sure you are aware, it is not." The judge picked up his gavel. "This case has no merit and is dismissed." He slammed the gavel on his desk with an anger that startled the crowd, then rose and left.

Reporters pressed toward Cord and his mother. Cameras flashed in every direction. Though Amy wanted to run to Cord's arms, she couldn't see him for the crowd. She stood on tiptoe, trying to see over all of them. His head emerged above the crowd. Their searching stopped as they spotted each other. Her face lit in a smile she felt from her head to her toes. There was an invitation in the smoldering depths of his gaze. She nodded. "Yes," she spoke aloud. Her one word seemed to bring the roaring crowd's attention to her. She felt her face grow hot. Everyone laughed.

The crowd split, allowing the couple room to get to each other. When they finally were together their arms wrapped around each other. She buried her face in his neck and breathed a kiss there. "I am so embarrassed," she whispered.

"Ahh, but you are so cute when you are embarrassed," he whispered back. Holding her tightly, he lifted her and carried her through the crowd and out into the bright sunlight.

She wrapped her arms around his neck. "You are my dream come true."

He galloped down the courthouse steps with her in his arms. "A dream that was meant to be."